IT HAD
TO
BE YOU

KATHRYN
SHAY

Kathryn Shay spent five years riding fire trucks with a large city fire department, eating in their firehouses and interviewing hundreds of America's Bravest. Read the books that resulted from her intense relationship with firefighters!

Reader Praise for It Had To Be You

"Wow...Such a well written, emotional, heartbreaking read. I just loved it. I was hooked from the start by such wonderful and lovable characters...these characters broke my heart."

"I loved Beck's character and I loved him with Lela. Kathryn certainly put their relationship through the emotional ringer!!"

"I never realized the extent of PTSD and how horrible it would be to have this. You also got in the mind of the firefighters and what they feel and see during a fire. It was also a different romantic story than usual."

"I found this book very down to earth. As a past navy wife, I could relate to the feelings of the different personalities of each character. This is portrayed as real life with the ups and downs. I also cried when reading it."

"I loved it! This book brings awareness to the very difficult reality of war vets with PTSD. It also shows the struggles people go through for love and how fate can bring you together."

IT HAD
TO
BE YOU

By KATHRYN SHAY

Published By Kathryn Shay
Copyright 2012 Kathryn Shay
Cover Art By Patricia Ryan

CHAPTER 1

"HELL, IT'S HOTTER in here than it was in Afghanistan!" Beckett Sloan mumbled the words, but his radio mic must have picked them up because he heard his captain, Gabe Malvaso, chuckle through the line.

"At least it's chilly outside for April," Gabe responded. "Thank God for small blessings, Beck."

Not gonna happen. To Beck, *blessings* and *God* had become irrelevant words since he'd taken his first tour in Iraq over twenty years ago.

Instead of dwelling on war experiences in Iraq, which still woke him in the middle of the night, he focused on his current job.

"How you doin' back there, probie?" Felicia White tossed out. The tall, slender woman had a core of steel.

Intentionally this time, Beck snorted into the radio. "Just fine, Lieutenant." For most of his adult life, Beck had held officer's rank—from second lieutenant all the way to colonel. No more. Now, thanks to the Hire Our Heroes initiative, he was rookie in the Hidden Cove Fire Department, which suited him fine. The fire service was basically a paramilitary organization, with the same slogan as the armed services: *Duty, Honor, Country.* It was as close to the army as he could get

1

without IEDs going off in his path or the slaughter of innocents happening right in front of him. At least now he was trying to save people instead of kill them.

A timber crashed down in front of Gabe, and all five members of the Rescue Squad jumped back. Sparks flew in every direction and a few embers landed on White, who was in front of Beck. They'd kept him close to officers for the first year. Immediately, he reached out to brush the glowing shards from her helmet. Embers under their Nomex hoods were nasty.

Into his mic, Gabe asked, "Condition of the fire, Chief?"

"Getting worse," their battalion chief shot back, with a note of concern in his voice. "You're close to coming out." The voice belonged to Cal Erikson, who was operating Incident Command.

"We're on the second floor. Let us check the bedrooms."

"Do it fast."

Gabe ticked off orders. "Sands and O'Malley, left. White, go with them. Sloan, you're with me."

"Yes, sir."

Following his officer into a bedroom straight ahead, he dropped to the floor when Malvaso did. It was a furnace in here as heat rose. "Check the left side."

Blindly feeling the wall, Beck connected with a steel post. A bedstead? He reached beyond it and found a soft spongy mass—a bed. Which, when pressed, bounced. "Got one, Cap."

"You carry him out, Beck. My side's clear. I'll be right in front of you to lead the way."

Thankful he didn't have a superior officer who took over when things got tense, Beck identified legs first, a torso, a head. Scooping up the body, he determined the person weighed about two hundred pounds. And had a lot of muscle.

Pitching the guy over his shoulder, Beck stood into even hotter air, which could burn the lungs. Using the wall again since he could only see outlines, he slid his hand along the sheetrock until he reached the door.

Stepping into the hallway, he slowly made his way down the stairs, careful to balance his heavy load. His pace was also hindered by the traditional gear of heavy clothing and a breathing apparatus, which weighed about sixty pounds. Halfway there, the horn blew, calling all firefighters to evacuate.

"Pick up the pace, Beck."

"Yes, sir!" Beck tried to quicken his steps, but his balance started to give way; sweat seeped out of him inside his turnout coat; the weight pressed over his shoulder had him stumbling to the exit.

"I'm right ahead of you," Gabe called out. It was pitch-black down here, and Beck couldn't see anything. "Follow my voice."

A bracing rush of cold air, clean air, hit them as they exited the house into the night. Two paramedics from one of the ambulances rushed to Beck, took the body and strapped it onto a gurney; when they left, Beck dropped to his knees. Every one of his muscles pulsed, and his breathing was ragged. Ripping off his head gear, he sucked in deep breaths. Again, he recalled the hot, fetid air he'd been forced to take in after a skirmish in Iraq or Afghanistan.

Brody O'Malley approached him. "Did good, buddy."

"Thanks."

"Gonna hurl?" A woman—Sands or White?—asked. "I have. It's okay."

Once more, he was overwhelmed with these people's *kindnesses*. When a member of the elite Rescue Squad,

Tony Ramirez, had been promoted to lieutenant on a different group at the house, they'd pulled Beck up from his six-month rookie position on a pumper. He knew why. Purple Heart. Silver Star. A variety of commendations for his performance on the battlefield. Though those things meant little to him, they gave him an opportunity for a career that suited him. And he'd always admired firefighters for the actions in 9/11, just as they admired soldiers.

"I think I'm good." Sitting back on his haunches, he surveyed the scene. Three alarms, which meant three firehouses were called. Five trucks. Two ambulances. Turning, he saw the structure engulfed in angry yellow-and-red flames. They'd had a close call.

He'd had closer.

"Need a medic?" This time, Gabe came over and asked the question because Beck still hunched on his knees.

White answered. "He says no."

Finally able to stand, Beck felt himself wobble. The lieutenant slid her arm through his. "You should be shaky, Beck. You carried a lot of weight in sweltering conditions."

"I'm okay." He moved away from her.

"Suit yourself."

"We heading to the trucks?" he asked.

"In a minute." Gabe perused him closely, his dark gaze searching, then turned to cross to Erikson.

The others wandered off to get water. Beck started toward the Rescue rig, passing the Midi, a two-person medical truck, which carried supplies. Someone stepped out in front of him. Zach Malvaso. Though he was a nice guy, he was more extroverted, more cocky than his brother, Mitch. "Doin' good, Beck?"

The origin of that question was different from the others' queries. Zach Malvaso was a firefighter with PTSD. "Yep, good."

"You going to the meeting tonight?" All the firefighters in Beck's house knew of his problem, which was necessary because something could happen on the job.

Afraid so. "Yep."

"Good." Malvaso grabbed his arm. Zach and all his family were touchers. "The group isn't so bad. I still go occasionally, so I knew about the one that's starting up tonight."

"Sure, yeah. I'm down with it."

After he told the lie, he strode quickly to the truck. Luckily no one was nearby. Circling the end of the rig so he was out of sight, he leaned his forehead against the cold, red-painted metal and closed his eyes.

His attendance at the Trauma Survivor's Group bothered him more than the experience he'd just had inside the burning building. The last thing Beck wanted was to be part of a specialty *support* group, set up by the fire department for its members and including veterans from all walks of life. Society was trying to help the wounded warriors who returned from the Middle East and Asia. One of the conditions of his employment in the HCFD was attendance at the sessions, but it had taken the department about nine months to set up this particular class because of scheduling problems. Then the doc running it had a family emergency, so the new group had kept getting put off.

Beck thought about his PTSD—the emotional shrapnel left in him by war—mostly centered around depression and nightmares, with the occasional flashbacks. The fire department officials believed he could learn to *manage* his symptoms. But he had no inclination to deal with the very thing that had cost him his marriage, his kid and, to a degree, his sanity.

• • •

LELA ALLEN KNEW she was in a dream, struggled to surface from it, but she couldn't. Instead, pain rocketed through her. The slam of her head against the wood-paneled wall radiated to her nerve endings, and her vision blurred. "Please, Len, don't."

No response from the man she'd married. Just a grunt as he wedged his arm in her windpipe.

She gagged. Choked. "Len, please. It's me, Lela."

Sometimes yelling her name pulled him out of the fog. Thank God, this was one of those occasions.

He blinked.

His eyes widened.

Then he fell to his knees and buried his head in his hands. Began to weep.

Her struggle to breathe, combined with the wrenching sound of his crying, had Lela bolting up in bed; she was gasping for air for real. Slowly, she became aware of the firm mattress beneath her, the cool April breeze on her arms and the scent of laundry detergent from the bedclothes. Tugging the quilt to her chest, she uttered the familiar mantra: "It's a dream; it's over; he can't hurt you anymore."

The first two points were true. The jury was still out on the latter. Maybe once the divorce came through, she wouldn't be as affected by his problems as much as she was now.

Hating the impotence those dreams engendered, she flung off the covers, grabbed a robe and padded to the bathroom off the hall. Ten minutes later, she crept down the steps, walked through the big living room, noting that it needed dusting and vacuuming. Once in the small but efficient kitchen, she made herself a cup of coffee. Sitting at the breakfast nook, she glanced at her watch. Five p.m. She had two hours to eat and dress for tonight. She calmed herself with slow sips of coffee. And thought about the invitation that had come to her. Her friend and colleague at Memorial Hospital, Sophia Ramirez, had offered it when she told Lela about the spouse-concerns group she attended at the Anderson County Fire Academy....

"Now that Jack Harrison is available" — he was the department shrink — "he's starting another group in a few weeks for sufferers of PTSD and their families."

Lela was confused. "I don't have PTSD. Len does."

"I know, and it's amazing you escaped the malady after what *you* went through in Afghanistan."

Now Lela was a trauma nurse in the ER, but for five years, she'd been a medic, stationed in Afghanistan in a small medical outpost that treated soldiers right off the battlefield. She'd seen some hideous injuries: limbs blown off, faces unrecognizable, evisceration of torsos, as well the vacant look of death in soldiers' eyes. But for some reason, Lela had been spared PTSD. There were three-hundred thousand returning vets with the condition. No one seemed to know why some combat personnel developed it and others didn't. In that area at least, she was lucky.

Sophia had continued, "The group is open to veterans *and* their families."

"That's an odd combination to treat together."

"What, the spouses and the sufferers?"

Lela nodded.

"Jack thinks having people on both sides of the condition together in one group will increase understanding of what each person goes through." She smiled. "And you know how much I adore the man." Sophia had confided in Lela what she'd gone through with her husband last year. She'd gradually become unable to bear the danger Tony was in every day and her fear had almost destroyed their marriage.

"Why is the fire department including veterans?"

"There's a big initiative out there for organizations to help returning soldiers in any way they can. Maybe you should give the group a shot...."

So, after she'd tried to get Len to join instead of her and he'd refused, Lela had enrolled. What could it hurt?

When she'd erased the aftereffects of the dream with high-test coffee, a quick sandwich and a shower, Lela dressed in blue jeans (her Southern mama would have had a fit) and a nice, deep maroon sweater, which brought out the red highlights in her hair. Driving to the Fire Academy made her tense, so she did some shrugs and stretches to loosen her shoulders. All too soon, she arrived at the big glass-and-brick building, servicing several surrounding towns as well as Hidden Cove. Lela had moved to the town, about a hundred miles outside of New York City, after she'd left the service, because Len had grown up here and had wanted to come back home when he'd gotten out. She'd thought being with family and friends might help him. Though Len had moved into his childhood house after their separation almost a year ago, he was still in bad shape.

Lela had visited the Fire Academy once for a refresher training on sunken chest wounds, given by a paramedic. The building held offices, but its main purpose was to train firefighters from several counties. As she approached the entrance a second time, her heart beat a wild tattoo in her chest at what she was in for tonight.

From her right, a man came up flush to the door when she reached it. He was definitely the armed forces. She could spot them anywhere. Impossibly erect posture. Still-short hair. This one had chiseled features, but his eyes were world-weary.

"Ma'am," he said in short clipped tones.

"Sir." She responded unthinkingly to the greeting.

He cocked his head and stared at her a minute. "Army?"

She nodded. "Nurse turned medic. Kandahar. You?"

"OCS, twenty years. Iraq. Afghanistan."

Wow, Lela thought. Len had only been in ten years. *This poor man's wife.*

Together, they took the elevator to the third floor. He gave her a little smile. "Don't much see Southern belles who turn into army medics."

He must have caught what remained of her accent. "My mama would have agreed with you. God bless her heart. But I joined after both my parents died."

He chuckled. The sound was deep, masculine. When they reached the third floor, he held the elevator door so she could exit before him. Chatter drifted out from the first room on the left, so she headed for it, with him behind. As they entered, Lela noted the muted lighting and how the chairs were arranged in two half circles, not one with chairs that would back to the door. The soft blue walls and grass-cloth paper soothed on sight. "I see somebody knows what he's doing."

"Ma'am?"

"Please, call me Lela. Ma'am makes me feel like your mother."

For a brief second, his eyes perused her in anything but a parental fashion. "Lela. Beckett Sloan. I go by Beck."

She held out her hand and they shook. His palm dwarfed hers and his clasp was firm. Since they'd reached the chairs at the same time, he stood while she took one, then dropped down next to her. Sitting, he seemed bigger. Taller. But for some reason, maybe his manners, she didn't feel threatened.

Not so of everyone who had assembled. As she glanced around, she saw in a couple guys' expressions, and one woman's, the confusion and acute anxiety she'd lived with for years. Without her conscious intent, she leaned in toward Beckett Sloan.

Promptly at seven, a good-looking man with a full head of dark hair graying at the temples, entered the room and pulled up a chair facing them, his own back to the door. "Hi, all. I'm Jack Harrison. You can call me Jack, Doc or Dr. Harrison. Behind my back, I hope you're kind."

A bit of laughter.

"I've been the psychiatrist for the fire department for close to two decades. Thanks for coming to this very first meeting of our Trauma Survivor's Group this year. Whether you're a sufferer or related to one, you're all survivors."

Before Dr. Harrison could go further, the door slammed open and Lela gasped. In the entry stood her soon-to-be ex-husband, Len Allen, once again crazy-eyed and, from the looks of him, drunk.

• • •

UNRUFFLED, JACK HARRISON turned and glanced over his shoulder. Then he stood and asked pleasantly, "Can I help you?"

The man said, "Staff Sergeant Len Allen, sir. I came for the group."

Harrison scanned the clipboard he held. "I don't see your name here, Len. Did you enroll?"

"No, but I changed my mind." His gaze scanned the semi-circle. "I wanna be here with my wife."

A quick intake of breath from the woman next to Beck.

"I'm sorry, Len." Again Harrison spoke calmly. Almost gently. "We don't allow spouses to take the sessions together." He looked to Lela. "You're signed in, right?"

"Yes, I'm Lela Allen."

Harrison fished something out of his pocket. When he gave the card to the soldier, the guy's hand shook. "Here's my number. Maybe we can schedule some individual counseling."

"Don't wanna. I'm stayin' here."

"No, I'm afraid you're not."

Jack wisely didn't touch Allen, just moved in closer. "Let's go out into the foyer, Len."

The man stood his ground. He sported a medium build, but his physique consisted of a roadmap of corded muscles. Beck remembered working out till he dropped, trying to conquer the demons. "No."

Harrison hesitated and Len started toward the group. Beck took another glance at Lela. Her lips had thinned and her jaw was tight. But she held her head up to face down whatever was coming.

Rising, he stepped between her and her husband. "*Attention*, Staff Sergeant Allen. Colonel Beckett Sloan here."

Reflex kicked in. The guy halted, stood straight and saluted, just as Beck suspected he would.

"We're going into the hall. That's an order, Staff Sergeant."

"Yes, sir."

Turning, he followed Allen out of the room. Harrison said to the others, "Be right back," and went with them.

In the corridor, Beck hadn't forgotten how to lead men. Standing over Allen, he donned a stern expression. "Have you been drinking, Staff Sergeant?"

"Some."

"A lot, from what I can see. Hand over your keys."

"Excuse me?"

"I want your keys. You aren't driving home."

"What do you mean?"

"We'll get you a cab."

The man's chin raised. Expecting belligerence, Beck leaned in some.

"I wanna go in there. I need help."

Beck glanced at Harrison, who had let him handle the situation to this point. The psychiatrist spoke softly. "Yes, you do, Len. Call me and we'll set up an appointment."

"I wanna be with my wife." He sounded like a little boy, and it angered Beck that the disorder could turn good soldiers into whiny children.

"I remember her application now. She said she asked you to come alone, and when you said no, she decided to attend. She also said you're legally separated and soon to be divorced."

"Don't want it." The man began to waver on his feet.

Beck moved in closer. "Come on, Staff Sergeant, I'll get you in a cab. We can talk some more while we wait."

Harrison nodded. "I'll call one of our staffers. He'll drive the Staff Sergeant home."

By the time they reached the elevator, Len Allen was slumping onto Beck's shoulder. He murmured, "It's fucking hard. Sometimes I don't wanna live anymore."

"I felt the same from time to time. You can get better."

"Tried."

"I know what I'm saying for a fact."

"Then why're you here?"

"Requirement of my job." They reached the parking lot, and a fire department Jeep pulled up in front of them. A uniformed firefighter got out. "I'll take him from here."

"Okay." Beck hesitated, then took Harrison's card, which Len still held in his hand, and scribbled on it. "Here's my cell number, too, if you need to talk to someone who's been there."

"Thanks, Colonel. Sorry about the scene in there. See if Lela's okay, will you?"

"Just go sober up. And get help."

Beck watched as the car sped off, then headed inside and took the elevator to the third floor. He walked into the room, and the person speaking halted.

Harrison said, "We're giving our reasons for being here. We've only covered three people, and I'll catch you up later, Colonel."

Beck nodded and took his seat next to Lela. She looked over at him and her eyes were bleak, but she hadn't cried or left. She was tougher than she looked. But, of course, she'd been an army medic. "Thank you," she mouthed and he nodded.

The spouse of a female marine spoke next. He was a big teddy bear of a guy. "Dennis Lewis. My wife's not the same person since she got back. Actually, I'm afraid to leave her alone with the kids. We need help, big-time. And she's not going to be the one to get it."

Two firefighters talked about having been trapped in an elevator that was about to plunge fifty feet. "I didn't think we were gonna make it out," the younger one said. "I can't sleep because of the nightmares."

Next was Lela. Her face was flushed, but she spoke clearly. "First, let me apologize for Len. I'm embarrassed."

Harrison took a bead on her. "Lela, listen to me. Your husband's behavior is no reflection on you. He's sick and needs help."

"Well, y'all know my circumstances. Len's why I'm here. We *are* getting a divorce." She nodded to the husband of the marine. "My son's afraid of him. He won't spend any time alone with his father, and it breaks Len's heart. I encourage him to go to Len's parents' house, so they can supervise, and that's what Josh does now."

"How about you, Lela?" Harrison asked. "What do you do?"

"I'm a trauma nurse at Memorial Hospital. Sophia Ramirez told me about this group. I was an army medic for five years, too, and made NCO status. I met Len over there. I left the service when I got pregnant, but Len stayed in for five more years. He's been home about two years, and things have gone from bad to worse."

"A lot to contend with," Harrison commented. His gaze transferred to Beck. "Colonel?"

Beck's heart started to gallop. His brow got sweaty. Subtle physical reactions happened whenever he talked about his experiences in the war. "Beckett Sloan. People call me Beck. Career soldier. Now a firefighter. Haven't had an episode since I joined the department, but before that, I was..." he glanced to the door "...a lot like the Staff Sergeant."

• • •

"CAN I WALK out with you, Beck?" Lela addressed him as soon as the group ended. His face was lined with more fatigue than when they'd arrived.

He gave a small smile. "Yeah, sure."

They walked side by side to the elevator, stood silently inside until they reached the foyer. Under the florescent lamps, she looked up at him. His eyes were a color green she'd only seen on people wearing contacts.

"They're real," he said sardonically.

"Excuse me?"

"The color of my eyes. No contacts. Everybody asks."

She wanted to say how beautiful they were but figured the remark was inappropriate. "Thanks for what you did."

"You got no business being embarrassed."

"Still, I appreciate you taking charge."

"Can't seem to get over that."

She gave him a smile. "Must be hard being the rookie on a squad, then."

His expression was questioning.

"I see firefighters all the time at the ER. Let's just say *one-upmanship* is a kind way to describe them."

Now a full-bodied laugh escaped him. It was a rusty sound. "I get you there. And I bet they flirt like hell."

She could feel the flush creep up her neck. "Nah, they call me ma'am, too."

"I highly doubt that." His gaze darkened. "I'm sorry for what you've gone through."

They locked gazes for a moment. Something subtle, an all-male scent, drifted over to her.

Then he said, "I gave Len my cell number. Maybe I can help him."

"That was sweet of you."

Huh! "I don't know as though anybody has ever called me sweet. Certainly not the soldiers under my command."

Reaching out, she squeezed his arm. "Well, you are, Beck. Thanks again. Good night."

He didn't accompany Lela to her car and she was glad. She'd had a strange reaction to him. She didn't examine it too closely, because for a long time, she'd wanted any reaction to any man to be nonexistent.

• • •

LEN BOLTED UP in bed. What the hell? It was dark in the barracks. Quiet. He grasped on to the mattress. The thing was too thick. When the clock's lighted dial winked out three a.m., he realized he wasn't in Afghanistan. But it took him a minute to get that he was back in the States, in the house where he grew up. Fuck!

Sliding out of bed, he stumbled to the bathroom down the hall, hoping like hell he didn't wake up his mother and father. He'd already put them through hell, and besides, they'd only rag on him about his drinking. He took a piss, brushed teeth that felt like he'd eaten camel dung, and splashed cold water on his face. But when he looked in the mirror, he cringed. Not because his hair was shaggy, a beard roughened his jaw, or his eyes were the color of cherries. He remembered what he'd done tonight.

Poor Lela. He'd hurt her enough. To barge into the Fire Academy and make a scene had embarrassed her. He could still see the shame on her face. The colonel had to drag him out. Jesus.

Once he got back into his room, Len lay down and listened to the sounds of crickets drift in through the open window. When the world stopped spinning, he did what he always did—he made a list in his head of what he needed to do to get better. Go to therapy. Maybe with that Harrison guy who didn't seem like too much of a dick. His mother had also given him AA pamphlets. He'd been to a few meetings before, and a lot of the guys were like him. Vets. Drunks. Bums.

Yeah. He'd do that tomorrow.

But when the dial on the clock clicked to 4 a.m. and then to 5 a.m., the demons came and ate up all his promises.

You're a worthless piece of shit. You never deserved her. She didn't know you bought black market liquor and how much of it you drank over there or when you got back. Go have some more. You don't deserve any better.

As always, he listened to the voices in his head. He slid off the bed, and this time went to his top dresser drawer. Out of which, he pulled a pint of vodka.

He gulped a swig back. And another. The taste was tart and cool. By the time the last drop touched his lips, the demons were gone.

CHAPTER 2

RESCUE 7, GROUP 3 gathered at the scarred oak table in the kitchen of their firehouse. Jenn Malvaso was sitting with them. She was pretty with dark hair and eyes like her brothers. Like Gabe. He'd heard she'd decided to take a year off from firefighting after she'd had twins a few months ago.

"So that's about it. We've almost filled the slots at Hale's Haven's big camp. But we're gonna need some volunteers for the junior camp we're opening this year for four-to-seven-year-olds." She stood. "Think about it."

Hale's Haven was a camp for kids of slain firefighters and police officers and was built, run and fully staffed by the fire and police departments of Hidden Cove and surrounding areas. It was held for two weeks in the summer at their property on the lake. Jenn had been in charge of running the very worthy cause since their opening, but rumor had it, she wanted back on the line. Beck had heard about the camp when he first started in the fire department, and knew that most of his colleagues on his crew worked there at some point during the summer.

"We'll spread the word, cuz," Gabe promised her with a hug when she started to leave.

Zach approached them. "Come on, sis, I'll walk you out."

"No, you won't. You'll just try to talk me out of going back on the line. It's not fair you guys are ganging up on me like this!"

The grapevine also contended that none of her brothers wanted her back in action.

"Hush. Let's go."

The Quint and Midi members, who were also housed at Station 7, headed outside, too, so that left the five members of the Rescue Squad at the table. As Beck looked around, taking in the gleaming appliances, the spic-and-span floor, the Windex-proud windows, he noted that the place itself was as perky as every single one of his group. Jesus, the department had nicknamed this particular shift Happyland. Though Beck appreciated being picked for the squad every-body wanted on, sometimes their sheer joy in life drove him nuts.

"What's the matter, Beck? You're scowling." This came from Brody O'Malley, a paramedic and all-around nice guy — if somewhat cocky. Beck had met his brother, Ryan, a cop, and liked him, too.

"Somebody's gotta counteract all the bliss in the air." His words bore no ill will, though, in tone or intent.

"We know."

Beck glanced over to see the battalion chief, Cal Erikson, had come into the room and now poured coffee from a big urn. Sometimes, when coffee burned, its scent triggered a PTSD attack in a sufferer. Thankfully, the smell didn't have that effect on Beck, but he knew it was one of Zach Malvaso's triggers.

"We decided everybody's just jealous of our *bliss* and laugh at them." The BC sipped from his mug and took a bead on Beck. "You jealous, Beck?"

"Yep." Hell, why had he said that? He was trying to keep his personal life out of the firehouse, but these guys seemed to share everything and Beck fell into it sometimes.

The other group members shifted uncomfortably, then Gabe said, "You're divorced, aren't you?"

"Uh-huh."

"How long?" White asked.

"A year."

"Got kids?"

That did make him smile. "One boy, ten. He's a great kid." But Tommy was getting in trouble at school these days—especially since Beck had left the house.

Sydney Sands, a top-notch firefighter whose pulled-back hair and absence of makeup didn't detract from her attractiveness at all, seemed to be the most sensitive one. She said, "I think it's time to baptize Beck into the Joke Jar."

He rolled his eyes. The Joke Jar was established by the captain years ago. Each of them brought in firefighter jokes—White said they were stupid and sexist—and the group read them when they were down or bored. If you could guess who put the one read into the jar, you won a money pot. He'd heard the only time they'd *never* used it was after 9/11, when things in the fire departments around the country were pretty bleak.

Crossing to the jar, Sands picked the decorated jug up and brought it to the table. She shot a glance at Brody and he winked at her. Something else was going on here.

"We're going to skip the guessing and winning part and just read some." Her dark eyes twinkled with mischief. "For you, Beck."

He knew he was in for it now. And was glad. The guys hadn't hazed him like they usually did probies. Hell, they probably thought he was too old for that. "I can't wait."

Sands began to read:
Q: What's the national bird of Iraq?

A: DUCK!
Stupid. But cute.
Q: What's the fastest way to break up a bingo game in Baghdad?

A: You shout out, "B-52."
Now he did laugh.
Q: What's the classic Iraqi Air Force motto?

A: I came. I saw. Iran.
"Hey, they aren't bad," Beck quipped, playing along. I heard your firefighter ones are pitiful."

Several hours later, the house firefighters were no longer joking when the PA sounded at 4 a.m. Beck awoke with the others to hear, "Car accident at Pine and Browncroft. Rescue 7, Quint/Midi 7, go into service."

The five of them jumped out of bed, dressed in their uniform pants, as they wore T-shirts and shorts to bed, and hurried to the bay. When they reached the big garages, they donned their bulky turnout pants and boots, which were set up like little soldiers on the concrete floor, ready to go into action. Then they climbed onto the truck. As the rig sped to the scene, Beck's heartbeat escalated like it had before his unit stormed an enemy outpost. He took a few deep breaths to calm himself. White, next to him, looked over. "You okay, Beck?"

"Yep, just preparing for battle."

She gave him a knowing smile.

The scene when they arrived was not what he'd expected. He saw through the rig's window two people lying on the ground. Gabe jumped off the truck first and headed to Incident Command; the others demounted amidst the noise of the rigs present and the smell of exhaust. They started to pull out equipment. He'd learned fast nobody went into a fire empty-handed. Gabe spoke with the commander—not Erikson but the legendary Mitch Malvaso.

Their captain jogged back over. "An SUV was hit by a sports car. The man driving the former is sore, and his companion has a concussion, but the other driver is trapped. The Quint will get the guy out, but we have another situation. The ambulance has just the driver on scene because the other medics are at a bad fire out near the lake. One of us has to go in the ambulance, and another has to drive the midi over to the hospital. Zach, you're in the ambulance." He scanned the group. "Beck, you take the midi over to pick up Zach and help with the patient once you get there. It'll be good experience."

"Sure." He liked new experiences. They kept him on his toes. And from thinking about the bodies around him. And other bodies that he'd seen too many of.

The front end of the blue Corvette looked like an accordion; the roof had also imploded. Quint 7 guys had already set up equipment, and the Hurst tools gleamed in the light from the huge halogen lamp already in place. A generator rent the air, buzzing and teeth-rattling.

Beck felt himself tense. Loud sounds affected veterans. But he focused on Casey Malvaso, who jumped onto the hood of the car and grabbed the Jaws of Life. She was poetry in motion and cut through the metal like butter. Again, his teeth hurt at the screeching sound. Holmes, from the Quint, joined her; someone handed up a backboard. In no time, they had the collar on the victim, slid him onto a board, jumped off the car and headed toward the Midi. Beck and Zach followed them.

When the group reached the ambulance, Zach said, "Thanks, babe." Then he gave her a peck on the cheek.

The woman's slate blue eyes snapped with frustration. "How many times do I have to tell you not to do that at work?"

Before he climbed into the ambulance, Zach quipped, "God, I love to do that to her."

As Beck headed to the Midi, he just shook his head. The whole damn house was on cloud nine. And as he'd told Gabe, he was jealous of all their relationships.

• • •

WITH HER WAIST-LENGTH, black hair and sparkling dark eyes, Sophia Ramirez was one of the most beautiful women Lela had ever met. She'd had a baby girl five months ago and just this week had returned to work at Memorial part-time. Lela had missed her when she'd been on maternity leave. Lela had no siblings, but had been close to the other women in theater. Now, she had only a few friends, mostly from work, and Sophia was the one she spent the most time with.

Sophia asked, "So, did you go to the support group?"

Lela sipped her strong coffee, much needed after a night shift, which would end in an hour. "Uh-huh."

"How was it? I adore Jack Harrison, so I'd be surprised if he wasn't great with you."

"He was, but Len showed up at the Fire Academy."

Sophia's brows raised. Months ago she'd noticed Lela's bruises and wormed out of her the entire, sordid story of the effects of Len's PTSD. After Lela described his behavior the night before, Sophia sighed. "That won't make you stop going, will it?"

"No."

"Meet anyone interesting?"

Unusual green eyes came to mind. "Yeah, a former soldier turned firefighter."

"Would it be Beck?"

"Beckett Sloan, yes. How'd you know?"

"He took Tony's place on the Rescue Squad when Tony made lieutenant and went to Group 2." Now the woman's eyes danced. "Beck's a looker."

"Oh, you should talk, married to America's most beautiful man in the world."

"Did I hear my name mentioned?"

Both women glanced up to see Tony standing before them in his light blue uniform shirt. He was startlingly handsome with dark hair and eyes and a smile to die for. "Hello, *carina.*" Bending over he gave Sophia a not-so-demure full-mouthed kiss. For a moment, Lela was stunned by the notion that she hadn't been kissed like that in a long time, if ever. They seemed to absorb each other.

Straightening, he smiled at Lela. "Hi, Lela."

They made small talk, then Lela's cell rang. "Lela here."

An on-duty nurse in ER said, "Incoming, bad car accident."

"Be right there." Lela disconnected and stood. "Gotta go. Car accident. Take care." And she was off.

She made it to the ER just as two firefighters wheeled in a stretcher. One guy—Zach Malvaso—said, "Give the report, Beck."

Oh!

Beckett Sloan began without hesitation. "Vehicle accident. Victim was trapped. BP 150 over 200. Cuts and bruises, lacerations on the face. Possible head injury."

24

"Got him," Christian Singer, a calm and dependable doctor, said. He was one of her favorite coworkers. "ER 4, Lela." He looked at the firefighters. "Thanks, guys."

Lela and a second nurse pushed the gurney to ER 4, followed by the firefighters, who needed their equipment back. Once they retrieved the gurney, they left the room.

"Okay, Lela, check his vitals again." Christian's blue eyes twinkled at her. "Not that I don't trust America's Bravest."

"Yes, sir," she joked.

"Oh, Lord, can the *sir* stuff. It makes me feel old."

Christian was easy to be with, too. He was forthright, had a great sense of humor, and he was particularly sweet to her.

A half hour later, the injured man went up for surgery on his spleen. Christian accompanied him, to make sure they got the right information, and Lela made her way back to the ER. Surprisingly, she found Beckett Sloan at the desk. "Hey. You stayed?"

"Yeah, we phoned the station house. We only have a half hour left on our tour, so they said we could go to a call from here if we had to. We, um, wanted to see how the victim made out."

"CT showed no brain injury. He needs to have his spleen removed, though. He's in surgery right now." She glanced around. "Where's Zach?"

"He found somebody he knew and went to get coffee. I said I'd text him about the patient." Beck shook his head. "I swear, those Malvasos are friends with everybody in town."

She smiled. He returned it. "Where's your coffee?"

"I was hoping you'd take pity on me and get me a cup." His eyes danced a bit, and Lela was surprised at the taciturn man in good humor.

"I'd love to."

Beck pulled out his phone. "Let me text Zach first."

Nodding, she said to the desk, "I'll be in the lounge."

They headed down a corridor to the staff room. Compact and clean, the space was about twelve by twelve, painted light blue with comfortable sofas and chairs. "Black?" she asked as she went to the pot.

"Yes." Like she took hers.

They settled on adjacent couches. For the first time, she noticed he was in a navy T-shirt and bulky pants. He looked…good…though his face was somber. "Any fallout from last night?"

She shook her head. "No, Len didn't come to my house or contact me. I'm glad because when Len makes a scene, it hurts Josh, my seven-year-old."

"I have a boy who's ten." He scowled this time. "My episodes did the same thing to him."

"I'm sorry. I'm coming to see that it's hard on both sides."

He glanced at the clock. "Who watches him when you work?"

"I have a night sitter. Mrs. Campoli. She's a godsend."

"No family in town?"

"No family at all. I'm an only child. You?"

"My parents live near West Point, where my father consults. He was army, too. I don't see them much, but my brother is here." Now he smiled, and it did something to his whole visage. His eyes crinkled at the corners, their unusual green color twinkling in the overhead lights.

Her insides turned soft. "You love him."

"I do; but more so, I owe him my life. He's helped me…a lot with this…thing."

She thought of how hard it must be for such a strong, brave man to be out of control sometimes. But she said, "Family can be invaluable. I'm glad you have him."

Lazing back, he crossed a knee over his ankle, revealing rubber boots. The gear seemed dwarfed by his big frame. "So, what time do you get off?"

"Seven."

"What will you do after work?"

"Go home, get Josh on the school bus, shower and go..."

When she hesitated, he arched a brow.

"I volunteer at the Veteran's Outreach Shelter on Collins Ave. It houses thirty-eight vets."

"Do you volunteer as a nurse or regular helper?"

"Nurse. I do screenings for diabetes and blood pressure, dispense some over-the-counter medicine and treat minor cuts and bruises."

"That's a big thing to tackle with a kid and a full-time job, which apparently requires some night shifts."

She shrugged. "Yeah, but I really like being there. And I can help. There's a young man who assists me in the clinic. He's not making any progress with their counselors, but he opens up a bit to me. I worry about him."

"Any specific problems? Injuries?"

"Severe depression, which caused him to leave his home with his wife and move into the shelter."

"That's too bad."

"It gets worse. He got close to an IED in a backpack an insurgent was carrying. Nick lost his foot." She bit her lip. "And his face is badly scarred."

Contrary to moments ago, the bleakest eyes she'd ever scene stared back at her. "I hate those stories." He sighed. "Did you ever hear one of those go off?"

She nodded. "It sounds like a tornado."

"I know soldiers are injured just from the effect of the blast, even if they don't get blown apart by one." Just then

27

his cell rang. "Must be Zach." He seemed relieved to end the gloomy topic. "Sloan…okay…uh-huh." Clicking off, he stood up. "Gotta go."

She nodded. He crossed to the door but turned after he opened it. "Thanks for the coffee. And good luck today. It's great that you're helping our guys."

She said inanely, "Thanks for what you did over there, Colonel."

"Back at you. And make it Beck."

When he walked out the door, Lela stared after him. What an interesting guy. She thought of Sophia's words. *Yum-my. He's a looker.*

Well, that too, though she hardly noticed men that way anymore. But she'd noticed him.

• • •

EXHAUSTED, BECK DROVE home slowly from the station. Too bad he wouldn't sleep after the shift. That was his nemesis now. He'd read the literature—a common symptom of PTSD was insomnia. Interesting, though, he slept at the firehouse when he was on the night shift, with only occasional nightmares that made him get up at three a.m.. Something about belonging, about security, a shrink would say. Maybe he'd bring it up at the PTSD group.

As he went in through the garage of his two-story condo, set his keys precisely where they belonged in the dish he'd placed next to the phone, he noticed the blinking light on the answering machine. Crossing the small galley kitchen, he pressed the button and leaned against the countertop. "Hey, buddy, it's me." His brother Linc. "Just checking in. We miss you since you moved out. Want to get a beer tonight? Call me back."

Linc was a software engineer at a local company in Hidden Cove. He had two boys and a darling wife. When Beck had first gotten divorced from Patty, Linc had insisted Beck move in with him and his family. Having a loving family around him had been a godsend, but Beck had made sure to leave before he'd become a nuisance.

Next message: "Beck, it's Patty. Tommy got detention after school again. Think you could call him at supper time to talk about it?"

Beck swallowed hard and closed his eyes. Mostly to block out the image that ambushed him: his son cowering in the foyer closet while Beck had a flashback to Afghanistan and broke a mirror, the hall coat tree and his right hand. It was hard for him now to be around the boy. Was it because he didn't trust himself?

"End of messages."

Instead of returning the calls, Beck left the kitchen, bypassed the large living room, with nothing out of place, and took the stairs to his bedroom. He headed for the shower and yanked on the faucet as hot as he could stand it. Water always seemed to calm him, maybe because there was so little in the desert.

Afterward, he lay down naked on the lake-size bed, which you could bounce a quarter on, and stared at the ceiling fan. Sometimes, he'd give his right arm if he could fall asleep easily.

One shrink had told him, "Think of something pleasant."

Huh. What was pleasant in his life? Linc. The group at the firehouse. The people who'd risked hiring him. For some reason, his mind went to seeing Lela Allen this morning. She'd looked cute in her pink scrubs, hair coming out of a braid and a little fatigue showing in those pretty, brown eyes. He kept that image in his head and soon his eyes closed.

• • •

TWENTY-THREE-YEAR-OLD NICK DEBLASIO stared out the window of his new home, counting to one hundred. Sometimes, occupying his brain was the only thing that got him through the hour. He used to say, *One day at a time*, but the length that he could stay sane had shrunk over the six months since he'd come back from theater. Images of war had bombarded him from day one when he arrived on American soil, whether he was awake or asleep, rested or exhausted, stoned or sober. He and his buddy, Billy, who'd died in that fucking hellhole, used to get high before they went to theater, and Nick had begun smoking joints again when he first got home. He hadn't been stoned since he'd been at the Veteran's Outreach Shelter, and he wasn't sure which was worse, the hazy drug-induced state turning into the bitter disappointment of reality and even physical sickness, or facing his problems head on. In any case, he'd chosen to come to the shelter after living at his house for only a week got to be too much for him.

"Nick, hi."

For a minute, he pretended the voice came from Amy, his wife, even though he'd screamed at her the last time he saw her that *he didn't need her fucking help* and to *leave him the hell alone*. Problem was, he did need her help, and a lot of others'. Too bad he couldn't force himself to accept it.

Turning, he found one of those *others* behind him. Lela Allen, R.N. Dressed simple in blue jeans and a pretty pink top, she brought sunlight into the room with her. "How are you today?" she asked.

"'Bout the same." One promise he'd made to himself was that he'd be honest here. But not whiny.

"Bad night?"

He nodded. Little Afghan boys with missing limbs and hopeless eyes had paraded through his unconscious all night long.

"I'm sorry."

"Were you on the graveyard shift?" he asked, noticing the smudges under her eyes. "You look tired."

"Afraid so." She nodded to the clinic set up for her on her twice-a-week volunteer days. She did routine checkups, helped plan the menus in a health-conscious way, dealt with minor things like skin rashes or referred the men to doctors. And Nick's chore (all the residents had some) was to help in this clinic. He'd get things ready and stay with her throughout the morning because the staff here thought she shouldn't be alone with the men.

He didn't mind the task. He couldn't work yet because he wasn't rehabilitated and still went to physical therapy. Not that he had much of a future anyway. A gimp couldn't get a job in the blue-collar world and businesses wouldn't hire him because his face looked like it had gone through a meat grinder. Besides, the jobless rate was staggering among vets. Limping, he followed Lela into the small room and didn't look down at the prosthetic at the shin of his right foot. The sight of it disgusted him almost as much as the raw and bumpy skin, which was all the best the doctors could do after he'd been ambushed by an IED carrier.

As Lela got out supplies from a row of white cabinets near a big window, and he changed the paper on an examination bed, she talked. "We had a bad car accident victim come in last night. It turned out okay, though. The fire department medics had done a good job."

He nodded. She didn't seem to mind if he didn't talk, and her voice was soothing. He imagined she calmed a lot of injured guys over there.

"One of the firefighters was in Afghanistan."

Nick's head snapped up. "They let him work as a fire-fighter?"

"Yes. It's part of the Hire Our Heroes national push."

He glanced away. He was no hero. None of them really were.

"Ironically, I met him at a support group for PTSD suffer-ers and their families."

"You said you were gonna go to that. How was it?"

She met his gaze and wrinkled her nose. "Really hard."

Nick liked that she didn't bullshit him. "Yeah, I bet. I'm sorry you got an ex with this thing."

"I know. That means a lot to me."

Cocking his head, he took a seat on the stool. "Why, Lela?"

Her brown eyes widened. "Because you can see my side. I'm wondering why you can't see Amy's."

Again, he looked away, regretting he'd confided in this woman so much. "Oh, I see her side as much as yours. It makes me sick to my stomach to think about her living with this," he pointed to his face, "And this." He motioned to his foot.

"She wants you in her life."

He shook his head. "Tell me more about the firefighter guy. I like success stories."

Which was true. Nick enjoyed hearing about men who'd come back from war who weren't so broken like him—physi-cally and emotionally—that even all the King's men couldn't put them together again.

CHAPTER 3

"CAN WE TALK about our kids?" a firefighter asked at the third PTSD support group meeting. The guy had gone down to work at the pile after 9/11 and afterward, had horrendous flashbacks.

Jack Harrison surveyed the members, most of whom nodded. "Go ahead, Paul."

"I had an attack at home when Shelia was using the hair dryer and the smell was like burning flesh. We'd had a charred body the week before in a bad fire. I was making my kid breakfast. She freaked." He went on to explain how his daughter had been remote since then and wouldn't let him hug her.

"Anyone else deal with issues like this with their kids?"

Pretty Lela Allen, dressed in a blue-and-brown skirt, which flowed around her calves, and a brown blouse, spoke first. "I have a boy. Josh. He's seven. He's, um, one of the reasons I'm divorcing Len. In the midst of a rage, my husband knocked me across the room. Josh saw it. I made Len move out the next day."

"How's Josh now?" Harrison asked. "You've been separated more than a year, right?"

She nodded, visibly shaken by the memory. "He's remote with everybody but me. Mostly with adult men." She rolled her eyes. "Not that there's been any in my life since my separation. But he had a male teacher and we had to switch him to a woman." Her lovely, brown eyes clouded. Beck could see her reaction from across the room. "The school recommended he have a few sessions with the school counselor, but he wouldn't open up. I tried taking him to a professional therapist, but he hid under a desk the whole time." She nodded to Paul. "It breaks my heart."

Though his own heart started to beat at a clip, Beck forced himself to speak. The least he could do was match the others' honesty. "I, um, have a boy who's ten. He's got behavioral problems and is remote, too." Beck's head began to spin. "I'm not sure I can get the reason out."

Discomfort trilled around the semicircles.

Finally, someone spoke up. Lela. "What's his name?" she asked.

"Tommy."

"Maybe you can do it for Tommy."

He drew in a heavy breath. "It'll make everybody here who's got family cringe."

Another man, a father of a soldier, said, "I don't care. Insight into people who have PTSD and those who don't is one of the reasons this group is combined with sufferers and survivors. I wanna know what's going on in your head."

When more members encouraged him, Beck found the courage to open up. Hands fisted in his lap, he said, "I had a flashback two years ago. In the foyer of my house. I'm not sure what triggered it. Suddenly I was running into an enemy camp and got tackled from behind. My arms began to flail to buck him off. I was kicking. Shouting."

He could feel the weight of an insurgent on top of him, and the taste of sand, gritty in his teeth. "Turns out it was

Patty, my ex, trying to confine me. When I came to and looked around, I couldn't believe what I'd done. I'd flung my wife against the wall and sprained her shoulder. The foyer was trashed. Mirror broken, a table upturned. I'd used a coat rack to pound a hole the size of Wyoming in the wall. Worse, Tommy had been hit by debris and he'd crept into a closet to get away from it. His face was bleeding. Our relationship went downhill from there. Stopped, really, after I moved out."

When he dared look at the others, he saw revulsion on a few faces but mostly there was…familiarity. It hit him then—other people had either done these things or seen similar actions in those they loved. It seemed stupid, but that made him feel better.

Harrison spoke. "I'm sorry, Beck. It must have been a horrendous scenario. It would help if you remembered the trigger."

He shook his head.

"I wonder if we could go around and discuss what triggers our own, or our family members', attacks."

"Before we leave the subject of kids, can I ask a question to the group?" This from Lela, who'd moved to the edge of the chair.

Harrison nodded.

"How many other people have children who've been adversely affected by PTSD?"

About ten group members raised their hands. She transferred her gaze to Harrison. "Since not everyone here has kids, any chance of getting you to hold a couple of separate sessions for us that do? I know I could use some help reaching my child."

Harrison agreed readily. Would Beck have to go to these, too? He left hurriedly after the meeting, vaguely distressed.

• • •

THE NEXT AFTERNOON at three, dressed in his navy pants and light blue shirt for the night shift, Beck went to visit his son. He found him in the backyard tossing a ball up and down.

"Hey, Tommy. Want to play catch?"

His son turned. At first, a hint of joy sparked in the boy's eyes. Then as if he physically quelled it, the expression was gone. "Whatever."

Retrieving a mitt from a tub they kept outside, Beck jogged about twenty feet away. Tommy hurled the ball at him. It flew through the air, fast for a ten-year-old, and Beck jumped up to snag it. "Great throw, Tom."

The boy shrugged. Often his responses these days were gestures, grunts and occasional mumbles under his breath, which he refused to repeat. The spitting image of Beck himself, his son represented one of Beck's greatest failures.

They tossed more pitches, and Beck felt almost normal in the warm April sunlight that trickled through the trees. But after ten minutes, Tommy dropped his glove in his mother's backyard—which used to be Beck's too—and headed inside.

Beck called out, "I thought we might go for ice cream. I got another hour before work." The boy halted, then shook his head without even turning around.

Damn it! He just didn't know how to reach his son. Since the incident in the foyer, which had caused Beck to move out, the kid wouldn't relate to him or anybody, really, and had begun acting out. Maybe he'd go to this new group with Harrison and get help finding a way back to his son.

After picking up Tommy's mitt, Beck sat down on a picnic bench, closed his eyes and let the spring weather soothe him. A few minutes later, the door slammed and Patty entered the yard. She was a pretty woman with light brown hair and hazel eyes. Beck knew she had a boyfriend. He just hoped this guy deserved her.

"Didn't go so well?" she asked, setting down coffee in front of him. Gratefully, he picked it up and sipped the almost-bitter brew. They got along a lot better now that they were divorced.

"Same as last time. He'll do stuff with me but then stomps off."

"I'm sorry. He's warming up to Mick, though." The beau.

Another paradox. Beck was glad his son liked Patty's boyfriend, but that Tommy turned to another man knifed Beck in the gut. These days, it often felt the knife stayed lodged there and twisted at will. He said only, "Well, good."

Patty snorted. "You don't have to pretend it doesn't hurt. I hated when you did that when we were married."

Briefly, he squeezed her hand. Before the divorce, they hadn't touched for six months. "I know. I'm sorry."

"Did you talk to him about his incident at school the other day?" Tommy had refused to do an assignment, somebody picked on him about it and he punched the perpetrator. Just the week before, he'd stood up for a boy littler than him to these same kids, so his actions were contradictory but involved conflict, just the same.

"No. I'm sorry I was working when you had to go get him. For what it's worth, my captain said if that happens again, I should leave and he'll find coverage."

"The fire department seems pretty amenable." She sipped from her own mug. She'd gotten a few lines around her eyes that weren't there before the divorce. Constantly handling Tommy's issues wasn't easy. "Is the support group helping?"

"Yeah, we're having a few extra sessions on dealing with kids."

Facing him, he saw acceptance in her eyes — something he *really* didn't deserve. "That's great, Beck. Really."

Beck slid off the table. "I have be at work in an hour. I'll go find him to say good-bye." He studied the woman he'd fallen for all those years ago. "I don't know if I ever said this, Patty, but thanks for being so nice to me."

"I'll always have a place in my heart for you."

"Same here."

Heading into the house, he felt an overwhelming sense of loss. It increased when he found Tommy at the computer in a den Beck himself had built off the family room. There had been hope then, for them as a family. "Hey, son."

Tommy stiffened and clicked out of a site. Beck saw that he was on FacePage, a social media venue.

"Your mom let you go on that site?" Beck had heard some stories about things happening online to kids. And Tommy was only ten — and impressionable.

He swiveled around. "Fifteen minutes a day."

"Hmm. You got a page?"

"She says no. I'm too young."

At least the boy was talking. "The fire department has a page." And the women had a blog, but Tommy was too young for that. "Want me to call it up?"

"No, I can do it if I want to."

"Try it. I post sometimes."

The boy went back to mumbling. Familiar frustration coursed through Beck. "Before I go, your mom wanted me to talk to you about the trouble you had at school last week."

"Some kid said some stuff. I didn't like it."

"What?"

Again, Tommy turned his back. "I don't wanna talk about it."

Beck decided to wait until he met with Harrison again before he pushed Tommy. A longing so powerful — to hug the kid — surged through him, so he crossed to the computer. But when he tried to put his arm around the boy, Tommy squirmed away from him. Instead, Beck settled his hand on Tommy's shoulder. The smell of sweat, but also of the shampoo he remembered using when he bathed the boy, wafted up to him. "See you Thursday, son."

"Whatever."

As Beck headed out of the house and to his SUV, the heavy feeling of failure engulfed him. *Please don't let this be forever,* he prayed to a God he didn't believe in. *Please.*

• • •

NINE OF THE ten people with kids from the original group showed up at the first of three sessions on the effects of PTSD on children. Lela entered right as the session began, and the only seat open was next to Beck. She'd purposely sat away from him at the regular meetings because his proximity disturbed her for reasons she chose not to examine. He gave her a weak smile when she dropped down into the chair. Today he was dressed in khaki shorts and a green-gold shirt that made his eyes look like cat's eye marbles.

"Sorry, I'm late," she said to the group. Josh had clung to her, quietly, like he did everything these days, and begged her not to go. Mrs. Campoli had had to pry him away.

Harrison smiled. "You're not late. We were just about to start. Hi, everybody."

Nods, hellos. The members attending looked more anxious than usual. No surprise there. Lela's stomach was on rinse cycle at the thought of analyzing what happened to their kids because of PTSD.

"I'd like to begin by having you describe what's going on with your kids; what caused you to sign up for this group. Lela, you said Josh's remote. Beck, you described Tommy's behavior issues." His gaze transferred to the next person in the semicircle. "Want to go next, Mark?"

"I got a teenage girl," the burly vet said. "She's into *causes.*" His lips thinned with irritation. "She told me we had no right to be in Afghanistan. That America's a bully, pushing its views on a nation that wanted to be left alone."

"That must be tough to hear after your service." Jack's voice was sympathetic.

Two more parents cited behavior problems. Three, remoteness. One, night terrors.

One mother, a former army lieutenant, said, "My kid's eleven. He...steals. He doesn't need to. We have plenty of material things and he gets an allowance. No one can figure out how to stop it."

After the survey of the room was completed, Harrison's face grew grave. "I'm going to say something, but before I do, I want you to know that this isn't a statement of blame. I'd like to see a nod from everyone that you'll try to view what I have to say without judging."

Nods all around. Next to her, Lela felt Beck's body stiffen. She had the urge to touch his arm in comfort but refrained.

Harrison continued. "There's some research that says when a parent has PTSD, a child sometimes *gets* it. By that, I mean he or she will exhibit the same symptoms as the parent."

Lela gasped and all eyes turn to her. "Oh, God, no. This is my fault for living with Len so long?"

"Lela, I said, no blame." Jack's voice was stern.

Still, her eyes welled and she looked down. She couldn't dam up the overwhelming feeling of responsibility that swamped her. She felt something — Beck's arm — circle around her. She didn't realize she was crying until he tugged her to him; clutching his shirt, she sobbed into it. Her boy had gotten PTSD — or at least exhibited some of the symptoms — from Len because Lela had stayed with him long after she knew he wasn't well.

A while later, she calmed and drew away from Beck.

"Feel better?" he asked softly.

She nodded. Embarrassed, she glanced around and saw everyone watching her.

"I wish I could cry like that," one of the former soldiers admitted. "I got a lot to bawl about, too."

His comment made it easier on Lela for not being able to control herself.

Harrison ran a hand through his hair. "All right, so much for my warning. Let's tackle the topic of guilt first."

• • •

WHEN THE MEETING broke up, Beck was waylaid by the firefighter, Paul. "Hey, Beck, just wanted to say hi. You leave the main group sessions as soon as they're over."

He gave the man a weak smile. "Yeah, I'm bummed after them. You?"

Nodding, the guy shoved his hands in his jeans pockets. "I hate this. I've always been the strong one. Now I feel like a wounded puppy."

"This condition levels us. I hate it's got that power."

From the corner of his eye, Beck saw Jack Harrison had pulled Lela aside. Man, when she'd started crying, it had called forth every protective instinct he possessed. He'd put an arm around her in a reflex action he couldn't say he regretted. She felt warm and womanly. Her hair smelled like lilacs.

Beck let Paul talk, listened and kept an eye on her. When Paul noticed, he said, "You two friends?"

"Um, no. I met her in the group."

"Huh. She sure is pretty."

Beck had noticed the tan jeans that fit her well and a loose, striped top that highlighted her coloring. "Yes, she is." When she finished talking with Jack, he said to Paul, "Let's get together for a beer sometime. I want to talk to Lela before she leaves."

She didn't leave. Instead, she approached him with a smile and he introduced her to Paul.

"Can I talk to you a minute?" she asked Beck.

When he studied her closely and saw her red eyes, his gut clenched. "Sure. Call me about the beer, Paul." He drew her away. "You okay?"

"Yeah. Sorry I blubbered all over you." She bit her lip, and the small show of vulnerability did something to his insides.

His smile was genuine. "I've been blubbered over before."

"Well, I don't blubber over anything. Never did. A nurse, an army medic has to be tough."

Somebody bumped into her and sloshed the water she held. Little droplets splattered on his shirt. He glanced around. "Listen, would you like to go get coffee with me?"

Her eyes widened. Then she glanced at her watch. "I've got another ninety minutes with the babysitter. I was planning to go grocery shopping."

Wondering why he'd made the offer, he just stared at her.

"Sure," Lela finally said, "My treat, though. For blubbering."

They arrived at the same time at a coffee shop down the road from the academy. When he gave her his order—decaf because of his sleep problems—he snagged a table and sat facing the door. Idly, he wondered if he'd get over the need to be ever-vigilant?

"Here you go." She sat. In this light, the wine color of her shirt highlighted the red of her hair. Deep red. Auburn, he thought somebody had called it once.

"That was quite a session, wasn't it?" she asked.

"Yeah. It kills me to hear my kid is reacting to me being sick."

"I like that you say that out loud. Len would never even admit there was something wrong. I stayed with him too long, living in denial."

Reaching across the table, he squeezed her hand. "I understand. I feel horrible that I, you know, sort of gave this to Tommy, too." He shook his head, seeing the perpetually glum face of his boy. "It's so ironic. In trying to protect my kid, I did more damage. I should have left earlier, too." He trailed off.

"We make a pair."

Leaning back in the chair, he crossed a leg over his knee. "Tell me something good about Len. I only hear the bad stuff from everybody in the group about guys like me."

She sipped her coffee, thinking. "We met in the army. I was a medic and he was a supply officer for our outpost. We were together after only a few weeks. Things happen fast over there."

"Yeah, I know."

"After about a month, he remarked that he'd never seen me in anything but army green and combat boots. When I told the other women that, they put together an outfit."

She smiled, and for some God forsaken reason, Beck was jealous of Len Allen. "It was a simple, flowing, white skirt and dark top, which was" — here she blushed — "a little tight. They did my hair, scrounged for makeup, put ballet slippers on my feet. Len's mouth fell open when he saw me." As if from far away, she said, "That was the first night we slept together."

"Lucky Len."

She sighed. "Tell me something nice about…Patty, is it?"

"Yeah. She was a saint when I got back. I couldn't sleep — still have that problem — and she stayed up with me, held me after I woke her up with my nightmares. She listened, understood."

"What happened?"

"She got tired of me not getting any better. She met someone at work, didn't cheat but told me about him and said she wanted a separation. I agreed because she'd put up with enough crap from me."

"I'm sorry you lost her."

"Yeah, me too."

"Beck, has Len ever contacted you? I know you gave him your card."

"No."

"I'm not surprised. The first step to recovery is admitting you have a problem. I really admire you for seeking help."

"Don't admire me too much. I was required to come by the fire department." Though he had gotten counseling in the past.

"No, you're involved. Even when you don't say anything, I can tell how absorbed you are."

So she'd been noticing him. At least he wasn't the only one…interested. "Thanks."

She glanced at the clock. "Wow. I have to go already. Time flew by."

"I'll walk you to your car."

"I'm an army medic, Beck. Despite my meltdown tonight, I'm made of stern stuff."

"I can tell."

Still, he walked with her to her car. The April night had turned cool and she tugged the sweater she'd put on before she'd left tighter around her. The action accented her full breasts, and for the first time in months, Beck felt his body stir. Jesus, he'd been lamenting the loss of his libido, and now he got juiced up by...the wife of a PTSD sufferer who just moments ago admitted she shouldn't have let her kid live with a man with the condition. What an idiot Beck was!

He tried to control his reaction to her when they reached her car, a sensible Civic hatchback. "Thanks for inviting me out, Beck. It was fun."

Her admission didn't help his *circumstances*.

"And thanks for sharing good memories with me."

"We remember too much of the bad." He shook his head self-effacingly. "Said the guy with PTSD."

The quip made her laugh.

Then she shocked him by standing on her tiptoes and kissing him on the cheek. "You're a good guy, Beckett Sloan. Try to remember that."

He said good-night and watched the car pull out of the parking lot. As he walked to his own vehicle, he was startled—and dismayed—by how much he wanted to respond to the friendly kiss, maybe grasp her to him, bury his face in that lilac-smelling hair and forget all about reality. Jesus. This had to happen with a woman in her circumstances? He'd ignore it, of course, even though he knew the situation was going to come back to bite him in the ass.

CHAPTER 4

BECAUSE BECK RARELY felt safe anymore—another after-effect of the war—he didn't put himself in unfamiliar social situations. But when Ryan O'Malley, Brody's twin, got promoted to lieutenant in the police department, Felicia had made a point of inviting Beck to join them at Badges, the local firefighter and police hangout, to celebrate. Beck had declined, but Felicia had badgered him into coming. So now he sat with a dozen people at a table in a small backroom that was paneled in cedar and sporting big windows on three sides. Firefighter and police memorabilia covered the walls, which Beck got a kick out of.

"So, O'Malley, you gonna stop wearing the uniform now?" The question came from Gabe as he lounged in his chair, his arm circling his stunning wife—whose rounded belly indicated she was about midway through her pregnancy. Every once in a while, Rachel Wellington Malvaso would lay her head on his shoulder in a tender gesture.

"I'll have to, for the most part." Reaching out, Ryan put his hand on Felicia's knee. Beck still had trouble seeing her so *girly* with her brown hair down and sporting a pretty, light purple blouse. Ryan grinned. "Though Licia said she wants to use it to play dress up in the bedroom."

"In your dreams, pal." Felicia made the quip, but her expression was so loving it took any sting out of her words. Beck had to quell a spurt of longing as he scanned the room of happy couples.

Dressed in a short, gray skirt, which showed off legs Beck didn't know could be so long, Sydney started teasing Brody about being a staid homeowner. Beck tried to relax and enjoy the banter. Gabe interrupted it by saying, "Ah, there he is. I was hoping you'd make it, *hombre*."

Beck craned his neck as Tony Ramirez entered the room, his wife behind him. *"Hola, todos ustedes,"* Tony said with a smile.

Beck was thinking about how the group referred to them as the Beautiful People, when Sophia dragged someone else out from behind her.

Ah! The woman who'd been occupying some of Beck's thoughts—and a couple of X-rated dreams—stood with her friends. He'd never seen her in a dress before, and this one was clingy and looked soft to the touch. It spiked his blood pressure. He'd had contact with her at least twice a week at the support group and a couple more times during a run to the hospital. But he'd never seen her in such feminine clothes. He was reminded of the story she'd told him about her husband having seen her only in army wear.

"Hi, guys," Sophia said cheerfully. "I talked my friend, Lela, into coming with me."

Greats and *more-the-merriers* abounded. Felicia's brother, who'd flown in from Colorado to share in his in-law's success, stood. "Over here Lela. Take my chair. I'll get another."

Nodding, she crossed to the man. The *attractive* man, who put his hand on the small of her back to help seat her. Lela scanned the table, said hellos, and when her gaze landed on

Beck, gave him a big, bright smile that might be able to eclipse the sun. It hit him square in the gut. "Hi, Beck. I was hoping you'd be here."

"Yeah?"

"You said you don't get out much." Her eyes were alight. "Me, either, which is why I let Sophia talk me into tagging along. I had a free night because Josh is with his grandparents'."

Garth White pulled up a chair, way too close to Lela. "So, pretty lady, what do you do?"

"I'm a nurse."

Felicia added, "She was an army medic, too, so she's used to fending off characters like you, buddy."

"I do not need fending off." He leaned in closer. "Yet."

Lela laughed as the waitress approached and she gave an order for straight-up, double malt scotch. Beck's brows raised and she caught his reaction. "Well, you didn't expect an army gal to drink something with a little umbrella in it, did you?"

"No, ma'am. Though I bet you had some of those mint-julep things down south."

She wrinkled her nose. "Too sweet."

"You from the south?" Garth asked. "Say something so I can hear the accent."

"I've lost most of it, but here goes. Y'all better watch yourself, or my daddy's gonna be on you like fleas on a dog." She'd dragged out some of the vowels.

Everyone laughed.

Beck sipped his own drink—a tart Manhattan—and watched the night unfold. It wasn't long before Chief Erikson arrived with a stunning dark-haired woman on his arm, who everyone addressed as Parker. So this was the famous journalist/blogger who'd sparred with the chief over fire-department matters, then unexpectedly fell in love with him. Beck hoped it worked out for them, but he didn't believe much in happily-ever-after. Again, his gaze strayed to Nurse Allen.

• • •

LELA TOOK SURREPTITIOUS glances at Beck—he'd changed into jeans and a gauzy, white shirt—as they ate some of the best pizza she'd ever had. Afterward, the group drifted out to the main bar area to dance and socialize with some of the cops who'd shown up. She'd thought about Beck over the two-and-a-half weeks since they'd met. Now she had the absurd urge to ask him to dance, but before she could follow it or quell it, Garth White dragged her out to the floor. The jukebox played a slow song, and Garth was a good dancer, so Lela enjoyed the twirl around the room. After they finished, Felicia rose and drew Beck up by the arm. "Time to dance, army boy."

"Uh, no, not me. I'm not the dancing type."

"Tough. You gotta learn to have fun, Beck."

When she had him standing, Felicia turned as her brother and Lela came off the floor. Garth said, "Hey, this is a swing dance. I was gonna ask you to do it with me, sis."

"Good news for me." Beck's tone was teasing.

"No way!" Felicia looked at Lela, who hadn't sat yet, and put her hand in Beck's. "You two dance."

The other couple left and Lela turned to Beck. "You don't have to do that. She pressed you into dancing with me."

"Nah, I want to. Let's see what we can do together."

First, he pulled her to him and held her close. They kept time to the music and he smiled down at her. Then, he twirled her out, and she came back easily. For such a big guy, he was light on his feet, fluid in his own moves as he repeated the steps and did variations on them. After the peppy song ended, a slow one began, and he watched Lela for a moment, then drew her into his arms.

"That was fun," he said as his cheek nestled next to her hair. She was distracted by the scent of him—woodsy with a hint of citrus. Acutely aware of his hand at her back, his other clasping her fingers to his chest, she had to resist the urge to lean into him and inhale the masculine scent. Instead, she looked up at him. From this angle, his chin was so chiseled she wondered why she'd never noticed it before.

"Wasn't it?" he asked.

"Excuse me?"

"The swing dance. Wasn't it fun?"

"You know, it was. I'm surprised I remembered how to do it. I rarely get out."

"Me, either, unless Linc and Sally drag me somewhere."

"Your brother?"

"Yep."

"You're lucky you have a sibling."

He nodded to Sophia, who was on the floor cuddling up to Tony like a teenager. "You and Tony's wife seem close."

"We are. She's been a friend for a few years, now."

"You said you had a night off."

"Tommy's staying with his grandparents and his dad. Going home to an empty house didn't appeal to me."

He tugged her a bit closer. "I feel that way a lot."

They talked a bit about where they each lived, how they liked the town. Beck had grown up here but left after high school for West Point. When they quieted, she gradually nestled into his granite-hard chest, listened to the Righteous Brothers and let herself enjoy the feel of him.

The unfamiliar sensation of being in a man's arms, held with tenderness and…a hint of desire.

When she realized what she was doing, she sobered. Oh, God, she was snuggling up to a man with PTSD! How dumb was that, especially since she'd learned about the effect the malady can have on children? No, she told herself, this was not going to happen.

As soon as the song ended, she drew away. "I, um, Beck, I think we'd better…" But he wasn't watching her.

Her words trailed off as she tracked his distracted gaze. Over her shoulder, she saw Gabe Malvaso stride toward them and the rest of his crew. "We gotta go, guys. There's a bad fire in a warehouse over on James Street. All available fire personnel are called in."

Lela wondered at the worry in his voice. The way the others stiffened. To Beck, he said, "We're gonna be on edge, Beck. Thirteen years ago, my cousins were practically buried in a warehouse fire when the ceiling fell. Nobody's forgotten it. So be on your toes."

"Yes, sir." He stepped away from Lela.

When both men started to walk away, Lela reached out and grasped on to his arm. Her earlier misgivings were muted by the danger he would soon be in. "Beck?"

"Yeah?"

"Be careful."

He gave her a somber look. "I always am."

She watched his retreating back with confusion. Her heart was racing and her pulse thrummed. Damn, she was worried about the guy.

• • •

BECK JUMPED OUT of the Rescue rig. Red-hot flames licked the roof and shot out from the tall windows of the warehouse; the air stunk like cow shit because of the angry, black clouds billowing from the building. Beck waited at the rigs and became aware of a conversation close by. Casey and Zach Malvaso were off to the side of the Midi, arguing, while the officers were determining their best use of firefighters called in.

"It's just like the last time." Zach's voice was tense.

"No, it's not." Casey sounded exasperated.

"Yeah, it is. I don't want you going in there."

Silence. Then, "Honey, it's my job and yours. Comparing this call to the Sinco fire is counterproductive."

Beck recalled Gabe's explanation earlier; the Malvasos had been buried by falling plaster and almost didn't get out, but they'd lost fellow firefighters.

"No, it's—"

"All right, everybody. Listen up."

Beck glanced over to see Gabe, with Captain Holmes of Quint and Midi, and Tony Ramirez lined up in front of the Rescue Rig. All three crews gathered around them.

The officers snapped out orders.

"Quint 7 is to slap water on the left quadrant of the building." This from Holmes.

Five people jumped on the Quint, and the vehicle headed to the back of the warehouse.

"Conklin and Thomas, you're coming with me." Though he was a new lieutenant, Tony Ramirez sound confident and in control. "We're going to assist with the Hurst tools. Some of the doors are jammed and there's reports of people inside."

Gabe gave the last directive. "We're on search and rescue for victims. We have the rear right-side entrance after Ramirez springs the door."

Adrenaline shot through Beck. His heart beat fast as they donned their SCBA, remounted the truck and circled around the structure. After Tony sprang the door, they walked inside, and thick, gray smoke closed around them.

"Jesus, how we going to search for anybody?" Felicia asked. "The smoke's almost opaque in here and the place is a cavern."

"With this." Beck could just make out a camera-like device, a thermal heat indicator, which Gabe held up.

They didn't always use thermal imaging, because it was cumbersome and because each station didn't have one, but they needed help tonight. Beck had used similar devices in Afghanistan for night missions because, if there wasn't a moon, you couldn't see your hand in front of your face. A term he'd heard ascribed to firefighting.

Gabe continued, "White, you hold this. I'll lead the way and you direct me."

The smoke turned to black as they plodded through the space—an indication that whatever was burning was noxious. Could be asbestos in the ceiling. The building was old. Beck kept his head up and his ears alert. They'd gone only ten meters when they heard a loud crack, then an ominous rumbling sound. Suddenly, he was engulfed by something hot and heavy. The last thing he heard over the mic was, "Jesus, it *is* just like before."

• • •

SOPHIA HAD PLUNKED down in a chair and wrung her hands together. "Could you stay with me, Lee? Everybody else will be here, but I'd feel better if you would."

"Of course." She took a seat next to Sophia. "Josh is with Len's parents for the night."

"My kids are with Mama." Sophia's beautiful face was pale and her eyes shadowed. "She took them to visit her sister in Camden Cove so they probably won't see this in the news."

All those left behind had returned to the backroom, where a local channel on the big-screen TV blared the coverage of the fire; Lela glanced around. Ryan O'Malley, who'd been joking with Felicia earlier, stood somberly in the back, leaning against the wall, his arms crossed over his chest. After refusing to go home, Rachel Wellington sat in the same chair she'd vacated earlier, staring at the screen, one hand on her belly. Lela and Sophia were only a couple seats away from Rachel, and the tension radiating from both women was palpable.

On TV, an anchor asked a grim-faced officer who'd just come on screen, "Captain Carlyle, can you tell us the status of the building?"

"We don't have any reports from inside yet. All the teams received their assignments and are implementing them."

From the corner of her eye, Lela saw a dark-haired, tall man stride into the room. O'Malley called out, "Hey, Max."

"Rye." He glanced at the screen as he crossed to Ryan. "Thanks for calling me. Any news?"

"They just went inside." Though Ryan's lips were thinned and his voice gravelly, he added, "I called you because I didn't want to be the only guy crying here."

Max clapped him on the back. "I hear ya, buddy." He shook his head as he watched the captain on TV tell the public absolutely nothing. "Fuck, I hate that Sydney does this for a living. Sometimes I have nightmares about 9/11."

"We all do." This from Rachel.

"Whatdaya mean, Wellington? You put yourself in harm's way, too."

"So do you, O'Malley. Put your life on the line. Doesn't mean spouses have to like it."

Quiet descended after a commercial break. The formerly poised announcer seemed rattled as he stared down at a paper and cleared his throat. "It appears the ceiling collapsed in the right side of the warehouse. Fears are that a group of firefighters conducting search and rescue are trapped."

Everybody gasped.

"What?" Lela asked.

Rachel got out, "Search and rescue is done by the rescue squads."

She thought of Beck, going into the fire, filled with stoicism and determination. The notion struck her out of nowhere: what would it be like to never see those beautiful green eyes, hear that low baritone, experience that kind smile again? She couldn't understand the fear because she'd only known him two-and-a-half weeks, but it was there, strong and potent.

The vigil they kept was excruciating. No official word came from the department on who was trapped. "Would they call, Sophia, if they could?" Lela finally asked.

"Not necessarily. They might be fine and just crawling through the smoke."

"Geez." The rescue sounded horrible. It had to stink to high heaven, though they wouldn't choke on the smoke because of their face masks. But Lela had read somewhere that sometimes the masks were knocked off in a fire. How long could they live in a smoke-filled room with the blaze sucking up all the oxygen? As a nurse, she knew it wasn't long and people succumbed to smoke inhalation fast.

Another ten minutes passed, then the reporter put his hand to his earpiece. "I have some news." He'd gained his composure back. "Five firefighters are trapped under ceiling plaster in the right side of the building. I repeat, five firefighters are trapped. Other crews have been sent in to assist them."

Lela was startled by a sharp noise. She turned to see Ryan O'Malley had punched his fist into the wall. She didn't blame him. His wife and the squad who'd gathered here tonight, eating, drinking, dancing might never get out of that building. Lela found it hard to swallow. Oh, dear God!

• • •

WHEN HE CAME to, Beck thought an IED had gone off in the school they'd been sent to protect in Kandahar, then he realized he was in a warehouse full of smoke. And he was covered with a chalky substance that tasted like plaster. Tasted? Jesus, he'd lost his helmet and face mask. A ragged bout of coughing ensued. And a stink as bad as the open sewage in Afghanistan filled his head. He moved his legs and pain shot through his body. Hell, was he hurt? If so, he wouldn't get out of here. Gingerly, he sat up. He was covered with layers of plaster and sheetrock; he tore at the pieces and shook some of it off. He still couldn't see and his eyes stung like hell. The relentless hacking continued. Fuck!

Feel your way when you can't see, his instructors had told him. Scrambling to his knees, he blindly brushed his thick-gloved hand side to side in front of him as he inched forward. Only a few meters away, he felt a pile. But how did he know if a person was buried under there?

Amidst the violent coughing, he wondered if should try to find his way out.

Don't forget, Beck, this isn't the army. You have to protect yourself first or you won't be any good to anybody. If it's between you and victim, choose yourself.

The hell with that. He didn't leave men behind. He came upon a rounded lump and began digging down into the mass. He closed his eyes to keep the smoke out and went by feel. He found an arm. It could very well belong to one of his crew. He dug like a beaver until he had the body uncovered. There was still a mask on him.

Share your air with your buddy or your victim.

Still not knowing who this was, he took the nozzle off and gulped in some air. There, now he could breathe. Settling it on the face of the downed firefighter again, Beck stood. Bending over, he secured the person under the arms and began to drag him. It wasn't a woman. The body was too heavy. Son of a fucking bitch, he thought as he backed up blindly; he had no idea which way was out.

• • •

LELA DRANK SO much coffee she knew she'd never sleep. It didn't matter, she wasn't leaving Badges, leaving these people alone with their terror, until news came of who was hurt and who wasn't. She forced herself to believe they'd all get out, just as she'd been determined to save every man who'd come to the makeshift hospital on the outpost, though she'd known it wasn't possible. Was this?

Again, images of Beck as he'd talked about his son came to her. Would that boy grow up without a father? Had Beck survived tours of the Middle East and Asia for years only to be felled by some stupid warehouse fire?

From the televised scene, a horn blasted the air. An over-voice narrated. "That's the evacuation call for the fire-fighters to leave the buildings. Still no word on injuries or casualties."

Immediately, three phones rang. She noticed Garth White, who'd flirted with her earlier, and who'd sat away from the group and stared morbidly at the TV, get up and stride to Ryan O'Malley. They all answered in unison.

"Hello."

"O'Malley here."

"This is Sophia."

"Sydney?"

Everybody else in the room held their collective breath.

"Hallelujah!" This from Ryan who jumped up from where he'd finally taken a seat. "My brother and my darling wife are okay."

Rachel yelled, "Gabe got buried under plaster. Beck pulled him to safety."

Lela blurted out, "Beck's okay?"

"Yeah," Rachel said, her eyes shining. "They all have a bad case of smoke inhalation, but they're gonna be fine."

Lela turned to Sophia. Her friend was quietly crying. Lela grasped her hand. "Soph? Is it Tony?"

"H-He's safe. I'm just relieved."

"They want us to wait here," Rachel said. They're going to swing by on their way to the hospital. Against orders."

Max and Ryan sprawled out in chairs, their bodies drained from hours of tension. "How do we do it?" Max asked.

"We have to," Ryan retorted.

Not Lela, though. She didn't have to keep this kind of vigil ever again. Nor did she want to. The immediacy of the rescue, the closeness of the scene was so much different than having a husband in war thousands of miles away, Lela was shaken by it.

She waited until the room settled down, then stood. "I'm going home, Sophia. You'll be fine now that Tony's on his way."

"Oh, don't you want to wait and see them?"

"No. This is an intimate gathering. I don't belong here. I'll see you later." Without saying good-bye to the others, she slipped out of the room. Noticing a side-door entrance to Badges, she swung it open, awash with conflicting emotions and needing to flee. There would be joy and celebration, she knew, but she couldn't be part of it. For one simple reason.

She'd worried too much about Beckett Sloan tonight.

As soon as she stepped out the door, the cool night air calmed her. Until she saw the big, red truck, blaring its horn, screech to a halt about twenty feet away from her.

She was caught.

• • •

MOVING SLOWLY, FOUR firefighters from the Rescue Squad dismounted the rig and traipsed into Badges. Beck stayed behind for a shitload of reasons. He jumped off the far side of the truck and circled around the back, dropped down on the fender and wished like hell for a cigarette. He knew firefighters smoked, and he'd inhaled his share of that or chewed tobacco in theater, but he didn't need another bad habit. Instead, he sucked down some water. His throat still burned, and his eyes stung, but he was really happy for the first time, in…he couldn't remember when. They'd all gotten out alive—and he'd been an integral part of the rescue.

Taking his cell from his pants—they'd removed their smelly turnout gear—he punched in the familiar numbers. First he tried Patty, but she didn't answer so he left a message that he was safe. The next call was answered on the first ring. "Beck?"

"I'm all right. I thought maybe you'd be asleep and I could leave you a message. Did you see the coverage?" Beck hoped not. His brother had worried enough when Beck was overseas.

"Of course I'm not asleep. Was it you? Were you buried?"

"We got some plaster on us. But, Linc, I saved somebody."

"Wait a sec on that. So you're not hurt?"

"No, but we gotta go get checked out at the hospital."

"I'll meet you there."

"You will not. I just wanted you to know I'm safe."

An audible sigh on the other end. "Okay. Tell me about the heroics now."

"I dragged my captain out."

He told his brother the story. When Gabe had regained consciousness outside the building, he was remarkably unhurt. And he'd been the only one buried. The others had been knocked out temporarily, which was why they were *supposed* to go directly to the hospital, but this little detour had to take place first.

"No, shit," Linc commented, amused. "They stopped to see their women?"

"Yeah. And their men. We got two female firefighters on our crew."

Once again, Beck was jealous as hell. He had no one waiting for him. And if he could have his choice of who to hug him, who to say *Thank God, you're okay*, he knew who it would be.

"Look, I gotta hang up. Go to bed."

"I will. But you come over tomorrow for dinner."

"All right." Linc had done this before, needed his brother's presence to assure himself Beck was all right.

Finally they disconnected. But Beck couldn't get rid of the images of Lela as easy as he got rid of Linc. The memory of her dancing in his arms came to him, and he could practically feel her curves against his body, smell the flowery scent of all that hair. She'd have gone home by now. Didn't matter anyway! He had no business thinking of her that way. She was divorcing a PTSD sufferer, and Beck would never inflict himself on anybody who'd gone through what she had. So he was confused by the intensity of these feelings.

Maybe they'd just spent time together in a highly emotional setting — like brothers banding in war.

Yeah, sure, Sloan, this is anything but sibling-like. Maybe he'd talk to Linc about it.

"Beck?"

Christ Jesus, he'd conjured her. But no, she was at the edge of the truck, standing there in that touch-me green dress, haloed by the light from the lampposts. He said, "Hey, what are you still doing here?" Hopefully, she'd think the rawness in his voice was from the smoke he'd inhaled.

She moved closer. "What are *you* doing out here?"

"Didn't want to see all those saps getting TLC from their significant others." He rolled his eyes. "It's embarrassing."

"I think it's nice." She came to stand close, in front of him. He wished she hadn't. Her eyes were wide and liquid, and the expression in them was so totally wrong for them both.

He shrugged. "So do I, really."

She watched him for a moment. "Stand up, Beck."

"Excuse me?"

"I said stand up, soldier."

"Yes, ma'am." He rose, curious to see what she'd do.

Reaching up, she stood on her tiptoes and encircled his neck with her arms. It took only a second before he moved in and drew her to him. Every single curve, ever single indentation of this lovely woman melded into him, even more than on the dance floor. She sighed and buried her face in his chest.

He pulled her even closer. For a few precious moments, she stayed there.

When she stepped back a bit so she could look at him — but not leave the embrace — she whispered, "I think you deserve some TLC, too."

"That's all this is, Lee?"

She stared into his eyes for a long time. Her face was shadowed by the night. "No, Beck, it's not. Which is why I shouldn't have done it."

The air was charged with her admission. "Why did you?"

"Because I wanted to, very badly."

"Lela, I—"

Her hand went to his lips to stop the dangerous admission. Her fingertips were soft and feminine. "No, don't say anything. Don't voice this, don't make it real. We both know it can't go anywhere."

He knew what she meant, and though it was a like a knife in the gut, he nodded.

"Just hold me for a minute."

When she went back into his arms, he held her next to his heart, which soon began to beat in unison with hers. If this was all he was going to have of her, he vowed to cherish it.

• • •

THE VIDEO GAME was giving Len a headache. Josh was enjoying it, though, so he kept at it as long as he could. Why the fuck did they make these things so loud? Of course, he let his kid win. Besides, his hands were shaking, and the screen went blurry sometimes.

When this game ended, Josh glanced over at him. "Dad, you okay?"

"Yeah, sure, why?"

"You seem funny."

"Nah. Wanna play again?"

"No."

Hell, what did the kid expect of him?

"You two okay in here?" His mother, the sainted Martha, poked her head in. She was a good woman and he wished he wasn't so mad at her and his father all the time because Lela said that they had to watch him with his kid.

"Yeah, Grandma."

When Len didn't answer, she stepped into the room. Walked over to them. "Son, you all right?"

"Goddamn it, Ma."

Martha straightened. "Josh, want to go make cookies?"

"Is that okay, Dad?"

"Sure. I'm gonna lay down some."

His mother reached out and touched his hair. He yanked his head away. "I'm outta here," he snapped, stood and made his way upstairs by holding on to the railing. When he reached his room, he fell into bed. The liquor he'd consumed before the kid had gotten here made his eyes close. But before he zonked, he heard, *Even your own mother doesn't trust you. Takes the kid away for his safety. He's too good for you. They're all too good for you. You're nothing after what you did over there!*

CHAPTER 5

JOSH LOOKED LIKE his dad, with blond hair and blue eyes, which were often so wary, it broke Lela's heart. Today, though, those eyes sparkled with excitement as they strolled through the Seneca Park Zoo hand in hand.

"Are you anxious to see the polar bears?" she asked her son.

"Yeah, they just came to the zoo."

"I know, sweetie."

Lela smiled as she raised her face to the sun and let it warm her. Mid-April was a bit chilly, but the snow had melted and a few daffodils and crocuses poked up through little patches of grass. She promised herself to enjoy spring this year, hopefully with less upheaval in their lives.

As they trekked down the paved path to the bears, she asked casually, "Did you have fun with Grandma and Grandpa yesterday?" She tried not to grill Josh about the visits, but him being around his father worried her.

"Uh-huh."

"What did you do?"

"Helped turn up the garden. Grandpa didn't care how dirty I got."

"Grandpa's cool. Was your dad with you?"

Josh shook his head. After a moment, he added, "He bought me a new game for my Xbox. We played for a little while."

Did he drink while they were together? She dared not ask.

"He had to go to bed after. He was tired. Grandma and me made cookies."

So Len did drink. Damn it! And she'd warned him about video games — they tended to be so violent.

"Hey, there they are. Aw, Mom, look they're sleeping together."

It was a beautiful sight, the two bulky animals, one spread out on its side, the other draped over it in a mound of white fur. Lela forced herself to banish thoughts of Len, who was unable to stay away from the booze even when his child was visiting. Thank God for the Allens, or Josh would never see his dad.

Though most times she wondered if that would be so bad.

• • •

BECK SAT IN the firehouse kitchen, reading *The Heart of Hidden Cove*, a paper produced by Sands' husband, surrounded by the pleasant scent of her bacon-and-eggs breakfast, when the doorbell rang. O'Malley went to see who'd arrived.

Soon, he heard behind him, "Colonel?" An address rarely directed at him these days. He turned and found Len Allen with Brody.

"This guy said you told him he could contact you any-time," his colleague stated. When Beck didn't respond, because he was surprised, Brody asked, "This cool, Beck?"

"Sure."

Brody left them alone. Beck stood. "Hi, Len."

"Hope this is okay." The man waved a hand around. His eyes were more bloodshot than white, and when Beck took a step closer, he inhaled that stale scent of beer and cigarettes.

"Rough night?"

"'Fraid so. 'S why I came."

"Let's sit outside." Where they'd have privacy and he could be upwind of the guy.

They left by way of the back door and walked into the crisp, clean, fresh outdoors. Still able to recall the heavy parched air in Afghanistan, Beck always appreciated the weather in New York State. "Sit."

They took places at a picnic table, on opposite sides, facing each other. In the clear light of day, Allen looked even worse. The dark circles under his eyes and the lines around his mouth made him seem old and worn. "Talk to me, soldier."

"I…" The guy scanned the area and shook his head. "I had Josh yesterday."

I know. Beck had been trying not to think about this man's wife. "How'd it go?"

"Good. For a while."

"Did you drink after he left?"

"No, while he was there. I passed out on the bed upstairs. I told the kid I had to lay down and never made it back." Even the tone of his voice was disgusted. Beck sensed this man did not like what he'd turned into. A spurt of anger for all vets who went to war and came back half the men they had been shot through him.

Bracing his arms on the table, he captured Allen's gaze. "You need help, Staff Sergeant."

"I tried to come to the Trauma Survivor's Group." Now his tone was whiny, which didn't bode well.

"Harrison told you that wasn't possible. He wanted to meet with you privately. Did you call him?"

Len shook his head.

"Not good. It's almost impossible to manage this thing alone."

Frowning, Allen's eyes narrowed. "You *had* to go to the group. I heard that."

"I got help before I became a firefighter, too. Look, Len, you can learn to live with the condition. You can have a good life if you take the proper steps to set it up right." The statement made Beck a hypocrite—his life wasn't good—but he believed it was possible.

"Lela's divorcing me."

"She has a right, if you were anything like I was. My wife divorced me." Though he hadn't objected. He'd been afraid of what he'd do to her and Tommy.

"No!" The guy pounded his fist on the table. "I won't accept her leaving me."

Beck realized the flare of temper he'd just seen was what had caused Lela to demand supervised visits. That and his drinking. Smart woman.

Since he sensed this conversation was going nowhere, Beck fished his cell phone out of his pocket. "Why don't you call Harrison now? Set up an appointment."

"I dunno his number."

Beck clicked into his address book, pulled up the psychologist's number and held out the cell. "There, take the phone and press send."

Allen stared at the instrument as if it was a snake ready to strike. "No." He stood, said, "Sorry to bother you," and walked out of the back area to the parking lot.

Beck watched him leave. This was not good. Sure, a lot of soldiers took a long time to get help. But Len Allen's decision affected Lela and her son's lives, so Beck didn't feel comfortable giving the guy space. He also had a deep concern for his fellow soldier who was on the skids big-time.

The door to the firehouse opened and Gabe Malvaso sauntered out. They were all a little sore from the warehouse cave-in and had taken yesterday off, but mostly they were good to go.

Gabe socked him in the arm. "How's my hero?"

"Hardly. And I been meaning to tell you, you should lose a few pounds. You were damned hard to drag out."

Gabe gave a hearty laugh. "Okay, I'll back off. Rachel probably won't, though. She thinks you walk on water now."

"Hence the goodies I get every day!"

"She bakes. Especially now that she's off the line." He rolled his eyes. "She's got three more months to go, so we'll both keep gaining weight, I guess."

"She's a real sweetheart, Gabe."

"And she adores you. She's trying to say thank-you with the goodies." Taking a seat on the tabletop, Gabe asked, "Who was the guy?"

"An ex-soldier. I met him at the Trauma Survivor's Group. He's in rough shape."

Gabe stared after where Allen had gone, too. "Hell of a thing. Like you guys didn't do enough over there. You have to come back and deal with this crap."

"You guys sacrificed as much during 9/11." A pause. "Anyway, we can manage it sometimes."

"And I hate that just as much. My cousin has his under control too until something goes awry with his wife. I imagine you have some triggers."

"Nothing I can really pinpoint."

Again Gabe watched Beck with warm acceptance in his eyes. "If you ever need to talk, wake me."

Beck pretended interest in the tulips lining the fence. "Huh?"

"I hear you get up at night. I know it doesn't happen regularly anymore, but if you ever want company, wake me. It'll give me a way to not be so freakin' indebted to you."

He thought about joking but didn't. "I might do that. Thanks, Gabe."

"You're welcome." Gabe checked his watch. "Now come inside. We need to train on the thermal imager. It has some new gizmos I didn't know about when we took it into the warehouse fire."

"Gotcha." Beck stood and thought once again about Len Allen. Poor Lela. She didn't deserve this.

• • •

"NICK, COULD YOU get that box of syringes off the top shelf for me?"

Lela always did this. Acted as if he could do what any other man could. Sometimes he liked it. Today her optimism left a sour taste in his mouth. Still, he didn't sass her. With a pole off to the side, he was able to slide the box to the shelf's edge, tug the cardboard down and catch it. But he lost his balance, stumbled backward and fell. His head hit the floor hard and syringes scattered every which way.

"Oh, dear, Nick!" She flew to him. Kneeling down, she searched his face. "Where does it hurt?"

"Hit my head. It's so hard, I didn't even feel it." Which wasn't true. An ache radiated from the back of his skull, but he hated to admit his weaknesses.

She slung an arm under his and helped him sit. She got up, put on gloves and examined the back of his skull. He flinched.

"A goose egg. The skin isn't broken, but we should put ice on it." Her tone was matter-of-fact. Professional.

"How come you never get upset here when something like this happens? A lotta people walk on eggshells around wounded veterans. Especially me, with the hoof-and-mouth thing."

"Very funny." She stood and offered him a hand.

"No thanks. There's a trick to this. Get me a chair, will you?"

As she watched him brace his arms on the chair and drag himself to a standing position, she answered his question. "I was over there, Nick, remember? I've seen worse than a fall."

"I guess." When he got to his feet, she bent back over to pick up the syringes, which were each wrapped tight in paper. He couldn't help her because his minor fall had exhausted him. Another thing he hated.

Just as Lela stood, Julie, the woman who ran the center, appeared at the doorway. Her bright red hair framed a face that was smiling. "Hey, there, buddy. You got a visitor."

Nick stilled. "Who?"

"That pretty little wife of yours. She wants to take you out to a romantic lunch."

Romance wasn't part of his life now and never would be. He didn't even think about it anymore and wished Amy didn't keep reminding him. "Tell her I'm doing chores."

"I did. She said she'd wait for you in the courtyard."

"I don't wanna see her."

"Nick…" Lela began, but Julie cut her off.

"Your choice," the director told Nick, "but then you have to have a one-on-one with Ken." The staff psychologist.

Anger built inside Nick. But he had to make a choice. Through gritted teeth, he said, "All right. Tell her I'll come down in ten minutes."

"Thataboy."

When Julie left, he faced Lela. "I don't want to see her."

Pulling up a stool, she sat down and faced him squarely. "I was very hurt when Len came back and didn't want to be with me. I'd waited so long for him, and it cut to the quick that he didn't want to spend time with me after we were apart for years."

"No shit?"

"No shit. Being ostracized from your suffering spouse is hard on us."

"So you think I should go out with her?"

Often Lela stayed neutral. "My opinion, as a spouse. Yeah, go somewhere and talk to her honestly about what you're feeling."

Ten minutes later, he limped into the courtyard and found Amy sitting at a table near the garden. God she was small. Delicate. His hands fisted. Breakable.

"Hi."

When she turned, the expression on her heart-shaped face was so full of joy it took his breath away. She never got that repulsed look on her face that other people did. "Hi." She tucked her blond hair behind her ear. "I'm so glad you wanted to see me."

He dropped down adjacent to her. "The nurse here is the wife of one of us, you know, who has it. She said she hated when her husband cut her out of stuff."

Amy straightened her shoulders and said simply, "I do, too." Her blue eyes mirrored her hurt.

He swallowed hard. A part of him wanted to fling himself into her arms and forget the world. But a larger part wouldn't let him. "I'll remember that, Ames."

The corners of her mouth turned up at the nickname only he called her. Actually, it was a pet name, murmured in intimate times.

"So, will you go out to lunch with me?"

God, please let me do this. Please.

But then she moved, and her sleeve pulled up. He saw the remains of a yellowish-purple bruise he'd given her in the throes of a flashback the last time they were alone. "No, I can't do that."

Swallowing hard, she looked away. God, the last thing he wanted was to hurt her. He needed to do something to show her how sorry he was. Slowly, he leaned in close, reached out and took her hand.

That was the best he could do today.

• • •

BECK CLIMBED OUT of his SUV and had reached the back of the vehicle when a car pulled up next to his. Lela's. Well, this was good. He knew he'd see her tonight at the Trauma Survivor's Group, but now he could give her the information he had about her husband before they went into the Academy. She exited smiling and rounded the trunk of her Civic to bestow her own brand of sunshine on him. For a moment, he let himself bask in the sight of her—pretty yellow blouse, tan jeans, her hair pulled up in some kind of knot with some curly tendrils escaping, accenting every feature of her face. Gold earrings dangled from her lobes.

"Hi, Beck," she said sweetly.

"Hi."

She eyed him critically. "You seem to be fine. No aftereffects of the ceiling incident?"

"None. Got checked out, too."

"Yeah, I heard."

He leaned back on the car and arched a brow.

"The nurses were talking about how you didn't complain a bit. All the other guys went after their sympathy."

"Yeah?" He wondered what her reaction was to the comments. Forgoing that line of thinking, he said, "I, um, came a little early, hoping you would, too."

Now fear shadowed those brown eyes. It killed him. She was waiting to be ambushed by life.

He rushed on to say, "Len stopped by the firehouse to talk to me."

"Oh, that's good isn't it? I was hoping he'd finally talk to someone."

"Yeah, and I'll spend whatever time with him he wants, but Lela, I can't do anything much but listen and encourage him to get help."

She studied him. "And he refuses, right?"

Beck nodded. "I even punched in Harrison's number on the phone and handed it to him. He walked away."

"I'm sorry. More than I can say."

She looked so sad, Beck's heart went out to her.

"Do you know he drank when he was with Josh the other night?"

"Yes, Len's dad and I promised we'd be honest about what happened in these visits. At least Len went upstairs to drink."

Beck couldn't help it. He reached out to take her hand. She let him. Clasped it as she stared into his face.

Something over her shoulder distracted him. A woman and her boy had exited the Fire Academy and started toward the parking lot. They were Afghan, both dressed in drab clothing.

Suddenly, the air around Beck shimmered. Suffocating heat surrounded him and there was no breeze....

"Bet you hate this, huh, Cap?" Sergeant Jason Kono, the combat engineer asked the question from the driver's seat in a Husky land-mine–detection vehicle. The million-dollar truck had wheels like a tractor, on top of which sat a steel cab that resembled a small tank. Its best feature was that it could detect IEDs, and if necessary, survive their explosions. "No problem."

"Sorry, Compton's sick."

Beck's sergeant had a bad case of diarrhea, so Beck had gone on this tactical mission.

Ahead of them, something appeared out of the sun. A mirage. A small figure and an even smaller one, coming toward him.

Kono stopped the Husky. "You see that, Cap?"

Without answering, Beck swung open the door and jumped down the ten feet to the ground. He started toward the pair but was head-locked from behind before he covered any distance.

"Hold on, Colonel," Kono shouted. "It's a trap."

"Let me go, Sergeant. That's an order."

"No. It's…"

Suddenly, their surroundings exploded. Kono pushed Beck to the ground and jumped on top of him. An ear-splitting blast reverberated around them. Shock waves shook the ground and shrapnel rained down on them, piercing their skin in many places. When it stopped, Kono slid off him. Beck tried opening his eyes, but the dust was so thick, they stung too much. After a bit, he tried again, and his vision cleared. His gaze caught on something next to him.

At first, he didn't know what it was. Then reality hit, harder than the shrapnel. For some reason he reached out, grabbed it, felt its tiny weight.

He was holding the child's hand.…

"No, no, no...."

"Beck, Beck, it's me, Lela."

"No...not this..."

Strong fingers gripped his head. Shook him. "Beck, you're here, at the Fire Academy. You had a flashback...."

Beck became aware of hard ground beneath him. He was staring into dark brown eyes, framed by an angel's face. Other times in theater, he thought he'd seen an angel, but...

He looked around; he wasn't in Afghanistan now.

There was pavement beneath him, the air was clear. A cool breeze fanned his face. He could smell the rich loam of the earth. Hear the sound of chirping birds. No wind, no soil like this, or wildlife, existed in theater.

Bile rose in his throat. He choked it back. "Oh, God."

Now she pulled him to her breasts. He grasped her hips when he realized she was straddling him.

"Fuck!" he said this time.

She soothed down his hair. Kissed his brow. "It's okay. Really. I understand."

When he could lift his head, he asked, "What happened?"

"You dropped to the ground all of a sudden and started yelling. Thrashing. So I climbed onto your lap."

Swallowing hard, he said, "You knew what to do. From experience."

Her face was so close he could see...not repulsion but relief in her eyes. "I was an army medic, Beck. I saw plenty of PTSD attacks. Len used to go off, too. I...subdue pretty well."

He didn't want to let her go, so he kept his hands on her. "I haven't had an attack in nearly a year."

"What triggered it? I didn't see or smell anything."

"I caught sight of an Afghan mother and her child leaving the Academy."

"And it took you back to the war."

He nodded.

"Tell me."

"No, I can't give you that image."

She grasped his head again, only her hands were gentle on his cheeks. "Don't do that. Don't stuff it. I've seen horror, too. Tell me."

He blurted it out. "We were looking for IEDs in a Husky. Out of nowhere, two people appeared." He felt his eyes well. "They blew up, Lee. And the kid's hand…"

He couldn't finish. Again, he buried his face in her breasts.

She tugged him even closer. "Oh, God, I'm so sorry. So, so sorry."

He tried to gulp back the emotion. But couldn't. Nor could he speak again. What was there to say, anyway?

• • •

IN THE SPACIOUS room, still set up in two semicircles, Lela sat next to Beck when they joined the Trauma Survivor's Group room. Tension radiated from his body, and his hands were fisted. This poor, poor man. He'd tried to retreat, go into himself.…

"I don't want to go to the group," he'd said when he'd sobered from the attack.

Conscious of her position on his lap, she slid off him, stood and held out her hand. He took it and climbed to his feet.

"I never want to go in there," she said softly, holding on to him. She studied his face. "Any nausea, dizziness, disorientation?"

A smile broached his lips. "No, Nurse Lela. It all passed."

She found the ability to smile, though she ached for him. "Then we should go inside. You don't have to talk about what happened. I won't bring it up."

He swallowed hard. Stood close. Held on to her.

"But here's my medical opinion. You *should* talk about it. You should tell everybody what happened."

Briefly he closed his eyes. "I'm not sure I can get the words out."

"All right. But don't leave. Please. It hurts me to think of you alone now."

Finally he'd agreed....

"So, how is everybody?" Harrison asked in his usual congenial manner. The atmosphere in the room tonight was different from before. More somber.

"Just peachy," Zach Malvaso commented. He hadn't shown up at other meetings.

"Ah, yes, I heard about the fire similar to Sinco. Were you hurt, Zach?"

"No, but the ceiling fell on us again. On Casey." The man's face crumbled and his hands fisted like Beck's. "I told her not to go into that building. That the fire was too much like Sinco. She got mad."

"Of course she did," one of the others stated. "She's a firefighter."

"You can't keep her safe." This from the man whose wife was a combat leader. "You can't keep anybody safe."

"I had an attack," Zach admitted. "Later, when we got home. Luckily none of the kids were there."

"How'd Casey react?" Harrison asked.

"Like she always does. She knew what to do."

Beck glanced at Lela. She searched his face and he gave her a sad smile.

Zach said, "You know, I just want this to stop. I can manage it now, but I hate the whole thing. It's gone on so long."

No one spoke for a moment. Then Beck said, "Me, too. I hate it, too."

Zach faced Beck. "You have an episode lately?"

Beck snorted. "Yeah. Just now in the parking lot."

"Hell. You okay? I'm a wet noodle after I have one."

Beck gave a sardonic laugh, but Lela noticed his body relax somewhat. "That about describes it."

His honesty called for others' stories. Harrison let everybody talk. Then he scanned the group. "So what's the consensus? You ever going to be able to control the attacks?"

A statuesque woman with blond hair and blue eyes spoke up. "No, never." She looked more like a Barbie doll than a lieutenant. "And as much as we hate it, most of the time we can only manage the fucking symptoms."

"Beck?" Harrison asked. "What else can we do?"

He sighed heavily. "I guess we can talk about it. I wanted to go home. Lick my wounds. But being here turned out to be better for me. And I hadn't had an attack in months, so I guess that isn't too bad."

The discussion went on until time was up. "Beck and Zach, you want to stay after and talk?" Harrison asked.

Both men shook their heads. Beck said, "I just want to sleep."

Zach was going to go home to Casey.

And a stark truth hit Lela. She wanted to go home with Beck. To hold him, comfort him with words. And her body. The urge was nearly overwhelming.

As they filed out, several people approached the two men who'd made big confessions tonight. A couple of women hugged Beck. Guys patted him on the back. Lela noted that no one mouthed platitudes. She waited off to the side until everyone left, then stepped up to him.

"I'll walk out with you."

He nodded.

He was silent on the trek to the bottom floor and after they got outdoors. So she didn't talk, either.

Turning when they reached her car, he grasped her shoulders gently. She swayed toward him. His touch felt so good she wanted to weep. "I don't know what to say except I'm sorry. And thanks for riding it out with me."

An image hit her. Of sitting on his lap, holding his head close to her breasts. That she wanted to do that again, in far different circumstances, flooded her with feeling. But she said only, "You're welcome."

He stepped away. She reached for the handle of the door but looked over her shoulder before she slid inside. And lost the battle. "You sure you're okay? I could, um, follow you home."

"That's a very bad idea, Lee. Very bad. Now get inside and start the engine so I know you're all set."

Always the protector, even when his world had exploded a few hours ago. "Good-night."

"'Night," he said and walked away.

Lela did as he asked, backing up and heading out of the lot. In the rearview mirror she saw him standing there, hands in his pockets, watching her leave.

It just about broke her heart.

CHAPTER 6

BECK SAT TALL and straight in Cal Erikson's office, waiting for the battalion chief to arrive. His secretary had let him inside. The space was roomy, but…homey, too. Firefighter prints decorated the walls, the conference-table furniture comfortable, as Erikson rarely sat behind his desk. Beck noted the picture of his wife on the sideboard—his wife, Parker Allen Erikson. Allen, as in Lela. Damn, he'd never made the connection.

No, don't think about her. About how she felt straddling your lap. About an offer she made in a moment of weakness that took all your remaining strength to refuse.

He focused back on the photo. Everybody around him had a happily-ever-after. Beck wondered if he'd ever find one for himself. For a man like him, he didn't think so. Unless…

Don't think about her.

The chief strode through the door and to the table. He appeared rested—lucky him—this morning, which Beck envied. The sun caught the battalion-chief bars, which spoke of a long and fulfilling career, on his crisp, white shirt. Once, Beck had worn bars like that signifying his time in theater. "Hey, Beck. My secretary said you were here. I'm late. Problems at home."

Beck frowned. "Nothing serious, I hope."

"Damned serious to us." He shook his head. Then an Olympic-size smile spread across his face. "I might as well tell you. I'm breaking the news to my groups today. Parker's three months pregnant."

Beck's heart lurched in his chest. He remembered the time he'd heard those words from his own wife. He'd been pole-axed. "That's terrific, Chief. Congrats."

"Thanks. I just wish I didn't worry over every little bout of morning sickness and fatigue."

"I hear those symptoms are common."

Erikson took a bead on him. "You have a kid, don't you?"

"Yeah, but I was stationed in Iraq during the pregnancy."

"Well, that sucks. You were deprived of so much, to fight for our country, Beck. I admire your willingness to serve."

Time to change the subject. Beck said glibly, "Now— what?—that makes you and Malvaso prospective parents. Ramirez just had one in November. Hell, is that going to be contagious, too?"

"Probably. But I know what you're feeling. I remember when all this went down with my group. I felt like I was on the happy planet. Then it happened to me."

It wouldn't happen to Beck. Ever.

"So, what's got you looking like you committed murder, Firefighter Sloan?"

He squeezed his hands tight and watched his knuckles turn white. "I, um, had a flashback last night."

"I'm sorry to hear that."

"I thought you should know. I haven't had one since I came on the department, but this wasn't at work."

"Good." Erikson studied Beck with intensity that made him want to squirm. "Do you think I'm worried about you?"

"You should be."

"I'm not. If you have an attack at work, we'll deal with it. The same as we do with the others on staff who experience symptoms of PTSD. In case you don't know, we had a hell of a time in this department after 9/11 since we're so close to the city. We aren't giving up on our own guys, or veterans, because of what happened to them trying to protect others."

Beck didn't know what he'd expected with this visit, but it wasn't unconditional support. He didn't remember the last time he'd felt so accepted, so warmed by it, as he did right now.

He was saved from responding, which was good because his throat felt too tight to talk, by the PA blasting out, "Accident on Broad and Main. Quint/Midi 7, Rescue 7 go into service. Bus hit a biker."

Both men bounded out of their chairs. This was likely to be a gruesome scene. And Beck didn't need any more gruesome to remember. Still, he blanked his mind and did his job.

Twelve firefighters met in the bay. Beck jumped into his turnout pants and boots but left off his coat, like the others. Climbing onto the truck, he took his seat next to Felicia. She turned to him. Over the wail of the siren, she said, "It seems stupid to prepare you for this, after what I know you must have seen in Afghanistan, but it's my job. This isn't going to be pretty."

"I know, Lieutenant. I'm ready."

They rode to the scene in silence. All three trucks reached the site simultaneously. Gawkers stood off to the right, on the sidewalk, as the firefighters descended from the rig. A strong scent of gasoline filled the air. Exhaust still puffed out from the vehicle. Beck steeled himself against what he saw. A bus had hit the concrete wall in front of a big building. It had traversed the sidewalk, and the front looked like an accordion. About ten feet away, a two-seater motorbike sprawled on the ground; two bodies had been thrown farther. A man and a woman. Young.

Chief Erikson said somberly, "Zach, you and O'Malley take the bikers until the ambulances get here." They were both paramedics. "The rest of you wait for instructions."

Erikson approached Mitch along with Gabe Malvaso and Holmes, the captain of the Quint/Midi. While they conferred, Beck heard moans coming from the inside of the bus. Then a scream.

Erikson hurried back. "Beck and White, get the chocking out. Quint 7 has the right wheel. You brace the left side. Sands, you're going inside with Gabe. The Quint will set up a ladder after the bus is stabilized."

Like a well-oiled machine, firefighters flew into action, dragging out blocks to wedge the wheels to keep them from moving. In minutes, the huge vehicle was steady, the ladder stable, and Sands climbed up it, followed by Malvaso.

The loud sound of the engines, still running, and the shout of victims created a cacophony around them, but Group 2's attention was focused on the bus rescue.

Erikson yelled out, "Beck and White, get ready for victims." Holms, captain of the Quint, gave the same order to LoTurco and Waterman from the Quint/Midi.

Minutes later, Beck accepted the first body from Gabe—that of a boy—and carefully placed him on a backboard. The kid had lacerations marring an unlined face, and his arm hung limply at his side. O'Malley and Malvaso were waiting to tend to him. When Beck took charge of a woman, probably the mom, he got her on a backboard, too. Sirens rent the air as the ambulances and another set of trucks reached the area.

The third victim Beck received was deadweight. As in *dead*. He was an older man with a shock of white hair. Beck turned away from the ashen face and lolling head after he set the man on the ground.

A fourth person came out, screaming and kicking. She was a teenager with a huge gash on her forehead. White set her down near the triage and spoke soothingly. Finally, the girl quieted.

Another one. Oh, hell! Beck took a baby, of not even a year, into his arms and saw he wasn't breathing. Setting him down quickly, Beck called out, "Got a baby here. Needs bagging." Meanwhile, Beck bent over and covered the child's mouth with his own. In. Out. Jesus, he'd never worked on someone this small. In, out. But just as a medic delivered the miniature bag, the tiny chest began to move. A cheer went up. Beck joined the chorus with a punch in the air and a happy, "Yes!"

A half hour later, the bus had been cleared, the victims in ambulances speeding to the hospital. He wondered if Lela was on and if she would have to deal with the gruesome aftermath.

Adrenaline crashing, Beck dropped down on his ass next to White, who sat with her knees drawn up and her hands linked between them. He said, "Well, that was hell."

"We get 'em once in a while. No time to think. We just react." She punched his arm. "You did good, probie."

"Thanks." He shook his head. "We lost the old man."

"Yeah. It's tough. But you got a baby breathing."

A genuine smile. "I did."

After a few minutes, they boarded the rescue rig and headed back to the firehouse. Traffic swirled around them and horns blew, but inside the truck, everyone was quiet, lost in their own thoughts. Beck had been surprised the first time this had happened, because this group was boisterous. But he guessed they all needed time to process what happened.

Inside the kitchen, Gabe went to a cooler, opened it and tossed everybody a bottle of water. "You did well today," he began just as the PA clicked on. "House fire on Addams Street. Rescue 7, go into service."

With a heavy sigh from each of them, the group turned and quickly strode out of the kitchen. Though he rued the circumstances, Beck was glad they were busy. It gave him less time to think.

About anything...or anybody.

• • •

LELA HAD BEEN a wreck all day thinking about what had—and hadn't—happened with Beck last night. At least he'd been sane enough to reject her ridiculously dangerous offer. So she was glad when the ER got busy again. Called to the desk, she watched an ambulance crew wheel in victims, but firefighters weren't helping this time. Good. The last thing she needed was to come face to face with Beck, whom she'd held intimately last night and would have done more with if he hadn't been so strong. Mind blank, she strode to the two victims on gurneys and met up with Christian, who'd just come from a nap in the on-call room after the night shift.

The EMT gave them the run-down. "Bus accident. These two were on the bike that got hit. Female, in early twenties. BP 60/80. Labored breathing." Hence, the oxygen mask. "Right leg bone protruding. We suspect internal bleeding. Face banged up." The EMT stopped. "Jesus, she's in bad shape."

Christian turned to the nurse behind him. "Call all available personnel. There's going to be a lot of injuries."

Lela squeezed The EMT's arm. "Thanks. We'll take it from here."

They wheeled both patients into a double room, followed by other nurses and a brand new intern. Lela and Christian tied masks on and donned gowns. He looked over at her. "Boy's coming around. I'll take him. Lela, you're in charge of the girl."

They turned to their patients. Lela took out her stethoscope. As she checked the girl's vitals, she noticed her leg. The medics hand bandaged it, but the gauze was soaked through with blood.

Behind her, Christian snapped out orders for his patient, which the nurses followed. As he worked on the boy, he asked, "Status on your patient, Nurse Allen."

She said, "Heart rate thready. Pulse erratic and really slow. I think her leg needs immediate attention, Doctor."

"Patient conscious, here. Mark"—the intern—"take over."

Christian crossed to assess Lela's patient. Slowly, he undid the bandages on the girl's leg. Lela stared unflinchingly at the bone sticking up and the torn and mutilated flesh. There were murmurs of "Oh, God, Oh, no," from others.

"Get an OR stat, Lela. Jenny, call Neuro and Ortho to meet us there. We need a trauma staff assembled ASAP."

Lela rushed to the phone on the wall and called Surgery. They agreed to free up a room immediately. She was monitoring the girl's vitals when the phone buzzed. "OR4 free," the orderly told them.

Suddenly, the monitor on their patient gave off a deadly, even beeeeeep. Everybody stopped. "Coding!" Singer said.

"Lela, be ready for chest compression." Jenny was already getting the paddles.

When the equipment was in place, he called out, "Clear," and zapped the young girl's chest.

Nothing.

"Go to two hundred.… Clear!" A loud buzz as the body bucked.

Nothing.

"Three hundred. Clear!"

Stillness. Nothing.

"Start chest compression."

Lela mentally calculated, "One, two, one two…" as she pressed hard on the girl's chest.

Christian gave an order for an eppie.

Still nothing.

And, later still, nothing.

Ripping off his face mask, Christian stepped back and checked the clock. "Time of death, 8:05 a.m.."

Leaning against the rails of the bed, Lela drew in a heavy breath, struggling to calm herself. After a few seconds, she helped take care of awful details necessary after a patient died. When she finally walked out of the ER, she was drained. Death was a part of this job, but wrenching in one so young. Really, nobody had time to waste.

Leaning against the nurse's desk, entering some information on a chart, Christian looked up when she approached. "Let's take a break, Lela." He set down the file. His eyes were sad and his mouth grim. "Get some coffee."

"Okay. I can't keep going without some energy boost."

Silently, they headed down to the staff lounge. When they arrived, Christian poured them both mugs of coffee, then pointed to the TV. "Want to see how this happened?"

"I do."

The bus collision was prime time in the local news. A TV crew had been downtown for a speech by the mayor, and although they didn't have footage of the crash itself, they'd caught the whole rescue on tape: trucks screeching to a halt. Firefighters pouring out of trucks. Close-ups of the bikers, then the cameras were shooed away from the ghastly sight of two kids, one now dead.

The bus was fair game, though, and the video was right there. Several uniformed firefighters whose names she knew were in various stages of the rescue; she recognized three names scrawled across the backs of turnout coats: G. Malvaso, White, Sands. Then the camera shifted off to the left.

To Beck. With a baby in his hands.

Dear God, she prayed, *please don't let the baby have died!*

• • •

THE DESERT DUST gritted through his teeth. He tried to keep his face covered with a kerchief, but it kept slipping as he trekked through a maze-like, mud-walled compound searching for Taliban fighters in the Helmand Province. He was almost blinded by the thick, gray curtain, and the air around him was unnaturally still. He imagined that he could feel the sand fleas bite his ankles. Then the world exploded.

"Nick, what...? Nick, where are you?"

He tried to shake off the Afghan who had him by the arms. But the fighter was strong. Nick bucked. "Get off me."

The soldier didn't move, only held Nick down. Rummaging for his gun, he felt the cold metal and knocked the guy off him with its muzzle.

"Ow! Ouch! Jesus!"

Why was that a feminine voice?

"Nick, it's me, Lela."

His body began to calm and sweat cooled on his skin. It took him a minute to open his eyes. Fuck! "What…what'd I do?"

"It's okay," she murmured softly. Just like Amy used to. "You had a flashback." She muttered something under her breath about this happening a lot lately. Nick scrambled to a sitting position, gripping the TV remote, and Lela hunched back on her legs. "You all right now?" she asked.

"Yeah. What happened?"

"I don't know exactly. I came in on an off day to take inventory in the clinic, and you were in front of the TV. Something must have been playing to trigger an attack, because suddenly you started yelling. I rushed out of the clinic to find out why."

Clearing his mind, he thought back to the show he'd been watching. "A documentary about the Marines was on. They were in Kandahar. I knew I shouldn't watch it but…" He gulped in a breath. "Hell, I thought I was looking for insurgents in a dust storm and you were the Taliban."

"If I had a nickel for every time I've heard *that* line."

He gave her whatever kind of smile he could conjure. "I hit you."

"Yeah, clipped me with the remote. Don't worry, I was knocked around on the front."

Studying her, he felt the darkness encompass him. He hurt people all the time without his conscious intent. "Your…your neck is bruising already." He winced at the discoloration.

She touched the space between her jaw and shoulder. "I'll put some ice on it. Get up and sit on the sofa while I get a pack."

She left and returned with the ice. They took places on the couch. He wanted to move away from her, but he couldn't manage anything more than dropping down on the cushion.

"Want to talk about it?"

"No."

Her brow furrowed. "Geez, you guys are all alike."

"Excuse me?" Was she mocking him?

"I was with an army colonel this week and he had an attack in the parking lot of the Fire Academy."

"He from the PTSD group you go to?"

"Uh-huh. He didn't want to talk, either, or go inside to the group afterward, but he did and he told everybody what happened."

Nick looked away. "He's a brave man. Braver than me."

"Oh, I don't know. Walking in a dust storm looking for terrorists counts as brave in my book."

Feeling okay about her comment, he shrugged.

She stared at him. "Nick, would you talk to the army colonel? It might help."

"Nah, there are vets here I can talk to. And the shrink."

"Do you?"

He shook his head.

"Then this is kismet, don't you think? I happened to be with two men who had an attack within a few days."

"I don't know."

She waited. Then said, "Just once. If it doesn't help, I won't ask again."

He glanced at the clock. "Now?"

"If he's available. I could call him."

"Okay."

Lela reached in her pocket for her phone. She called 411 and was punched in to the House 7 phone. It was well after five. Beck was working yesterday, so hopefully he'd be on today. And still there. "House 7," a familiar voice said. "Firefighter Sloan speaking."

"Hi, Beck. It's Lela."

Quiet. Then, "Hi. I'm surprised to hear from you." He didn't sound displeased.

"I took a chance you were still at work and getting off duty soon."

"I am. My replacement just came in. What's up?"

"I was wondering if you could come to the Veteran's Outreach Shelter on Collins Avenue. It's not too far away from where you are."

"Why?"

She explained the circumstances.

"Damn it. Are you okay?"

Her hand went to her neck. "I'm fine. Can you spare an hour?"

"Of course. I'll leave right now. See you soon."

When she hung up, she faced Nick. "He's coming."

"I heard. Seems like you can talk anybody into anything."

She decided to take the jibe lightly. "And you best remember that, young man. Now, y'all come into the clinic and help me take stock of what we need while we wait for Beck."

"Yes, ma'am."

Fifteen minutes later, Beck followed Julie, the woman who ran the clinic, up the stairs. "I'm glad he agreed to see somebody, Colonel. He won't talk here, even in the required counseling sessions."

Beck said, "I'm glad, too," still surprised that Lela had called him. "I hope I can help." Julie walked him down the hall to a big conference room off of which was the clinic. "You take it from here."

Beck stood in the doorway watching Lela and the soldier. They were working without talking, writing down inventory, with some soft rock seeping out from a jukebox. Despite the gravity of the situation, he took a minute to notice how the khaki of her cropped-off pants clung to her nicely toned bottom and how her shirt rose just a bit when she lifted her arms. A small patch of delicious-looking skin peeked out.

He cleared his throat. "Hi, there."

Both turned. Lela's expression was one of pure pleasure. The soldier's was not. She said, "Hi, Beck," walked over to him and took his hand. Her touch skimmed along his nerve endings. Until he saw the dark mark on her neck. It took all his reserve not to comment, which would hurt the boy. "Come in and meet Nick."

Pivoting, Nick nodded to him. "Colonel."

"Just make it Beck. We're out of theater."

The boy relaxed. "Yes, sir." Habits were hard to break, Beck knew.

He glanced at Lela.

"There's an empty office down the hall. You can go there. I'll finish up here."

"Can you stay until we're done?" Beck asked. "I'd like to talk to you."

Soon, Beck and Nick settled into comfortable office chairs belonging to one of the case managers. A veteran flag and an American flag stood post in the corners. The desk was piled with papers. A good-sized window let in the late afternoon sun.

Beck watched the guy for a minute. God, he was young. He'd probably been a teenager when 9/11 happened.

When Nick didn't start talking, Beck did. "So you just had an attack?"

He nodded.

"They're horrific, aren't they?"

Finally Nick spoke. "Yeah. Lela said you had one this week."

"You think it's a full moon?"

The boy laughed. Then sobered. "I hate them. And I can't control them. It kills me."

"I'm with ya there, kid."

"How do you function?"

"One day at a time. If it's any comfort, they do abate the longer you're back. If you get help, that is."

He motioned around the office. "I'm here."

"But Julie says you don't talk to anybody about your PTSD."

He looked away, out the window; Beck tracked his gaze, saw a hawk fly by. "If you only knew what I've done in the middle of them."

"Let's see. Hit your wife? Hurt your kid? Endangered the lives of those you love? Yeah, Nick, I've done it, too. But you gotta manage this thing or it'll win. The fucking terrorists will win. We didn't go over there to fight so they could win once we got back in the world."

Huge tears welled in Nick's eyes. Beck remembered trying to battle those back, as Nick was. "I can't do it."

"Yes, you can. You don't want to be the statistic that says every eighty hours, a vet commits suicide."

Nick stared down at his hands. "I understand why."

Hell. He wasn't equipped for this, though he'd put in place some counseling in theater for his men and women. "Are you suicidal, Nick?"

His head rose and he met Beck's gaze straight on. "I think about it. Especially when my buddy Billy died three months after I got home. I didn't want to live anymore, either."

"Sorry about your friend. And my guess is more vets think about suicide than we realize, especially initially. Do you have a plan?"

"No. I just want to die sometimes. When something bad happens or I think about Billy."

"I understand. I had several friends who died over there. Can you talk to the therapist at the shelter? I'm not qualified give you the clinical advice you need about those feelings."

"I could."

"What's stopping you?"

A heavy sigh came out of him. "It hurts to think about what I did."

Beck chose his words carefully. "Life hurts in general. More when you just get home. But it can get better. It did for me."

"You had an attack this week. Lela said you go to the same support group she does."

"I did, and it just about kills me when I have them, too. But you must know you never get rid of the condition."

"Yeah, Lela says that, too. You just manage the symptoms."

They talked a while longer, then Nick slumped back in his chair. "I'm whipped. I want to sleep."

"Good idea. Will you see the shrink here, Nick?"

"I will tomorrow."

"Fine. I'll let Julie know. I have to tell her about your feelings."

"I hear ya. I guess I don't care if she knows now. What I'm doing isn't working so far."

After he stopped by to see the director, who put Nick on a suicide watch, Beck returned to the clinic. He found Lela, sitting on a chair, an ice pack to her neck, eyes shut. Some romantic song was playing on the radio and he shook his head. Quietly, he closed the door and leaned against it. "You've had a hell of a week."

She looked over at him, gave him a sad smile. "Yep, I have. You, too."

He dropped down on a chair opposite her. "You know about the fire. The baby and old man."

She nodded. "I worked on the young girl." Her throat worked. "It was heartbreaking."

"Hell of a thing. So much death around."

"It makes you want to live your life better. More fully."

He watched her. At a crossroads, he knew a lot depended on what he did now. But she was right. Life was short. Rising, he went to her, drew her up from the chair and lightly gripped her shoulders. The ice pack fell to the floor with a thud and she grasped on to him, too.

"Which is why I'm going to do this…" Leaning in, he inhaled the scent of soap and shampoo and maybe some lotion she used. Then he brushed his lips gently over her bruise, whispered, "…and head out, before we both do something we regret."

He'd done harder things than leaving her alone in that small room. But as he jogged down the steps to the first floor, Beck couldn't remember any of them.

CHAPTER 7

AT THE THIRD meeting of the offshoot, Survivors with Kids, Harrison had said, "Research shows that groups which get together people with similar problems increases healing among its members significantly. I'd like to try it with your kids."

Which was how they ended up at Sea Breeze Amusement Park on the outskirts of Hidden Cove. Thankfully, the May morning had dawned bright and warm, though they'd chosen a Sunday, so the place would be crowded later. Lela watched from a distance as Harrison spoke to his little charges about why they were here. The twelve of them—a good mix of boys and girls—concentrated on Jack like he was the most popular video game available.

"It's something, isn't it?"

Lela turned to find Beck had come up to her. She'd purposely not searched for him in their group after she arrived. And—no fair!—he wore sage-green shorts and a T-shirt to match that made his eyes the color of jade. Truth be told, she, too, had dressed carefully, in a coral-pink-and-white sundress that swirled at her knees. "Um, what did you say?"

Giving her a questioning look, he answered, "It's amazing how Harrison has the kids mesmerized."

"The topic interests them. I think PTSD is on their minds all the time, even if they can't identify it for what it is."

"I guess. Even Tommy didn't give me any grief about coming. How about Josh?"

"Josh does about anything I ask him to."

"Lucky you."

She shook her head, her loose hair brushing her shoulders and back, like a lover's caress. "Not so much. He could use a little rebellion."

Talk ceased and Beck stood next to her, arms folded across his chest, as they watched the goings-on. He must have just showered, because Lela could smell his soap mixed with man, and it brought all her senses to red alert.

"Did you have to wear that dress?" he asked when Harrison got the kids laughing at something he'd said.

She didn't pretend to misunderstand. "I was just thinking the same thing about your clothes."

"At least we're on the same page." His tone was sardonic. "Right? About our feelings…"

Glancing up at him then, she found that his green gaze, directed full wattage at her, had darkened. She wondered if his eyes did that when he… She halted the thought. "Yes."

He jammed his hands in his shorts pocket. "Why the hell do the fates keep throwing us together?"

"The fates are cruel."

"Hmm. Our kids will probably meet up today and become best friends, then we'll have to deal with that."

She chuckled. It was better to joke about their situation than to be on the verge of tears over their inability to be together.

As Harrison continued to explain how the day would go, Lela noticed Josh sitting alone. Damn it, she wished he'd socialize. Finally, the talk ended with an admonition to have fun and mingle. Heads popped up and turned, kids looking for their parents. Soon, two little boys raced toward them. One must be Beck's son. In fact, he was a miniature Beck, adorable in a green shirt and denims. "Can we go on the roller coaster?" he asked Beck.

"Where's your manners? Tommy, this is Mrs. Allen." He bent down to look a shorter Josh in the eyes. "And you must be Josh."

Literally, her son hid behind his mother's skirt.

"Hi, Tommy," Lela put in. "Josh, this is Mr. Sloan."

"Everybody calls him Beck," Tommy told them.

Beck ruffled Tommy's hair, and the boy backed away a bit. Then he turned to his son. "Sure, we can go on the roller coaster." He rolled his eyes. "My favorite."

"At least it's not the flume ride," Lela put in, "where you get wet."

Tommy's eyebrows rose. "There's a ride where you get wet?"

"Let's go before Mrs. Allen gets me into more trouble."

Lela watched him walk away, feeling an incredible sense of loss. Josh took her hand. "Why do you like him, Mom?"

Uh-oh. "He's a nice man. And he served his country, like your dad."

"Is he sick, too?"

Stopping, Lela asked, "What do you mean?"

"Grandpa told me dad's sick."

"Well, yes, he is. Beck isn't as sick as dad, but you heard Dr. Harrison. We're all here for the same reason."

"Can we go to the games?" Obviously, he'd gotten enough information. "I like Skee-Ball."

"Sure, honey. We can do anything you want."

It turned out Skee-Ball was so popular, each kid had to take a ticket and wait for his turn. Josh said he wanted to get in line alone, and Lela thought that was progress for her shy son; she retreated to a bench in the shade, where she could keep an eye on him. She noticed Josh say something to the girl ahead of him, which was great.

Five minutes passed and Josh had moved up to about halfway in line. Raising her face, Lela took pleasure in the sun, the warm breeze and the cloudless sky until she sensed someone watching her. She opened her eyes to find Christian Singer transferring his gaze to a little girl. The child also got in line. Christian pivoted and a smile spread across his face as he headed toward her. "Hey, Lela. Small world, I guess."

"Yes, it is. You brought your daughter to the park?"

"Umm. That's Kayla." He shook his head, and his face got somber. "I hate that I only get her on weekends."

Rumor had it Christian's wife had cheated on him and left him. Rumor also had it that he'd wanted to keep the marriage together, but she hadn't. None of the nurses could believe the woman had abandoned him, because they thought he was *yummy* and was such a romantic—he'd sent flowers and had nice lunches with her in his office. Lela knew not to assume anything about people's marriages by what you saw on the surface.

"What about the summer? Can you see her more then?"

"I hope so. I've got a lot of vacation time and I'm going to spend it with her." He nodded to the line. "Which one is your boy?"

"One, two, three…ten back."

"Ah." Gesturing to the bench, he asked, "Mind if I join you?"

"Not at all. I'd love the company." Too bad Lela had another male here at the park on her mind. But she liked Christian, and maybe he'd distract her.

They chatted about work and kids until Lela noticed a commotion in the line. Josh was first up now but another boy—oh, no, it was Tommy Sloan—had slid in front of him.

The other kids objected.…

"No fair."

"Wait your turn."

"No cutting."

Tommy ignored them. He just stood in front of Josh. In her peripheral view, she saw Beck head toward them. Before he reached the line, Josh tugged on Tommy's shirt. The boy turned and said something to Josh. Then her son shrugged and handed his ticket to Tommy.

When Beck reached them, he spoke to the boys. For a moment, they talked, then Josh trudged to the back of the line. Beck stood there as if deciding what to do. Finally he turned and spotted Lela. He strode over, but when he got closer, his gaze landed on Christian. His face was impassive when he reached them. But his eyes were full of thunderclouds.

"What happened?" she asked Beck.

"Hell of a thing. Tommy cut in line, but I wasn't surprised. It seems he does that stuff on purpose. I spoke to the boys in line. Your son said it was okay; Tommy could have his ticket. When I asked him why, he said Tommy's just mad because of me."

"Oh. I, um, I don't know what to say."

"I'd say Josh's just like his mom." At Christian's remark, Beck turned angry eyes on him. "And you are?"

"Christian Singer. I work with Lela."

"I see. You two planned to meet here?" There was ice in Beck's voice.

"No!" Lela said a little too quickly.

Christian smiled easily. "Not for want of trying, I'll tell you."

Really? Christian was interested in her? She'd had no idea. Had he been flirting with her since his divorce?

Beck nodded. "I'll just go wait for Tommy."

"You can keep us company," Lela suggested.

"Wouldn't want to intrude. Nice meeting you, Doctor, is it?"

"'Fraid so."

"Lela." Beck strode away. He didn't stalk, but she could tell by the stiffness of his shoulders he was angry. Damn it, not angry.

Beck was jealous.

• • •

SO WHAT IF she was keeping company with the handsome doctor? She should. Maybe now Beck would take Rachel Wellington's suggestion that she and Gabe double-date with her sister, Alexis, and Beck. Yes, this was for the best.

Then why did he feel like punching the fence he leaned against while waiting for Tommy. He watched his son leave Skee-Ball—must be they were allowed only a certain length of time to play—and spot Beck. The boy sauntered over.

"Have fun?" Beck asked neutrally.

"Yeah."

"Was it worth cutting in line?"

For a minute the boy's eyes flared with mutiny. Then his expression was replaced by...embarrassment? "I shouldn't have done it."

Beck squatted down. "Why did you, son?"

"I dunno."

"I think you do."

Tommy shrugged. "I'm mad all the time."

That was exactly what sweet little Josh had said.

"I'm sorry. Want to talk about that?"

"Maybe. Sometime."

Wow, this was progress.

"Not today, though. I wanna have fun with you."

Hallelujah! "Okay, just don't cut in again. But we'll have fun on the rides."

Tommy turned to look at the line. "The kid's still waiting."

"I know. It's Josh. You just met him."

When Tommy looked up at Beck, his expression was confused. "Why'd he give me his turn, Dad?"

"He said because he knew you were mad."

"Isn't he? All the kids here have dads or moms like you."

Beck swallowed hard and tried to ignore the sting of his kid's statement. "His mom says he isn't mad. He just feels so bad about his dad that he doesn't talk much with other people."

Tommy nodded and looked back at Josh.

Beck did, too, though his gaze wandered to Lela. And the doctor. Fuck!

Two hours later, lunchtime rolled around. Beck had liked traipsing all over the park with Tommy, seeing him enjoy himself, but he was ready for a break. They headed to the pavilion about noon. He spotted Lela right away, alone at a table with Josh, who probably didn't want to sit with anybody.

None of your business.

"Let's get a—"

"There's Josh and his mom, Dad. Can we sit with them?"

Come on, God. Gimme a break. But he said aloud, "If you want to, Tom."

How could he not cooperate the only time all day Tommy had asked to do something with another kid?

They reached Lela's table; bent over, she was talking softly to Josh. Beck said as evenly as he could, "Tommy asked to sit with Josh."

When she glanced up, then to Josh, Lela's face held a wealth of understanding. "Would you like that, Josh?"

"I guess." More eagerly he said, "Sit next to me, Tommy."

Frustrated, Beck dropped down on the bench across from Lela. She'd gotten sun this morning, and her nose was red. The color made her cheeks glow, though. "What are we having?"

"Hot dogs and salads. I brought one for the group."

"I provided drinks."

Harrison called for all the little ones to get their food.

And once again, Beck and Lela were alone.

He said, tightly, and without preamble, "Singer seems like a nice guy."

Her face flushed. "He is."

"He indicated he'd like his relationship with you to be a lot more."

"Did he?"

Beck swallowed hard.

"You should follow up on that."

Her jaw dropped. "I should?"

"Yeah." He told her about Rachel's sister.

Temper flared in her eyes, surprising him. "So is this how we're going to handle things?"

"It's as good a way as any, don't you think?"

Her eyes moistened and she turned away. "Yes, I guess so."

"Fine." He stood. I'm going to the john. Can you keep an eye on Tommy?"

"Sure."

Turning, he strode away quickly, cursing the fates that it *had* to be her he'd fallen for. The sheen in her eyes twisted its way into his gut. He'd only seen her cry the day of the first kids' group when she'd said she felt guilty about staying with Len so long. She wouldn't cry over this standoff with him, he guessed. But her small show of vulnerability cut him to the quick and he couldn't be near her anymore.

• • •

"SPEND SOME TIME with her," Ken, the therapist at the shelter, had said to Nick two days ago. "Give yourselves a chance to get to know each other again."

And Lela had put in her two cents. "Just try, Nick. Please."

But it was Beck, the guy who'd come to talk to him that night he'd had his last attack and who'd stopped by the shelter today, who had convinced him. "You get over humps by scaling them, Nick. Giving up before you try isn't going to accomplish anything."

"Are *you* trying to get over your humps?" he'd asked. It wasn't a challenge, it was a genuine inquiry. He'd like to know this guy more.

"Yep. As a matter of fact, I got a date tonight...."

And so Nick had called Amy. She'd been so happy to hear from him that he felt like a jerk for putting her through this separation. But, in his conversations with Ken, he realized he didn't really want to die. So he had to start living.

That was how he'd ended up sitting out in front of the shelter in the late afternoon, with a special pass to break curfew, waiting for Amy to pick him up. Large oak trees lined the city street, but the sun peeking through the leaves warmed his face.

The car she'd bought while he was in theater because the other had broken down pulled up to the curb. It was a little blue sedan, but he could still get into it. He limped to the passenger side, wondering idly if he'd ever be able to drive again. He slid inside, with at least a little bit of grace, and closed the door. Turning to face her, he said, "Hi."

She'd dressed up for him in a soft, light blue blouse and a pretty, printed skirt. Her hair was shiny, and for the first time in months, he wanted to touch it. Even from over here, he could smell the flowery scent.

"I've been looking forward to this all day." Her eyes were full of gratitude and love. Did he deserve either?

"Me, too."

"Really, honey?"

"Really. Where are we going?"

"You said you didn't mind a restaurant."

"I gotta get out in public some time." He touched his face. Finally, the redness was starting to fade. "A small one, though. Okay?"

"You're on."

They drove to Enzo's near the shelter on Gains Avenue. At one time it had been his and Amy's favorite restaurant. He gulped back the shame when she let him off at the door—he used to do that for her—but when she returned and reached out for his hand, and he took it, he was glad he'd come. This felt…right.

Inside, everybody milling around the desk averted their eyes from his face. He expected the reaction and swallowed the lump their shunning caused in his throat. Then Enzo approached them, stared straight at him without gaping, and held out his hand. "Hey, Nick. Glad to see you're back. Sorry about what happened to you."

"Thanks."

"Where would be a good place for you to sit?"

Nick scanned the room. The place was nearly full, and the clatter of utensils and soft murmur of guests filled the air. "That table over in the corner by the window."

The owner led them through the diners, and Nick dropped down onto a chair with his back to the wall. Must be Enzo knew about vets. Oh, now he remembered, the guy had been in Vietnam.

From across the table, Amy smiled at Nick. There was something about the joy in her eyes that made him determined not to blow the night. "Do you want a drink?" she asked.

"Yeah, sure. They drug test us when we go back to the shelter after an outing, but Julie said I could have a beer."

Her pretty face darkened. She hated that he'd chosen to stay at the shelter instead of with her after he'd gotten out of the hospital in Kuwait, where they'd taken his foot and he'd done a stint in rehab.

Put the bad memories of the past out of your mind, son. Beck had made the comment. *Or at least try.*

Damn it, he *would* try. So when the waiter brought their drinks, he lifted his glass. "Thanks for bringing me here, Ames. I'm glad we did this."

Tears glistened in her eyes. "So am I, Nicky. So am I."

Nick almost meant the words he said to his wife. Someday, they would be true.

• • •

LELA FUSSED WITH her appearance. She'd washed and dried her hair until it fell in soft waves onto her shoulders and down her back. She'd dressed in a knee-length, baby-pink skirt and a white, silk blouse with a ruffle down the front. She had a date! Actually, she'd *initiated* a date when she realized her feelings for Beck were, in her heart if not in actions, out of control. She had to switch gears.

Also, she'd gotten her divorce papers in the mail. She'd signed them yesterday morning, sent them to Len, and promptly said to Christian Singer when she'd met him as she'd entered the staff lounge, "Would you like to come to dinner at my house tonight?"

Weeks ago, Josh had been invited to a birthday sleepover with a friend down the street, and Lela had insisted he go. So she'd picked tonight to ask the handsome doctor for a date.

Christian's flirty, blue eyes had sparkled and he reached out to touch her arm. "Now that makes my day. I'll bring the wine."

Hmm, maybe Beck had been right. Maybe Christian was more interested than Lela realized. *He indicated he'd like to be a lot more…You should follow up on that.*

"Well, Beckett Sloan," she said aloud as she poked diamond studs into her earlobes, "I'm taking your advice." Though she felt a clutch in her chest, she added, "You should see Rachel's sister, too."

The doorbell chimed so she headed downstairs. Smiling, she opened the front door, ready to concentrate fully on another man.

But she found Beck on the stoop. "Oh. Oh!" Her eyes widened at the sight of him. He wore nice, black pants, which fit his trim waist perfectly, and a gray, long-sleeved shirt, which molded to his torso, rolled up on his forearms. For a minute, her mind spun out a vision that Beck was her date, coming over for the night—where they'd eat and talk like normal people, then end up in bed. For a long time.

Jamming his hands in his pockets, he stared at her. "Sorry to drop in unannounced."

"Um, that's okay." She nodded to his clothes. "You're all dressed up."

"I have a date."

Damn it! "Ah. So do I."

He scanned her appearance and his eyes narrowed. "I hate that you gussied up for him."

Leaning against the door, she asked, "Beck, why are you here?"

He pounded the jamb with a fist. His eyes sparked frustration. "Because I don't want to go out with someone else."

"We agreed not to talk about that."

"Do *you* want to date another man, really?"

"Beck, don't."

Without warning, he reached for her. And God help her, she couldn't resist. She looped her arms around his neck and melded into him. His scent was something new, something spicy and woodsy at the same time; his body was hard against her. She met his gaze squarely.

He stared down at her.

Then he lowered his head.

The kiss wasn't rough, but it wasn't tender, either. His mouth brushed hers, nipped, then pressed in full force, making Lela's knees buckle. She met the intensity with her own and locked her hands tighter at his neck. His tongue probed her lips until she allowed him entry.

Then he devoured her.

And she devoured back.

She didn't know how long they'd stood there kissing—in the open doorway, for God's sake, but when he drew back, his eyes were full of hot desire.

Then, without a word, he turned and stalked down the brick pathway to his SUV.

• • •

WITH HER SLIGHT build, steel-blond hair and hazel eyes, Alexis Wellington was a beauty. They sat on the deck of Gabe and Rachel's condo on the lake, and the breeze coming off the water cooled Beck's heated skin. His *still*-heated skin—from a kiss that never should have happened. What the hell had he been thinking to go over to her house? To initiate a kiss that had knocked his socks off? He was an idiot.

With the discipline he'd mastered in the army—apparently absent when he was around Lela—Beck concentrated on Alexis's story. "So then I said, 'If you don't let me do surgery on him, he might die.'"

"You never were one to mince words, sis." Rachel, who had the exact same coloring as her sister, made the comment from where she was comfortably ensconced in a chaise. Gabe wouldn't let her get up to do anything, though she had a good two months to go in her pregnancy. They were grilling outside, and Alexis had prepared all the accompaniments. Beck had brought wine and beer.

Alexis scrunched her nose. "Well, geez, why wouldn't the specialists come right out and tell the parents the truth?"

"Malpractice?" Gabe suggested, sitting next to Rachel and holding her hand, sipping a beer. Dressed similarly to Beck, his captain was relaxed and at ease in his home.

"At least Sophia backed me up. She's a pediatric nurse."

"Yeah, we all know her." This from Rachel. "Do you, Beck?"

"I met her the night of the warehouse fire. She's a nice woman." As was the one with her that evening in a pretty, clingy dress. The one who'd kissed him just hours ago like she wanted to eat him up. Was she kissing Singer now?

"Do you know Christian Singer?" he asked Alexis before he could stop himself.

"Uh-huh. He's a great doctor." She winked at Rachel. "And a looker. But I don't mix my personal and professional lives."

Must be Lela didn't feel the same.

Shit.

Sick of his mind retreating to Lela at every comment, Beck excused himself to go to the john, then when he came back, Gabe was at the grill. Getting another beer, he crossed to his friend. "Can I help?"

"No thanks. Stay and talk to me, though. Steaks are at a stage where I have to watch them."

Beck leaned against the railing of the deck, trying to enjoy the beautiful, early May evening. The setting sun had turned the sky a pretty pink-blue.

"You seem preoccupied tonight," Gabe commented.

The Molson's he sipped went down cold. "I guess I am. I did something stupid earlier and can't get it off my mind."

Taking a quick glance at Beck, Gabe's dark brows rose. "I'm a good listener, if you want to tell me."

He nodded to the women, who were paging through a catalogue of baby things. "Not tonight. Maybe some time." He smiled. "So are you looking forward to impending fatherhood again?"

"I am, though I never thought I'd have another kid. It's a girl, you know."

"I heard. I never had a girl."

"Did you want one?"

He shook his head, sure of *that* answer. "I'm not a very good father."

Gabe set down the tongs and faced him. "You never had a chance to be."

"Hmm. I guess that's true. I missed a lot of years with Tommy."

"I hear your PTSD group took the kids to a gathering at Sea Breeze."

"Yeah. My boy misbehaved, then met up with somebody he liked, and we had fun the rest of the day."

"That's nice."

For Tommy and Josh maybe. He remembered joking with Lela, *Our kids will probably meet up today and become best friends, then we'll have to deal with that.*

"Gabe, come here and look at this high chair. It can have the baby's name carved into the back." Across the room, Rachel held up the catalogue.

"I still think Maria is too plain. Marietta, maybe?"

Rachel shook her head.

Rolling his eyes, his cap said, "Keep an eye on the steak, will you?"

His back to the others, Beck stared down at the grill, willing himself not to think about what he couldn't have. From behind him, he heard, "Sorry about the fix-up."

Turning, he found Alexis had joined him. She looked cute in a yellow, one-piece overall thing. "Excuse me?"

"Sorry about the fix-up. You don't seem happy to be here."

Pretty, competent *and* direct, something he valued in women. "No, I am glad to be here. I had an unpleasant encounter before I came, is all. It's taking me a while to shuck it."

She raised delicately arched eyebrows. "Okay. If you're sure."

Reaching out, he squeezed her arm. "I am."

Dropping down on a chair at the table across from the grill, she grinned up at him. "Then tell me about why you decided to become a firefighter after serving overseas. I'd think you'd done enough for society."

"Habit, I guess. The need to protect others." He slugged back more beer. "I love the job as much as I did the army."

She glanced over at her sister. "So does she. Drives me wild, though."

"I'll bet. The worry's hard on families."

"Seems everything is." She sipped from the wine glass she held, its contents ruby red. "Tell me about somebody you saved. Other than Gabe, so I can concentrate on the good that emerges from the risks she takes."

"You'll like this one." He gave her a genuine smile. It was easier than he thought it would be. "I saved a baby."

Beck was surprised how much he enjoyed the rest of the night. After supper, they played euchre, which was fun, and he was good at it because they'd had games in theater, where the competition had been fierce. When the evening ended, he was in a better mood.

Until he walked to his car and wondered how Lela's evening would end!

• • •

CHRISTIAN SINGER WAS good at everything. Cooking—he'd done the seasoning for the rice, which was delicious. Conversation—he'd told her about his med-school days with self-effacing humor, which she enjoyed because he always seemed so competent and confident at the hospital. And overall, he seemed comfortable with himself, something she admired in people. If Lela hadn't been distracted by the debacle earlier with Beck, she'd be enjoying herself. But the feel of Beck's hands, gripping her tightly, and the taste of him in her mouth, which the best wine couldn't get rid of, stayed with her the entire night.

Damn it, Lela, get over it!

They'd finished a dinner of salmon, green beans and rice and taken coffee out to the stone patio Len had built in one of his better times. They sat watching the stars, making idle comments about the locations of the constellations.

"You're a great cook, Lela," Christian said, sipping his coffee.

She gave him a genuine grin back. "I'm glad we did this."

"Are you? You seem sad tonight."

She'd tried to keep her feelings to herself and thought she'd accomplished that. But apparently not. "Did I? No, I'm not sad." Mad and frustrated, maybe.

"You sure?"

"Yeah, I guess I'm just worried about Josh. I had to insist on this sleepover."

"As a dad, and a doctor, I can tell you that sometimes children need a push out of their comfort zone."

"That makes me feel better. Tell me about Kayla. What kind of kid is she?"

Another brilliant smile crossed his face. It revealed dimples on both his cheeks, something that Lela had never noticed before. "She's a sweetie. Now *she's* sad I'm out of the house."

"Are you? Sad?"

"I was. But my ex had other ideas."

"I'm sorry."

"Do you know the story? It's all over the hospital grapevine."

"Some of it. I wasn't gossiping myself."

"I just wish I'd known she was so unhappy. That sounds trite, but she never once complained about my hours." He set his mug down. "She had other outlets, I guess. When she told me, it was because she wanted a separation. I was poleaxed. I really loved her."

"I'm sorry you had to go through that."

He took a bead on her. "Enough about me. How about you? *I* heard your divorce just became final."

"Yes, but we've been separated for a whole year. He didn't want the divorce, so it was hard. I got the official papers this week. I'm glad it's over, too."

"Listen to us, talking about our exes." He rolled his eyes. "Breaking the cardinal rule of dating after a divorce."

"You know you're right."

Sitting back comfortably on the wicker couch next to her, he slid his arm up on the cushion so his hand was near her hair. "Tell me what it was like to be an army medic. Honestly, I can't believe you did that job. You're so feminine and delicate."

"Nah, I'm tough. All kinds of women volunteered."

"Why did you?"

"I was an only child. When my parents died, I'd been working as a nurse for three years. I was bothered by what I saw on TV, unattached, and I decided I could help. Then 9/11 happened and that solidified it for me."

"How long were you there?"

"Five years. I quit when I got pregnant." She gave Christian a sideways glance. "After we were married."

"I—"

They heard the doorbell through the open French doors of the kitchen. Her heart leaped in her chest. What if Beck came back? She'd told him she had a date, but how did she know, really, what the man was capable of?

"Who might that be?" Christian asked.

"I don't really know. Stay here, though." She rose and walked quickly through the house to the foyer. When she opened the door, she found Jake Petersen's mother on the stoop, holding Josh's hand. "He wouldn't stay at the party," Sara Petersen began right away. "He said you told him you'd be home and he could come back if he wanted to."

Dropping down to crouch, she put her hands on Josh's shoulders. "What's wrong, honey?"

He stuck his fingers in his mouth, something he hadn't done for years. "Didn't wanna stay."

She gave him a hug, stood and drew him inside. "I'm sorry to trouble you, Sara."

"No, trouble. Got me away from ten screaming kids. They're playing war. Jake wanted a GI Joe-and-camouflage theme for his birthday."

Lela gulped back the remark she wanted to make about encouraging kids to play war. Did parents have any idea how combat ruined lives? "Still, thanks for bringing him home."

When they went inside, she said, "Josh, I have company."

"Dad?" he asked, his eyes both hopeful and a bit frightened.

"No, honey. A friend."

Just then, Christian came through the French doors and made his way to the living room. "Hi, Josh."

"This is Dr. Singer."

"You sick, Mom?" Josh's voice held panic.

"No, I work with him."

Josh watched Christian for a moment, then turned and ran up the stairs. Lela sighed. The night had just gone from bad to worse.

CHAPTER 8

LEN SAT IN his car, in the church parking lot, staring at his glove compartment. The darkness welled inside him and he pounded a fist on the steering wheel. He caught sight of his cell phone on the seat next to him. Picking it up, he held it to his chest. He'd started reading some stuff on the internet, and one of the sites for vets had said to call somebody when you felt like the black hole was about to swallow you up. Who could he call? His mother? No, she'd just get worried. His dad? Nope, his dad would get mad. Maybe Lela. Maybe she'd say she changed her mind, he could come home, she'd help him get through this terrible phase in his life. And right now he was sober, though the car stunk of stale booze; she hated when he called her drunk out of his gourd. He dialed the home phone.

"Hello," a small voice said into the receiver.

His heart plummeted. Lela hadn't answered. He'd gotten his son. But maybe he could still talk to her. "Hey, kiddo. How you doing?"

"Okay, Dad."

He scrambled for something to ask the boy. "How was the sleepover last night?"

A pause, then a soft, "I, um, I had to come home."

"Oh. That's not good. Why?"

"I got scared when the kids started playing war."

Jesus. For a minute, the interior of the car darkened.

All kids play war and your son can't stand it because of you, asshole. What good are you?

"I'm sorry, Josh," was all he could think of to say.

"'T's okay."

"Did your mom pick you up?"

"No, she was here having dinner. Mrs. Petersen brought me home."

Having dinner? What did that mean? Oh, fucking shit!

"Was…was she alone when you got home?"

"Uh-uh. How'd you know, Dad?"

"Lucky guess. Who was with her?"

"A doctor from the hospital. She wasn't sick. She said they're friends."

Red spots swam before his eyes. "Is she home now?"

"No, Mrs. Campoli is. Mom's running errands."

"Okay. Well, look, I'll see you soon, okay?"

"Yeah, sure."

After Len clicked off, he leaned back and closed his eyes.

Why wouldn't she have a date? She sent you divorce papers. You're a shit. You're worthless. She's moving on with her life and leaving you in the dust, boyo.

After listening to the voices in his head as long as he could, Len reached over and opened the glove compartment.

The gun was heavy in his hand. Not as much as the M4s in theater, but it would do the job. For a long time, Len just stared at the Glock, thinking of Lela with another guy.

• • •

THE BALL RAMMED into the front wall, ricocheted back and hit Beck in the leg. "Son of a bitch," he spat out, bending at the waist and rubbing his thigh.

"Sorry." Linc, his brother, didn't look sorry at all. "Besides, I don't complain when *you* beat the crap out of the ball, like you're doing now."

"Good, 'cause get ready for this." Mindless except for the game, Beck tossed up the ball in front of him, hit it hard, so it spun and zeroed into the left-hand corner. The tiny, blue sphere just missed the floor, hit right in the vee instead, and with a loud pop, spun out like a bullet. Linc couldn't return it. Not that he didn't try. Beck watched his brother take a slider across the floor. Damn, that had to hurt.

"You okay, hotshot?"

From his position on the floor, Linc laughed. His dark hair was dripping wet, and his clothes almost soaked, too. Just like Beck's. "Yeah, but we either gotta take it easy or quit. Sally said she'd kill me if I came home with any more bruises."

"Let's finish this round. I'm going to beat the pants off you."

Beck did beat Linc, but only by two points. When they were walking off the court, Linc glanced at the clock. "Come on, I'll buy you coffee. There's this little bistro next to the gym that has great fried dough."

They showered and bantered like they had when they were kids. Dressed, they took the short walk to the coffee shop. Once ensconced at a table, Beck was glad to kick back, listen to his brother and sip a double espresso.

Linc looked relaxed, too. "So, catch me up. I haven't seen enough of you since you joined the fire department. And emails don't count."

Beck filled Linc in on the firefighting excursions. The friends he'd made. How he sometimes even felt like he belonged. His brother nodded his approval as Beck confided in him.

"What about the PTSD group?" Linc's dark brows furrowed. "How's that going?"

One of the real tragedies of his condition, other than hurting Patty and his son, was Linc's constant worry over him. Beck loved his brother and didn't want to burden him. Jesus, he wished he could get rid of the thing.

"*That's* not as bad as I thought it would be. Talking to other people and hearing their stories is good for me. And that parents' group I told you about? It's helping me make progress with Tommy."

Linc's face lit up. He had the same green eyes as Beck, but his hair was lighter. "Beck, that's so good."

"I know. He was halfway decent to me at a gathering at Sea Breeze. He met a kid he actually liked." He told Linc about the line-cutting thing and how Josh Allen had behaved. Just like his mother would have. Beck's hands curled at the thought of her.

"You should try to get them together." Linc had two boys, now teens. He'd given Beck good advice over the years.

"Yeah, about that." Uncomfortable now, he nonetheless wanted to share his real feelings with Linc. He needed some help. "There's a woman."

Linc shook his head. "At the group?"

"Yeah, the other kid's mother."

"And?"

He shrugged a shoulder. "I like her. Oh, fuck, it's more than that. We got close somehow, fast. She's um, come to mean something to me."

"Where's the problem in that?" Linc had made no secret he hated seeing Beck alone.

"She just divorced a guy with a severe case of PTSD." Saying the words aloud made them real. And the situation clearer.

"Oh, shit."

"Yeah, oh shit."

For a while, Linc stared out the plate-glass window. "I don't have to tell you," his brother said quietly, "then she's probably off-limits."

"I know that."

"Wanna tell me how far it's gone?"

"Too far."

"Emotionally or physically?"

"Emotionally, too far. Physically, not far enough. Damn it, Linc, I think about her all the time. I can't wait to see her. And I only met her five weeks ago."

"You told me before, in certain situations, especially where you're pouring your guts out, all that's speeded up."

Drawing in a heavy breath, Beck let it out slowly. "I made an ass out of myself the other night." He explained their *dates*, his trip to her house and the kiss that haunted his dreams.

Linc chuckled. "Pardon me, big brother, but that is so much not you, I can't picture the scenario."

"I know it's not me. I can't believe I behaved so badly."

Linc socked his arm. "You're only human, Beck. Maybe it's good you let out some of what's inside you."

"That's what the shrinks say."

"What are you gonna do about her?"

"Try to stay away from her and discourage Tommy from seeing Josh."

"Too bad, bro, but I think that's for the best."

Beck shook his head. "Yeah, I know. I just wish I didn't feel so bad about what I have to do."

After they returned to their cars and Linc drove off, Beck was depressed from his talk with his brother, so he called Tommy. "Hey, son, how are you today?"

"Bored. Mom's busy with Mick."

"Are you alone?"

"No, Mrs. Elkins is here. Damn it, Dad, I don't need a babysitter."

Did he? Beck had no idea. He didn't like that he knew so little about parenting and vowed to do better at being his boy's father. "I'll talk to your mom about it. And don't curse. I'm off today. Wanna do something with me?"

"Like what?"

"I don't know." He watched the wipers go back and forth in their hypnotizing rhythm. "It's raining outside. Bowling maybe?" They'd done that a few times when Beck could coax his son to go out with him.

"Can I ask Josh Allen to come?"

Not once, ever, had Tommy sounded excited about spending time with Beck or asked for another kid to tag along. There was no way he could decline. Still, he cursed those goddamn fates he and Lela had mentioned. "Yeah, sure, if you want to."

"Can I call him?"

"Go ahead."

"You got his number?"

He'd noted her cell number when she called him at the house and for some God forsaken reason, had put in his phone. "Uh-huh. Just a minute, okay?"

As he searched his address book, he thought, *So much for staying away from them.*

• • •

LELA WATCHED SOPHIA wolf down a huge plate of frittata at a local restaurant they'd gone to for brunch on their day off. Lela hadn't wanted to leave Josh, but she needed to talk to somebody or she was going to lose her mind. And she didn't want to risk her son overhearing, so she'd invited Sophia out. Since Tony was with the kids, Sophia had jumped at the chance for some adult time.

Taking a sip of coffee, Sophia smiled mischievously. "So, is this about your hot date the other night? We haven't had a chance to talk about that."

Lela swallowed hard, her food untouched. "In a way. Look, Soph, something's been going on with me that I haven't shared with you." She glanced heavenward, hoping she was doing the right thing. "With anybody."

"Do you want to share now?"

"I have no choice. It's eating me up."

Beautiful dark eyes rounded. "You're not sick or anything, are you?"

"No, Josh and I are fine. It's an emotional thing. I've developed feelings for a man."

"Christian." She identified the doctor with certainty.

"If only it were that easy."

Thoughtful, Sophia set her mug down. "It's Beck, isn't it?"

At the mention of his name, at the notion of admitting her innermost desires aloud, her pulse rate doubled. "How'd you know?"

"From being around you two. There's not exactly sparks flying between you. It's more like a...link. Like you're tied together somehow."

"Well, there were plenty of sparks last night. He had a date. So did I. For some reason, he came over beforehand.

Asked if us dating others was *really* the way I wanted things to be."

"I don't understand."

"We've talked—actually we've talked around–the fact that we care about each other. In that messy male-female way. And every time we're together, there's so much going on, so much emotion in the air, we keep getting closer. I don't really understand why. This hasn't happened to me before."

"Tell me about the sparks."

The girlfriend-like inquiry made Lela smile. "When I asked him to leave, said that I didn't want to talk about us, he kissed me."

Which was a mild word for the explosion that had occurred between them.

"It was good?"

"Let's just say if what happened during a simple kiss was that hot, I can't imagine what making love with him would be like."

Sophia got a dreamy expression in her eyes. "It's been like that between me and Tony since day one."

"As if that isn't obvious to everyone."

Her friend concentrated back on her. "So what are you going to do about him?"

"Nothing. I don't plan to see him alone."

"I'm sorry. It's the PTSD thing, right?"

"Truthfully, I might risk a relationship for myself with him—he's so different from Len—but I'd never subject Josh to another man in his life who was sick with the syndrome."

"Sounds like an impossible situation."

"Uh-huh." She gave Lela a sad smile. "I just had to talk to somebody about it."

"I'm glad you chose me. But I have to say, I've been in what I thought was an impossible situation with Tony, and we got past it, dealt with it, to be together."

"You're married. You've been a couple since middle school. I've only known Beck for five weeks."

Lela's phone buzzed and she glanced down at where she'd set it on the table. "That's Josh's ringtone. I have to take this."

"Go ahead."

She clicked on. "Hey, buddy. You okay?"

"Yeah. I gotta ask you something."

"All right."

"Remember that kid Tommy I met at the park the other day?"

"Uh-huh." The back of her neck began to prickle.

"He just called and asked if I could go bowling with him and his dad."

"Do you like to bowl, Josh?" She'd never taken him to an alley.

"Grandpa takes me sometimes, remember? It's fun. Can we go?"

Lela stilled, but her heart rate escalated. "We?"

"Yeah, you and me. He said I could come alone, but I don't want to. I want you to be there with me."

"Oh, honey, that's not convenient for me."

"Why? You don't have to work today. You're only doing errands. Please, Mom."

Sophia's expression was puzzled. Lela rolled her eyes.

"Mo-om!"

"All right, I'll go. I'll call his dad for the arrangements."

"Thanks. I really like Tommy."

"Why, honey?"

"I dunno. I do."

"I'm glad. I'll be home soon."

When she clicked off, Lela buried her face in her hands. "You won't believe this."

"I got the gist of it." Sophia's tone was dry.

"I guess my son and I have a date with Beck and Tommy."

"You poor thing."

Lela nodded. But in truth, though she knew the decision they'd made to stay apart was the right one, she couldn't quell the spark of excitement at seeing Beck again.

• • •

BECK SWUNG THE bowling ball back with the grace of a natural athlete and sent it spinning down the lane. The big, black sphere smacked into the pins, leveling them all.

"Way to go, Dad!"

Though Beck was enduring the tortures of the damned at being around Lela, his heart was full as Tommy raced up to him and gave him a high five. "Thanks, son." He smiled back at Josh—shy little Josh who'd insisted his mother accompany them. "Your turn, Josh."

The boy had been up three times and gotten gutter balls. Beck had suggested they use bumpers, but Tommy had objected. When his son saw Josh's glum face as he approached the ball return, he whispered to his dad, "Can we still get the bumpers? I feel bad for Josh."

"Let's try one more thing first."

Lugging the lightest ball they could find, Josh approached the lane. Pins crashed in the background, and people laughed and cheered, but Josh was grim. Beck said, "Want some help, Josh?"

Josh shrugged.

"Tell you what, set the ball down by Tommy and stand just back of the line."

Like a good little soldier, Josh obeyed.

"Can I show you how to swing?"

"I guess."

Gently, he moved Josh by the shoulders so he was facing the pins and adjusted his stance. Then Beck placed his hand alongside the boy's and swung it back, then forward. He repeated the process.

Josh's face lightened and his body lost some of its rigidity. "I can do that."

"The other thing to try is throwing the ball on that arrow right in the middle of the lane."

"Down there" — he pointed to a second arrow — "or at the line?"

"Either, but I'd aim for the second one. I think that's easier."

"Okay."

Crossing to the side to get the ball from Tommy, Beck caught a glimpse of Lela's face. The profound approval there made him swallow hard and quickly avert his gaze. For once, he didn't feel like a total loser in the family department.

"Here you are." He handed the ball to Josh. "Try what I showed you."

Josh approached the alley gingerly, but he followed directions and concentrated hard as, with a thunk, he sent his ball down the lane. It rolled slow, slower, but straight on. Finally it hit. Pins!

"Holy cow, I got five." He pivoted around and did a little hop up and down. "Mom, I got five."

"I see, buddy. That is so cool. You're gonna beat me."

Tommy suggested, "Maybe my dad can help you, too, Mrs. Allen. Can you, Dad?"

"I guess." He mimicked Josh, but he knew his voice was hoarse.

He didn't watch Lela approach him in her plain, brown jeans and simple, tan T-shirt, which were anything but plain and simple on her. He tried not to inhale whatever-the-hell scent she was wearing as she lined up next to him. He ignored the throatiness in her voice as she said, "All right, Beck, have at me."

Sidling close, he leaned into her, much as he had Josh. "I'm sorry," he whispered. "I couldn't do anything about all this."

She sighed and peered up at him with huge, brown eyes. "You know what, fuck it! We're here; let's have fun. We'll deal with the rest later."

So he let his chin touch her hair—it was down soft and sexy. Aloud, he said, "All right, Miz Lela. Now, swing your arm back like this." His other hand went to her waist. And stuck there.

She whispered, "What are you doing?"

"Well, you said to have fun."

She chuckled. And managed a four-point gain.

When they finished their set, Tommy averaged 100, Beck 187, Josh a respectable 54. Lela managed a 75.

"Dad," Tommy asked as they exchanged their bowling shoes for their own, "Can me and Josh go play Monsters?"

"What's Monsters?" This from Lela.

"A video game. They got a sweet game room here, Mrs. Allen."

Beck explained, "Tommy's been to this bowling alley for birthday parties."

"Josh, do you want to go?" Lela asked.

"If Tommy'll help me."

"Then okay." To Beck she said, "Let's sit where we can see the room."

A table happened to be free across from the game section. Beck bought Cokes and popcorn, the kids ate a bit, then took off for their fun. Though the alley was crowded, Beck pretended he and Lela were alone in the cavernous space.

She stared over at him, as he did her.

After a while, he said, "It feels good just to look at you."

"I know. Same for me." She sipped from her soda and shifted in her seat. Because he'd stretched out with his legs in front of him, her foot came into contact with his.

"Sorry." Slowly, he moved both his feet and trapped one of hers between them. He watched to see what she'd do. She didn't squirm away. And her eyes looked like melted chocolate.

When she reached for popcorn, he stayed her hand. And linked a couple of fingers with his.

Her breath hitched. "Beck."

He held on loosely to her, but her touch burned him like a brand. "This is some predicament we've gotten ourselves into, isn't it?"

"The kids?"

"That, too."

"I'd be upset, because, you know, of me and you..." He squeezed her fingers. "...if Tommy wasn't so happy."

"Josh, too." She rolled her eyes. "I have a confession to make."

He scowled. Now what? "Oh?"

"I can bowl better than I did."

"Pretending for your son?"

"Uh-huh. And because we got to…touch." She shook her head, sending a few tendrils of it into her eyes. "We just can't seem to avoid each other."

"What are we going to do, Lee? I want to be with you."

"So do I. With you."

"All the time…" they said simultaneously.

He heaved a sigh; she frowned. But never once did he let of her hand.

• • •

LELA KNEW SHE should feel bad because she and Beck had gone back on their decision to stay away from each other, but whenever they were together, he filled up a hole inside her despite the circumstances. It was hard to regret that. So she let his feet imprison one of hers, let his fingers capture hers. No one could see their hands touching, because they were obscured by the popcorn, or their feet caressing, because the table precluded it; the dual connection made her heart skip beats. Once again, she allowed herself to wonder what it would be like to make love with him if just this tiny contact captivated her so much.

"Penny for your thoughts."

Again she shook her head. "X-rated."

"Jesus. Me, too. Doesn't it make you wonder what it would be—" Her phone rang, cutting off his confirmation that they were indeed on the same wavelength.

To prevent him from voicing the thought, she snatched her cell out of her purse. "Hello."

"Lela, I'm glad I caught you." Christian's smooth baritone came across the line—and did nothing for her.

"Oh, hi."

"One of my surgeries got canceled and I wondered if you wanted to go out on the boat tonight."

Oh, God. "I can't. There's no one to look after Josh."

"Bring him."

She shifted her body again, but Beck wouldn't let go of her hand. "I'm not ready to do that yet. I thought we discussed this."

"I could bring Kayla."

"No. Thanks, though. Some other time."

"I can't say I'm not disappointed, but I understand. We'll try it again when things are different." Before he disconnected, he said, "Think of me, at least."

When she clicked off and dared to look at Beck, his eyes burned with green fire. Hell, she was…aroused by his jealousy.

"It was your doctor friend, wasn't it?" Beck asked in a gravelly voice.

She nodded.

"You said no to a date?"

Another nod.

"Why?"

"Because it's too soon for him to meet Josh."

He arched a brow. An arrogant one. Could the guy be any sexier?

"I know." She sighed heavily. "We're here with both our boys. Sometimes this thing between us takes on a life of its own."

"Lela." Now his voice turned soft and coaxing. The verbal caress mesmerized her. "Maybe…"

Once more, her phone rang.

"I'll check the caller ID first to see if I have to answer this." She looked at her phone. "It's Len's father." Again she clicked into the cell. "Hi, Joe. Is everything all right?"

"No, Lela, it isn't. Can you come over here now? Without Josh."

Panic skittered up her spine. "Why, what happened?"

"I think Lennie tried to kill himself today." Her ex-father-in-law practically choked on the words.

"Oh, my God! Is he all right?"

"Unhurt, but far from all right. He's asking for you."

"Oh, Joe, I don't know...."

"This is my boy, Lela. Please."

"All right, I'll come. I have to make arrangements for Josh. I'll be over after I do that."

When she put the phone away, her hand trembled.

Beck's brow was furrowed, his eyes full of concern. "Honey, what happened?"

Somehow she got out the words.

"But he's not hurt?"

She nodded.

"What did he do?"

"Joe didn't say. Len wants to talk to me. Joe asked me to come right over."

"It's a crisis, Lela. You know you have to go."

"Yes, you're right. I don't know what I was thinking to object." She glanced toward the video room. "I have to find child care for Josh first."

"I can watch him."

"What?"

"He can come to my house with us. Tommy would love it."

"Oh, Beck, that's sweet of you, but he wouldn't stay at Eddie's party the other night. He probably won't go with you."

"Then we'll take him to your house. He'll be more apt to stay there with me in his own surroundings. It'll be better because it's after seven and you might be gone till bedtime."

She studied him closely. "You are a really nice guy. Damn you." At his questioning expression, she added, "It only makes you more attractive."

CHAPTER 9

THE ROOM WAS dim when Len woke up. He laid in the bed, staring up at the ceiling, trying to remember what had happened. But his mind was fuzzy. He recalled sitting in the car, talking to Josh.… Oh, fuck. Lela had had a date. Then he'd taken the Glock out of the glove compartment.

Had he eaten it? Was he in hell? He scanned the room. No, he was in the house where he'd grown up. And he didn't hurt any place. Must be he hadn't done anything to himself.

Too bad, shithead. Why don't you just end this misery?

He closed his eyes. The last thing he remembered was stopping at a liquor store and downing a pint of vodka in the parking lot. He didn't know what had happened after that.

Smart guy you are, Allen.

A knock on the door. He didn't want to see anybody. "Go away," he barked.

The door creaked open. He rolled to his side so he was facing the windows.

Soft footsteps. Then, "Len, it's Lela."

He swallowed hard. "Go away."

"Your dad called me. He said you'd asked for me."

Had he? What could she do for him? "I changed my mind. I'm fine."

"You were arrested, Len. Your dad had to go down to the jail and bail you out."

Holy mother of Christ. Turning over, propping himself up on the pillow, he found her standing before him, her hair back in a ponytail like she used to wear when they first met. He watched her pull a chair up to the bed with the gracefulness he'd always loved about her.

She asked, "Do you remember anything?"

"No, I blacked out after I drank."

"You probably had another PTSD attack. Yours seem to be worse with the alcohol."

He threw his forearm over his eyes. "What does it matter?"

"You don't remember what you were going to do?"

He shook his head.

"Len, you had a gun in the car. It had been fired."

So he did try it. Fucking first-class shit!

"Your dad says he thinks you tried to shoot yourself in the parking lot of a liquor store but were so drunk you missed. A bullet was embedded in the backseat."

"Jesus." He managed to sit up straighter and took a good look at her. She was so pretty and he wished like hell he could have her back. Then everything would be all right. "How much trouble am I in?"

"You were arrested for DUI. Apparently you have a permit for the gun."

He felt like the biggest loser in the world.

You are.

She fidgeted with the strap of her purse. "Len, do you want to die?"

"Why not? It's better than the alternative."

"What about Josh?"

"He'd be good without me. Then you and your guy could raise him and live happily-ever-after."

She stiffened. "You know about…What are you saying?"

"I called the house. Josh said you had a date last night with a doctor."

"Oh, Len, is that what brought this on?"

"No. I been thinking about it a lot."

"You need help."

Maybe he did. He either had to die or get out of this emotional hellhole. "From the fire guy?"

"We could start with Beck. But I heard at work that the VA hospital has a special program now for soldiers who are suicidal. It's, um, in-house."

"What does that mean?"

"You'd be admitted to a unit for six weeks and get extensive treatment."

Don't do it, asshole. Just throw in the towel.

Reaching out, she touched his arm. "Please, Lennie, I might be able to get you in. Do it for Josh."

Josh will be better off without you.

After a moment, Len rolled over on his side, and away from her. Nothing was clear and he didn't want to deal with reality anymore today.

• • •

BECK CLIMBED THE staircase of Lela's house for the second time tonight. The boys had wanted to go up and watch TV on her bed, together and without him, so he couldn't resist taking a look around.

It was a cute little two-story in a quiet part of town — just a small kitchen with a dinette in the back, a large living room and playroom in front. Upstairs were three bedrooms. She'd decorated the whole place with earth tones, microfiber couches and chairs, pictures of Josh all over the walls, some with Len and some with her. He hadn't found any of the three of them together.

Len. How was Lela faring through all that? His heart had gone out to her when she'd gotten the call. And though he knew better to feel this way with a PTSD sufferer, he was pissed as hell at the guy for putting Lela through this emotional trauma.

As he reached the top of the stairs, he heard a commercial about saving money with a local insurance company and headed in that direction. Initially, he'd checked on the boys to make sure they got settled with something appropriate on TV, then headed downstairs without spending too much time in her bedroom. Being in there did things to him, made him feel things he had no right to experience.

Now, at the doorway, he saw both boys sprawled out on the mattress—sound asleep. He glanced at his watch. Ten. They were facing each other, and for once, Tommy looked at peace. For some reason, Lela's son had gotten to *his* son with unbelievably positive results. What would happen if he told Tommy he couldn't see Josh again? The thought depressed him and he vowed no matter what happened to keep the boys together.

Still at the doorway, he studied the room. The walls and carpet were done in soft blues and greens with peach accents. Pretty, white furniture. Pastel prints of seascapes. Did she like the beach? The space suited her—feminine but strong. And man, she was strong. She handled everything fate shot her way, and fate had been cruel to her.

He stepped inside the room. After shutting off the TV, he crossed to the small mirrored vanity in the corner.

Bottles and jars lined the surface. He picked up an odd-shaped one, took off the top and sniffed. Immediately, he got hard. It smelled so much like her, he couldn't stop his reaction.

Quickly, he capped the jar, moved to the bed to cover the boys with a throw and left the room hurriedly. Ten minutes later, he was stretched out on the couch, reading a magazine, when he heard Lela enter the kitchen through the garage door. Soon, she appeared in the living room.

Her face was pale and her lips thinned. She stared at him silently. He rose and went to her. She put up her hand, palm facing out. "No, don't. I'll break down and I can't afford that."

"It'd make you feel better."

She shook her head firmly.

He stepped back. "Okay, then come sit on the couch."

When she did, he took her hand—her *ice cold* hand.

"Was it bad?"

"Oh, Beck, they think he tried to kill himself, but he downed a pint of vodka so fast, he missed. The bullet lodged in the backseat; its trajectory was about two inches from his head."

"Jesus."

She raised her free hand. "What do you do about something like this?"

"He's got to get help."

She described the VA program she'd learned about at work.

"Do you think he'd go?" Len didn't sound sane enough to make that decision.

"I brought it up. He didn't say yes."

"I can talk to him."

137

She nodded. "Maybe that would help."

Studying the lines near her eyes and the mauve smudges beneath them, he brushed his knuckles down her cheek. "You're exhausted. Do you think you can sleep?"

"I don't know." She glanced around as if a thought had just entered her mind. "Where are the boys?"

"They fell asleep on your bed, watching TV."

She sank back on the cushion as if fatigue had caught up with her. "Oh."

"I'll wake Tommy and take him home."

Silence. A long meaningful look from her.

"What?" he asked.

She waited, and he could see she was torn about something. "Do you think you could stay here tonight? Let the boys sleep on my bed. I'll go into Josh's room and you can have the spare room."

"Why?"

"I don't know. I just want you in the house." She bit her bottom lip in a rare show of vulnerability.

"Yeah, sure, I can do that. But I'll sleep down here on the couch."

She cocked her head in question.

"I don't want to be upstairs with you, Lee. I don't trust myself to sleep that close to you."

"I understand. That's probably best."

And probably one of the hardest things he'd have to do concerning her. He wanted nothing more than to sleep with her in his arms.

"Go on up now. Get some rest. We'll talk more in the morning."

"Thanks." Her hand trembled when he let go and he had all he could do not to clasp her to him.

Finally, she stood, crossed the room and disappeared up the staircase. Eventually, he lay down on the couch. He checked his watch; it was close to eleven. He rarely went to bed this early, but he closed his eyes and tried to block out the images of Lela suffering alone above him in her child's bed.

•   •   •

LELA BOLTED UPRIGHT. It was pitch-black in the room. She felt the space around her. A little bed. She sniffed scents of Play-Doh and crayons. Why was she in Josh's room at the back of the house? Josh. Tommy. Beck. Oh, God. Len had tried to kill himself!

She fell back onto the pillows and willed the tears that threatened away. She couldn't cry. She'd seen obscene things most people couldn't imagine. She wasn't going to bawl like a baby over the situation with her ex-husband.

But the images kept coming.

A gun.

A pint of vodka.

The city jail.

And Len, lying in the bed, telling her he didn't want to live anymore.

Then the recriminations began...if she hadn't left him... if she hadn't dated...if she was stronger and could make him get help...

Though she knew none of those were the root cause of his depression, her inadequacies plagued her until her thoughts became too much to bear. Throwing off the light sheet, she slid out of bed; the floor was cold against her bare feet as she walked out of the room. She was halfway downstairs when she realized she was braless, in a white T-shirt and navy pajama bottoms. Damn it, she didn't care. Beck was here and she was drawn to him.

The living room was cast in shadows, but light from the street lamps seeped in through the blinds. Tiptoeing across the carpet, she found him sound asleep on the couch—he was on his back, one arm thrown over his head. He'd unbuttoned the checked shirt he wore with jeans—which were also unsnapped—and Lela imagined a sprinkling of hair on his chest that was just a shade or two darker than his hair.

As she stood beside the couch, she was overcome with need—not lust—to be close to him. To have him shield her, for a little while, from the pain she felt over what had happened with Len.

The couch was wide but not wide enough to lie down next to him. So she perched on the very edge of a cushion and he came awake fast.

"What?" He didn't bolt up, though his body tensed.

"I'm sorry...I didn't mean to startle you, but..." she shrugged her shoulders. "I just...I wanted to lie next to you. I feel so bad." Her voice cracked on the last word.

"Aw, baby." Turning on his side, he slid farther into the pillows, making room for her. "Come here."

She stretched out on her side, too, so they were spoon fashion. His arms went around her and settled at her waist. She felt the brush of his lips on her hair, then a soft, "Better?"

Settling into his embrace, she nodded. "A lot."

"Go to sleep, then."

"Okay. You, too."

"You kidding? I'm gonna stay awake and enjoy this."

She chuckled. He laughed and then they quieted. Heavy, her eyes closed. But she felt safe for the first time all night and her last thought was, *Now, I can make it.*

• • •

FROM BECK'S PERSPECTIVE, Hale's Haven ranked right up there in his Best Things column, and had ever since he'd heard Jenn Malvaso talk about it at the firehouse. Gabe had encouraged Beck to come to this informational meeting for Junior Hale's Haven.

It's a good cause. We all work at one of the camps on our shift off plus furlough time. I think you'd like it, Beck.

That was Gabe, always trying to pull him into something. But how did he say no to a program so worthwhile? Besides, the meeting would keep his mind off sleeping with Lela in his arms last night.

"Hi, everybody," Jenn said to the volunteers. If we haven't met before, I'm Jenn Malvaso."

"O'Connor, woman!" someone yelled out from the group. Beck turned to see Grady O'Connor wink at his wife. Beck had worked with him a few times and found him to be one of the nicest guys in the whole department. But here it was again—that mile-wide-grin happiness that had infected the HCFD.

"Can it, O'Connor. You know the rules at work." She faced the group. "In any case, thanks to all of you for coming. As you know, we're going to put on an additional week this year for kids under seven. They can't attend the overnight camp because they're too little, but once again, we're modeling this program on the upstate New York Camp and calling it Junior Hale's Haven."

"You know all about kiddies these days," someone else said. Zach, Jenny's brother. "How are the twins, sis?"

Instead of putting him in his place, she smiled. "That I do, so listen up. We've identified ten kids in the area who qualify for this program and hope they'll all come. So we'll need ten volunteers at least: one for each camper, since an adult has to accompany the child everywhere. And I mean everywhere. They're little and they run away."

"Guess that lets Mitch out," Zach added. "He's too old to chase after babies."

"Watch your mouth." The comment came from a woman off to the side. She was pretty, with dark blond hair and blue eyes. This was Megan Hale, the founder of the camp. She'd come once to the firehouse to visit her brother-in-law, and Beck had seen her at a few social events. "Mitch can run circles around you any day, Zaccaria."

After the kidding stopped, Jenn scanned the room. "Any questions?"

Beck raised his hand. He'd thought about this off and on since Jenn came to House 7. "Firefighter Beckett Sloan, ma'am," he said formally.

"Yes, Beck. We're glad to have you in the department, and thanks for what you did over there."

He nodded. "I had an idea after you came to talk to us. There are some kids in Hidden Cove whose soldier parents were killed in the Middle East and Asia. Is there any chance we can include them in the junior camp?"

Immediately, Megan spoke up. "That is a terrific idea, Beck. Why didn't we think of it before?"

Jenn's face lit, too. "I agree. Though that'll mean more volunteers, depending on how many kids of soldiers we get."

"Maybe some vets from the Outreach Center will volunteer. They've got soft spots for the children of their brothers who died."

"Hmm. Beck, would you check that out?"

His brows rose in surprise. "Me?"

"Hey, don't make a suggestion around here. You get stuck with following through." This from a big guy, who he'd seen at Gabe's lake condo. Rick Ruscio, he thought, with some scandal in his background. He was holding hands with a pretty blonde.

She said, "I'm a volunteer in the hospital playroom. A lot of nurses and doctors talk about the camp. I bet they'd volunteer if somebody recruited them."

"Faith, honey, didn't you hear me about offering a suggestion?"

Ruscio was totally besotted—geez another couple in Happy Land—but it was Faith's question that made Beck moan internally. Jesus, he couldn't get away from Lela. Would they ask *her* to volunteer? Maybe she'd take a week at the big camp instead.

This morning, when they'd woken up together at dawn, she'd turned over, buried her face in his chest and said, "We can't do this, Beck. For a zillion reasons."

It had killed him to say, "I know...."

Still they'd lain there together, absorbing each other, cherishing the closeness that would never come to its natural conclusion.

Jenn interrupted his thoughts. "I'll count on you for that, Faith." She switched on a PowerPoint presentation. Now that we have all that to look forward to, let me outline what Junior Hale's Haven will look like. Each day we'll take the kids on field trips. Day one, we'll visit the Anderson County Zoo, then go to a movie. Day two will be at Play Station. They're closing the place just for us. For those of you who don't know what that is, it's a huge warehouse-like space filled with attractions like a rock-climbing wall, a variety of video and carnival games, and an outdoor area with batting cages and other games. We'll be there all day."

As Jenn continued to outline the movie they'd see, the amusement park they'd go to and a few other activities, Beck tried to focus on her. Still, his mind conjured lush, auburn hair that tickled his nose all night long, curves that tortured his body and the scent of the woman he cared for way too much.

• • •

"JACK, YOUR COUNT is too high again." Lela spoke quietly to the overweight man sitting on the examining table, who was having trouble keeping his diabetes under control. "What have you been eating?"

The kind but very troubled man rolled his eyes. "The pastries those church folks deliver every Monday here."

She arched a brow. "Do you only have one, like we discussed?"

"Um…"

She was exasperated this morning, and not because of guys like Jack. She knew it was because she'd slept with Beck last night, then he'd walked out of her life again. "Jack, we set up a nutrition program for you. You have to follow it." She put the blood pressure cuff on him and pumped the bulb. "Hmm, this is high, too. Have you been exercising?"

"Yeah, I been doing that. Honest Nurse Lela." He explained his routine to her.

"Good. But your pressure is still borderline. If it goes any higher, we'll have to send you to the doctor for pills."

He nodded vigorously.

When Jack left, she walked to the door with him and noted that there were no others waiting for her. She'd be here four hours so some guys were likely to straggle in.

Damn it. She wished they were busier. She needed something to occupy her brain. To stop thinking about Len trying to end his life. About Beck and how he'd totally been there for her, held her all night, made everything seem bearable if only for a few hours. They'd woken together and stayed very still, reveling in the feel of being so close.

"Hey, Lela." Nick came down the hall to the clinic entrance.

"Hey, buddy. I was wondering where you were."

He rolled his eyes. "I overslept."

"How wonderful. Insomnia's been a problem for you. You must be feeling good." He did look better. His eyes weren't brimming with fatigue. "And is that a tan I see? Been outside?"

"I went for a picnic on the lake with Amy yesterday."

"Good for you. Was it fun?"

"Yeah. Then we went to a concert out there and listened to some great band. It was outside, so there was no dancing." Automatically, he glanced down at his foot.

"Oh, Nick. I'm so glad you did that."

"Takin' one step at a time, pardon the pun."

Lela laughed. She knew as a nurse that patients who could joke about their condition, no matter how black the humor was, were making progress.

So she gave Nick a big smile, then led him inside to stock an assortment of creams and ointments they'd just gotten in.

About an hour after they'd started, she heard, "Hey, there."

Hell. Beck had said, *I'll try to stay away from you. I promise.* So why was he here?

When she pivoted around, she saw him standing in the doorway, dressed in khaki shorts, a brown T-shirt, with sandals on his feet. He looked…delicious.

"Sorry to stop by unannounced, but I came to see Julie and wanted to talk to you, Lela, for a minute."

Nick said, "I'll go get some coffee."

Beck held up his hand. "Before you do, I wanted you to know some vets here are going to volunteer at a camp for kids of slain firefighters and police officers. They're adding children of soldiers this summer."

"That's cool," Nick commented.

"I was hoping you'd volunteer, Nick."

"Me?" he said, his tone incredulous. He even backed up a bit. "I can't work at a camp. I can barely walk."

"There are a lot of jobs you could do."

"Like what?"

Beck went on to list several. Then he added, "Or you could be my assistant counselor and come along in a wheelchair."

Nick's face turned beet red. "No way, Colonel. No fuckin' way." He brushed past Beck and out the door.

Beck raised troubled, green eyes to Lela. "Did I blow that?"

"He said he'd never use a wheelchair. It's one of his main goals. You couldn't have known."

"Damn it. I should have checked with you first."

She shook her head. "No, Nick needs to be pushed out of his comfort zone. You've given him something to mull over."

She smiled sadly at him. "What did you need to talk to me about?"

"The camp is looking for volunteers, like I said, and somebody suggested drafting nurses and doctors. I came to tell you I'll be working Junior Hale's Haven in July."

"That's so sweet of you."

"I wanted to warn you. If you volunteer for a camp, you shouldn't pick that week."

Her heart plummeted. She just stared at him.

"Don't look at me that way, honey. If we're going to stay away from each other, then we have to do better than we have been."

"Of course. You're right."

He scowled fiercely. "I hate this." He hit the wall with his open palm. "All right, I'm getting out of here before I say something I regret. Take care."

"Yeah, you, too."

Lela sank down on a stool. Her insides were churning and her heart ached. She cursed herself, and him, for getting themselves into this position.

Then, she did what she'd learned to do in the ugly outposts when soldiers died on her. She turned back to her work and blanked her mind!

CHAPTER 10

"INCOMING," THE CHARGE nurse called out and Lela went running from the medicine room. The paramedics wheeled in a stretcher through the ER door, and Lela reached the gurney just as Christian did.

"Four-year-old fell into the river," the female medic said. "We found him twenty minutes after he was last seen."

Lela took the child's pulse while Christian checked his breathing.

"No pulse." She glanced at the woman—Sarah, her name tag read. "You said he was submerged twenty minutes?" That needed to be clarified.

"Yes. That's our best estimate."

Lela looked back down at the blue, rigid, little body. "The water could have been cold enough," she said to Christian.

"I agree. Get him in ER 1." He glanced up at the paramedics. "You did cardio resuscitation?"

"Yes."

"Good job." They were wheeling the boy away, but he added, "You could have saved his life, Sarah."

He and Lela brought the boy into the first room.

A half hour later, she walked out, drained. Christian was behind her.

Whipping off his surgical mask, he blew out a heavy breath and leaned against the wall. For support, she guessed. "Jesus, that was close."

"It's not over yet."

"No, but he's breathing." Christian's blue eyes were animated. It was a nice sight. "He might be in a coma for a while."

"Still, the family has hope." She nodded to two people who looked about fifteen, who were sitting with Sarah, the medic—obviously the parents. The frightened expression on their faces hurt to watch. "Go tell them," she said.

"You come, too." He grasped her elbow. "It's not often we bring people back from the dead."

"I can't. I have to make a phone call. I'm on break"—she glanced at her watch—"as of a half hour ago."

Lela made her way to the lounge and found one inhabitant on the couch. Sophia Ramirez. She held a cup of coffee, its strong scent permeating the room. "What are you doing down here?" Lela asked.

"I came hoping to have coffee with my friend."

Lela gave her a sideways look.

"You've been positively bleak since last week, and even though I know why, I'm worried."

Too tired to argue, Lela took her phone out of the pocket of her pink scrubs. "I have to call Josh." Which meant talking to Beck again. In the past week since she'd last seen him, Tommy and her son had spent time together twice. Once, Lela had taken them to the circus that was in town, and today, Beck had taken them to a movie in 3D.

Beck answered her call after the third ring. "Hi, Lee." His voice was husky but restrained. They'd both been determined to stay apart this time and had acted accordingly. They even stayed distanced when they had to talk on the phone. The whole situation had just gotten too painful.

"Hi, Beck." Her voice was full of soft approval. She couldn't disguise that. "How are things?"

"The movie was great. The boys had a good time."

"Did you?"

"Of course, I find Shrek fascinating." He chuckled, the sound masculine, sexy. "From-one-ogre-to-another kind of thing."

She giggled and wanted to flirt but didn't. "Good. I should be done in an hour."

"We're heading to my house as we speak."

"I'll swing by and pick up both boys and drive them to the Allens." Grandma and Grandpa had asked to take Josh to Six Flags Amusement Park in the Adirondacks for a couple of days while Len settled into the rehab they'd finally convinced him to go into. Josh begged to bring Tommy along. Since Beck's son wanted to go, it seemed harmless.

"You sound cheerful," he noted. "Good day at work?"

"A four-year-old boy fell into the river and was submerged for twenty minutes. We got him breathing."

"Ah, a save. There's nothing like it. Especially a kid."

Another thing they had in common—he understood life and death in the same vein as she did. "I have to go. See you soon." She clicked off so they didn't *bond* over this, too.

"Come sit." Sophia rose and poured another cup of coffee. She brought it to Lela and dropped down across from her. "Even a save like that didn't help ease the pain, Lee. It's written all over your face."

Beck had taken to calling her the nickname, too. "I don't know what to do about it. We've stayed apart as much as we can this week. Hell, I even skipped the PTSD meeting."

"And it's not better?"

"You know, it's worse. Maybe because Tommy and Josh want to hang out. I wish like hell it could be the four of us together."

Sophia was silent. Which was unusual, because she always had something to say.

"Soph?"

"I'm going out on a limb here, but I can't watch you suffer any more. I think you should give you and Beck's relationship a try."

Lela sighed and ran a restless hand through her hair, which she'd forgotten she'd braided. "As if I don't think about that all the time."

"But?"

"I could risk it for me, I care about him so much. But I can't risk Josh."

"You're risking Josh right now. By letting him be with Beck."

She bit her lip. "In certain situations. And for a contained amount of time. That's as far as I'll go. We don't really have a choice in the boys being together. It's brought both of them out of their shells. But having Beck around all the time? No. As a pediatric nurse, you know the stats on how PTSD affects kids. Beck and I have both seen it up close."

"I understand that. But I don't think you can do this much longer, Lee."

"I have to. We both have to stick to our plan."

"I'm so sorry."

She sighed. There was little else to say.

Her phone went off again. She checked the ID and the nurse at the desk said, "Come quick, Lela. There's been a bad accident. Lots of people. Heavy casualties. Kids, too. We're calling everybody who's available in."

Clicking off, she said, "An accident. Heavy casualties. Some kids. Let's go."

They flew out the door and raced to the ER, all thoughts of Beck and Lela's doomed relationship forgotten.

• • •

AS HE'D TOLD Lela, Beck had had fun at the movies. The story was cute and he'd enjoyed seeing Tommy and Josh laugh aloud at the antics of the ogre and his crew. Both boys needed more laughter in their lives. Now, as he drove them to his condo, he glanced in the backseat. Tommy held a comic book and was reading aloud to Josh. His heart expanded in his chest as he watched them together. Apparently Tom enjoyed being a big brother, and Josh liked having one. Maybe, just maybe, getting the two boys together was worth the hell he and Lela were going through to arrange it.

She'd sounded so sad on the phone, like she missed him as much as he missed her, that he wanted to rush over to the hospital and tell her they had to work this out. But he knew he wouldn't do it. They both needed to be strong.

Splat! Damn. A bird had flown overhead and dropped his business on the front window. It dotted the entire driver's side.

"Hey, Dad. That bird pooped all over your window."

"I see that."

"You should go to the car wash," Josh suggested. "I like when Mom goes through it."

Shrugging, Beck took a few turns and found the nearest car wash. Chatting easily with the boys, he pulled in line; a worker sprayed the car with water. Josh and

Tommy plastered their faces to a side window, and the kid obliged by spraying right at them. They giggled, making Beck grin.

Another worker motioned for him to move up, and that one took his payment, then soaped the car, giving special attention to the boys' faces. When the light flashed green, he put the car in neutral and sat back.

The first major spray coated the entire car. The boys whooped.

But Beck began to sweat. Being closed in was never easy for him and he'd forgotten how…confined the car was in this process. He breathed in through his nose and slowly let it out his mouth. Once the soap was washed off, his skin began to cool. The kids got a kick out of the blue belt-like brushes and pretended they were monsters from outer space. Beck looked down at the steering wheel. The belts reminded him of some-thing, but he couldn't place what.

On the second soaping, the car was even more opaque. And Beck's stomach began to churn. Oh, God no. Not now. He tried deep breathing as a counselor had taught him to do. Again the soap cleared.

The last part of the car wash was a hard spray of water on all the surfaces, glass included.…

Oh, God, the sandstorm had come out of nowhere. With his men behind him, he yanked the kerchief up to cover his mouth and pulled his goggles over his eyes. He hoped the men behind him did the same. They'd trained for this. Gales of sand rolled in like a tornado, and all they could do was stop and ride it out. He thought fleetingly of the sand fleas this would bring with it.

A loud clatter rent the air as the dirty cloud passed over them. The sand began to abate but blue cloth appeared before him. The clothes of the enemy. He lifted his gun…

There was pounding. Beck opened his eyes to hear, "Hey, Mister, you okay?"

Glass dripped with water, but he could see out of it now. One of the workers was standing close. Beck slid down the window.

"What's wrong?" the guy asked.

Mortified, Beck began, "I…I…look, I'm a vet. I had a…" Oh, Jesus. "Step back!" he barked and the kid did, just in time for Beck to bolt out of the car and vomit all over the pavement. When he finished, he wiped his mouth and noticed the four guys off to the side. They were teenagers and their expressions were disgusted. Hell. He'd made a mess and it stunk to high hell. When he turned, he saw Tommy's and Josh's faces pressed up against the window again.

He wanted to die at the abject fear in their eyes.

• • •

SITTING IN HER car, Lela stared at Beck's condo complex. The outside was well kept, with lush landscaping, mature trees and paved sidewalks. She stared at it, unable to move.

In the hour she had left on her shift, they'd lost two husbands, a grandfather, one three-year-old child and the cab driver. The scent of blood and death still clung to her, and her heart ached for the relatives of these people who'd been the victim of a man driving his pickup truck drunk. The guy hadn't had a scratch on him. A black pall had been cast over a group of people who, minutes before, had been overjoyed at saving a child.

She'd phoned Beck and told him she'd be late. He'd offered take the kids to the Allens', but she had Josh's duffle bag in her car. He'd sounded odd on the phone but said everything was okay.

Everything wasn't okay with Lela. Staring death in the face, as she had in the nightmarish scenario, had hit her harder than the time a squad of seven soldiers had been killed in an IED explosion and she'd had to patch up the remaining three. Maybe it was because one of the dead today was a child. Or because for hours she listened to the wrenching sobs of the grieving wives, whose lives had been unalterably shattered. Maybe it was going from such a high, saving the little drowning victim, to the abyss of so much loss.

And maybe it was because her reserves of strength had been depleted in the weeks she'd been trying not to fall victim to Beck's spell.

Now, in the depths of despair, she wondered why she avoided the joy they could have together. Sophia's words echoed in her brain. *I think you should give your relationship a try.* Followed by the slap of cold hard reality in her face: *we never have as long as we think we have!*

"Fuck it," she said. "I'm done with this. I'm going to take a chance." Whipping open the door, Lela exited her car, marched up the sidewalk and rang the front bell at Beck's condo.

He answered right away.

"Hi," she said breathlessly. "I've got something to tell you. Something good."

His face was pale and his eyes haunted. "Yeah, I've got something to tell you, too."

• • •

HAD BECK EVER felt any worse about himself? If he had, he couldn't remember the time or place. The thought of telling Lela what had happened to him in front of the boys made his chest tight as they crossed into the living room. The pressure kicked up to angina when Josh bounded off the couch and ran to her. He threw himself at his mother and held her in a death grip because Beck had scared the living daylights out of him.

"Hey, Josh." Lela held her son tightly. "What's wrong?"

"Beck got sick, Mom, like Daddy does sometimes."

Her gaze snapped to Beck's face. He said simply, "I had a PTSD attack in the car wash. It scared the boys."

She watched him. He was sure she was torn between worry about Josh and the desire to comfort Beck.

"I'm so sorry, Lee."

Standing, she touched his arm. It was a kind gesture, but the disappointment in her eyes knifed him. "Me, too, Beck. For you." Disentangling herself from Josh, she held him apart from her. "Honey, are you okay?"

"I got afraid, Mommy."

"I know. It's frightening when Daddy gets sick, too."

"I didn't like it."

"Neither did I, Josh." Beck knelt down so he looked the boy in the eye. There was none of the pleasure in Josh's eyes that he usually showed when he was with Beck. "I'm so sorry I scared you. The car wash scared me."

Josh peeked up at him. "It did? You're so big."

"Big people get afraid sometimes." He glanced over at his own son. Tommy, sitting on the couch, wouldn't even look at him. Had he just destroyed the fragile bond he'd been building with the boy?

Lela waited until Beck rose and put her hand on Josh's shoulder. "We should cancel the trip with your grandparents. Why don't you just stay home with me, baby?"

Tommy bolted up off the couch. "No, please, Mrs. Allen. I wanna go."

Josh remained silent.

Tommy crossed to him. "Don't you want to be with me anymore, because of my dad?"

Jesus, could this get any worse? Beck had to look away from the sight.

Finally, Josh spoke up. "I do. I wanna go on the rides with you." He looked at his mom. "Can we still go with Grandma and Grandpa?"

"If you want to."

Josh took Tommy's hand. "I do."

She transferred her gaze to Beck. He expected disgust, anger, accusation in her eyes. Instead, there was pity. It was almost worse. "Is it all right if they still take the trip?"

"Yeah, sure. Tommy's ready." He cursed the hoarseness in his voice, but he could barely speak.

"I've got Josh's bag in the car." She motioned to the boys. "Then let's do this, guys."

Beck watched as his son got his duffle and headed past him to the door. Josh followed suit. Lela called out, "Wait on the stoop, guys."

When they were alone, she turned to him. "Beck, Josh will get over this."

"Nothing I don't deserve."

"Oh, Beck, no. This isn't your fault."

"Of course it is."

"I don't want to leave you like this." He knew she meant the words, and that made things all the worse.

"Go, Lela. Now and forever. I'm no good for you. For your boy." When she hesitated, he said raggedly, "Please."

She watched him for a few excruciating moments. Then, standing on her tiptoes, she kissed him briefly on the mouth. Finally, she walked out of the house.

Beck closed the door behind her, and leaned his forehead against the cool wood. He stayed there for a long time, trying to diminish the almost intolerable pain he felt at his inadequacy.

• • •

LELA HAD SEEN atrocities in her life, both physical and mental. But the pain in Beck's eyes when his son walked out on him was so deep, she wanted to weep for him. She simply had to make him feel better.

So, after she dropped the boys off at Len's parents' house, she made a quick trip home and then headed out again. When she reached Beck's condo for the second time tonight, she found the windows completely dark. Still, she pulled into the driveway, got out of her car and checked the windows of the garage, where she saw his SUV. He was probably sitting alone in the dark suffering.

Not if I can help it.

At the front door, she rang the bell. No answer. She rang again. Still the silence. She tried the door handle and couldn't turn it. Looking around, she noticed a path on the far side of the garage to the back of the unit. She followed the stone, circled the end of the building and came upon an eight-foot-high fence. And found a patio on the other side.

He was stretched out on a chaise; a bottle of beer sat on the table beside him. One arm was thrown over his eyes, and his body was rigid.

"Beck?"

He bolted up, his hands gripping the arms of the chaise. "Lela? What...?" He raked his hand through his hair and stared at her for a few seconds. "Why are you here?"

All she'd known was that she couldn't leave him alone in such misery. "I needed to see you."

"I'm okay." He sank back onto the chaise. "You didn't have to come back over."

"Of course I did."

He studied her. "What's that?" He pointed to a bag she carried.

Though she'd faced down war and terror, her insides churned at the risk she was about to take. "Clothes, toiletries." She raised her chin. "Condoms."

She hadn't expected his face to darken, and anger to flare in those beautiful eyes. "No."

"No?"

"I don't want a mercy fuck."

She shook her head. "That's not what I'm thinking."

"What could you *possibly* be thinking to come here like this?"

Again, she went on instinct. Dropping the bag on the bricks, she moved to him. Slowly, she straddled the chaise. Straddled him. "Why, kind sir, my little southern heart is flutterin' at the thought of makin' love with you."

His hands gripped her waist. Clenched there. "Don't joke about this."

"All right." She covered his mouth with hers to stop his protests. His body hardened even more, but she pressed her breasts into him and deepened the kiss. It took only seconds for his arms to band around her. His mouth softened and he angled his head. She took the opportunity to open his lips with her tongue. They explored each other and the sweetness of it, the bridled passion just waiting to burst out made her melt into him. He moaned. But eventually he set her away.

"That better?" she asked.

He shook his head. "Lee, baby, this isn't good."

"It *is* good. We have to savor whatever joy we can find in life."

"What do you mean? You saved a baby today."

"Right after, there was a bad bus accident. Several people died in our ER. A child." She nosed into his chest, inhaling the male, alive scent of him. "It was awful."

His hand curled around her nape. "I'm sorry, but I still don't understand. You should be running for the hills from me."

"I ran toward you instead."

"Meaning?"

"I decided on my way here to pick up the boys that we should try out a relationship between us."

He gave an awful laugh. "Well, I sure blew that out of the fucking water."

She had to be honest. "You did. We can't be together. I know that now—again, I guess—after what happened to you and the boys' reaction. I knew it before, but I talked myself into giving us a shot."

He swallowed hard. Facing your flaws, particularly for a strong man like Beck, a leader and a savior had to be killing him.

"So why are you here?" He squeezed her hips. "Like this?"

"Because I want two days with you. The kids are gone; I'm off and you're off. I want this, Beck, even if it's all we'll ever have."

"I don't know, honey. Can you imagine how much harder it will be afterward?"

She leaned in and whispered, "Well, I'll be darned, sugar. All this time, I thought it got softer."

He laughed and the sound made her smile. "You're bewitching, you know that?"

"Am I?" She cupped his cheeks with her hands. "Please, Beck, give us this. You and I have seen death, seen horror, and we still do. Let's forget about it for two days, be together and enjoy what we can get out of life today. Afterward, we'll be strong."

He pressed his forehead to hers. "All right. Just for now."

CHAPTER 11

BECK BLANKED HIS mind as she slid off him and held out her hand. He refused to think as he took it, stood, stooped down to pick up her bag and led her into the house. He locked the glass doors rotely. Without saying anything, fearful that he'd ruin the moment, or worse, awaken and find her coming here was a dream, he went before her up the steps to the second floor and down to his bedroom. Once inside, he turned to her. Softly brushing his knuckles down her cheek, he whispered, "You are so lovely. You take my breath away."

She inhaled sharply. "No one's ever said that to me. Thought that about me."

"I do, love. I do." His fingertips flirted with the strap of the sundress she'd changed into. "This is nice. I like you in yellow."

"Take it off me, Beck."

"My pleasure." He chuckled at his joke. "Now and for two whole days." With as much gentleness as he could summon, he slipped the material from her shoulders. He tugged it over her breasts, then past her waist until the silky material puddled on the floor. Beneath it she wore a yellow strapless bra and, oh, dear Lord in heaven, a matching thong. "Good grief." He pressed his body against her.

"I see someone sprang to attention, soldier."

"Damn right. That's what you get for wearing this." He ran a fingertip along the scalloped top. "Though I can't quite see practical Nurse Lela buying it."

"I didn't." Her face flushed. "Sophia gave it to me for my last birthday after I confessed I loved sexy underwear but never get around to getting any."

"I love sexy underwear, too. Leave it on for a while."

"Anything for you."

Damn. Her words made his hands shaky as they went to the hem of the green T-shirt he wore.

"No, let me."

"Anything," he repeated. She pulled his shirt over his head. Stopping briefly to kiss his breastbone, her hands went for his belt, dispensed of that and his shorts. He wore navy blue briefs, which were now stretched to their limits.

By God, if she didn't kneel in front of him. "Lee, wait, what…?" But she was already tugging his underwear off. Soon he sprang free of the material, kicked out of it. Her palms cupped him. He allowed the massage for about two seconds. Then he tugged her up.

"Aw, no fair."

"Honey, it's been a while for me. Um, a long while."

Her eyes lit. "For me, too. A very long while."

"Let's go to the bed."

She fished some condoms out of her bag and followed him. He laid down first; she put her knees on the mattress, then draped herself over him. "Kiss me, Beck, like you mean it."

He flipped her over, covered her with his body and met her mouth with his. He pressed, probed, took. Then he soothed and started all over again. She squirmed restlessly beneath him. He felt himself harden even more and worried he couldn't prolong their lovemaking; he wanted to savor every minute.

Easing off her and to his side, he captured her gaze and removed her panties. Reaching around her, he unsnapped the pretty bra and tugged it away. "You are so incredibly lovely. I almost can't stand it." He cupped the flesh he'd bared, kneaded her. "Almost." He ran his hand along her torso, over the silky skin, raising goose bumps. "I don't know how you like this," he said, feeling momentarily unsure of himself.

"I'll love anything we do together. Don't wait, Beck. I'm ready. So are you." More softly, sexily, she said, "We can take our time later."

After one more look at her beautiful body, he snatched a condom from the nightstand and rolled it on. Facing her again, he poised himself at her entry and slid easily inside. She *was* ready. He lowered his head so their cheeks and chests touched; her legs went around his waist and he started to move.

Nothing in his whole life had ever felt this good. She moaned, and he pushed harder, picked up the pace. Only a few thrusts and she spasmed around him, called out, "Beck…" and came fast and hard.

His mind blanked at her orgasm; he pushed and pushed and pushed. Rockets went off in his head. Bright colors eclipsed everything as he found his own release.

They stayed as they were, hugging even tighter, breathing each other in. Then he knelt back and looked at her. "It was—" he couldn't find the words.

"Mind-blowing. I knew it would be."

He'd known that, too. Doubts about the wisdom of making love tried to penetrate his consciousness. He fought them back, lay down and tugged her to his chest. He wouldn't think about that for two days. There'd be enough time to face life without her after this was over.

• • •

LELA AWOKE IN Beck's bed, alone. Damn. She wanted to see his face the first thing in the morning, touch his skin, inhale his scent. After all, she wouldn't get a chance to wake up with him after tomorrow. Her throat closed up.

Don't think about that.

As an army medic and a trauma nurse, she'd trained herself to focus on the now and blank out the rest. So she glanced around her. His bedroom was masculine and trendy. She thought he might not be interested in décor, but he'd done a nice job with the sand-colored walls, beautiful landscape paintings in an impressionist mode. Oak dressers were flanked by two comfortable-looking, nubby, white chairs in the corners, both next to a stack of books. She wouldn't have pegged him as a reader, either. What kind of books did he like?

Spying a bath off the bedroom, she hopped out of bed to use the facilities, then she wandered around the room. A copy of a Tom Clancy novel sat on top of the stack of books. Loose change, a handkerchief and a pocketknife were spread out a dresser. Next to the door, on the wall, was an eight-by-ten engraved plaque of the raising of the flag by World War II soldiers at Iwo Jima. Adjacent to it was a second one of firefighters from 9/11 also raising a flag.

Because she wasn't ready to leave the cocoon of this lovely space yet, she climbed back in bed. Dreamily, she recalled how he'd touched her last night, how tender and sweet he'd been until passion claimed them both and things got wild. The second time had been slower but no less intense.

"Ah, you're awake." He stood in the doorway holding a tray. The strong scent of coffee and fresh pastries made its way across the room. "I brought you food. I'm famished."

"Me, too. We forgot to eat."

"We had more important things on our minds." He set the tray down on the dresser and yanked off his shirt and pants. He'd gone commando. "That's better."

"No argument from me there."

Bringing the tray to the nightstand, he climbed in beside her and kissed her. "Good morning."

"Hmm, that it is." She ran a hand down his cheek, now darkened and scratchy. Sexy. "Sleep well?"

"Better than I have since I got back from Afghanistan."

"I'm glad."

He nodded to the tray. "What do you want first?"

"Coffee."

"Black, right?"

"Yes." She pointed to the food. "Did you have all this on hand?"

"Hardly. There's a Starbucks right near here. I stopped for the fruit at a little store."

Propping herself up higher onto the pillows, she drank from the cardboard cup he handed her. He mirrored her position, took her hand in his and they sipped in silence.

After a while, she said, "I want some of the croissant," and moved to reach over him.

He batted her hand away, took a croissant off the plate, buttered it and faced her. Tearing off a small piece, he put it to her lips. She held his gaze and chewed. He smiled and took some for himself.

They ate again in silence. She briefly wondered if they were afraid to talk but pushed the notion away and simply let him feed her. Flaky bread. Succulent strawberries. Oh, there was a big fat apple fritter. They consumed that, too.

"Stop," she finally said. "Enough food." When he adjusted his position, she got a glance at the tray. "Oh, we forgot the orange juice."

"No, we didn't." He turned back to her with the glass in hand. "Now pull that sheet to your waist. I'm thirsty for juice." He winked at her. "And you."

"Yes, sir," she said and began to tingle all over when the cold liquid hit her breast.

• • •

"THIS WAS A great idea," Lela said, slipping her hand into his as they walked down Broadway. At nine, they'd decided on a day of fun in the Big Apple, and since the city was only an hour away, they'd made it here by eleven. She'd dressed in a denim skirt and simple, white T-shirt with canvas on her feet and he'd worn jeans and a short-sleeved, navy shirt.

Beck gazed down at her. The sight of Lela by his side, after an incredible night — and morning — of sex made him feel like he could scale mountains. When he remembered their tryst was only for two days, his heart hurt. "I thought it would be fun to do something together."

"Don't you love the feel of the city? The tall buildings, the scents of vendor food, the sheer aliveness of it?"

"Yeah, I do." He leaned into her because he could. "And it's the home of my guys."

"Your guys?"

"Yeah, the Bronx Bombers."

"Excuse me?"

"The Yankees, silly." He stopped dead in his tracks. "You *have* heard of the Yankees."

"Of course. My parents watched the Red Sox and they played the Yankees."

"Uh-huh."

The sun gleamed off her head, revealing some strands of blond in the auburn mass. "Besides I know a little bit about baseball. I saw the play *Take Me Out* on stage here a few years ago."

"Let me guess. It was about baseball."

"Yeah. About a rookie player who came out gay and the ramifications of his disclosure."

"That's good to hear. We need more positive views of gay athletes. And soldiers. I fought hard against Don't Ask, Don't Tell."

She smiled up at him and he could feel approval emanate from her. As they continued to walk, they passed the ad for a new play starring Kiefer Sutherland and Lela halted this time. "Oh, I love this actor."

On a whim, because he wasn't much of a play guy, he asked, "Wanna go?"

Her eyes reminded him of Christmas morning. "Do you mean it?"

"Sure." He glanced at his watch. "We still have time for lunch first." He scowled. "But I wanted to take you to a bookstore down here that's really cool."

"Honestly? Oh, Beck, I love books."

At least they had that in common. Not that it mattered after today. After today, she wouldn't be in his life.

Don't think about that.

She said, "We could have a hot dog from a vendor, go to the bookstore and still make the play."

"The box office isn't open yet."

"We'll take a chance and come back."

"Sounds good to me." He smiled, anxious to show her Mum's the Word, curious to what her reaction would be. "Let's go this way."

He led her down a narrow street of shops and stopped in front of a tiny store, tucked away as if it was one of New York's secrets.

When she read the sign, she began to laugh. "You're taking me to an erotic bookstore?"

"It's not porn." He shrugged and leaned into her. "Or maybe it's high-class porn. Come on."

The interior was classic Old World, with the requisite grizzled man at an ancient desk, the musty scent of books piled high on tables, shelves, chairs and the floor. "It's a lot more organized than it looks," he whispered.

They wandered around. Beck watched her pick up a heavy tome. "What's that?"

"A classic from the *Sleeping Beauty Trilogy* by Anne Rice. I met her once at a signing I went to because I love vampire books." She read the back-cover copy. "Not sure this is my taste, though." She moved farther down the shelves. "Ah, here's one by an author I love. She writes in several genres under pseudonyms, but she did a series of erotic books called the *Hidden Grotto* as Louisa Burton."

He scanned the book blurb. Wow. "You want these? Seriously?"

"Uh-huh." Her eyes twinkled and her cheeks were pink. "We'll read some scenes aloud together. Maybe it'll give us new ideas."

"I have plenty of ideas, lady."

"Did you find anything?"

"Yep." He held up a slim paperback.

She read the title, *The Fine Art of Erotic Talk,* and burst out laughing. "You don't need that, Beckett Sloan."

"No?"

"No."

He slid his arm around her. "Let's get it anyway. Along with yours. We can have fun with them both tonight when we get back to Hidden Cove."

"Sounds like a plan." She nodded to the older man who was watching them. "Go pay for it. I want to make a call."

"Really? To the boys? I thought you talked to Josh on the way into Manhattan."

Something flitted across her face. "Just go."

When they left the store, he took her hand. "We have an hour left. Let's go down that way."

"Nope. We need to get the car."

Cocking his head at her, he stopped walking. "Why?"

"I want to have a hot dog for lunch."

"Yeah, I know. We're going to find a kiosk closer to the play."

"I want to have mine at Yankee Stadium." Her face was filled with joy and he realized it seldom looked like that. "I just called the box office. They have good seats available that I reserved for us. We should get going because there'll be traffic."

And right then, in the bright sunlight of a Sunday afternoon, Beck had a revelation. He grabbed her. "I love you, Lela."

She stilled.

He stilled. But he didn't take back the vow.

Then she raised her eyes to him and bravely said, "I love you, too."

• • •

BECK ENJOYED THE game, mostly because he kept Lela close to his side. Robinson Cano singled in the first inning, Rodriguez hit a double in the fifth, and Derek Jeter had a grand slam in the bottom of the ninth; everything was more fun because she sat by his side. Neither mentioned what had happened on the street in front of the bookstore.

Now they were back at his place. The kids were returning tomorrow at noon, so Beck had about twelve hours left with her. She stood staring out the window dressed in a coral-colored slip of a thing; he came up behind her. "Want to talk dirty, using our new book?" He was trying to keep the atmosphere light.

She chuckled, but when she turned to him and stared up into his face, she whispered, "Why bother? I've heard the most romantic words in the world today."

There, she'd said it aloud. Truthfully, he wanted to shout it from the rooftop.

Her face reddened. "It just slipped out."

"For me, too. I'm not sorry. At least for that."

She put her hand to his mouth. "Shh. No depressing talk. Let's not ruin our last hours together."

Swallowing hard, he nodded and they crossed to the bed. He removed a condom from the dresser, and when he turned, she'd slipped out of the pretty gown and stretched out on the mattress. For a few moments he just stared at her, drinking in a sight he knew he'd never see again after tonight: The feminine contour of her hips. Firm, full breasts. The triangle of curls at the juncture of her thighs.

Filled with an unutterable sadness, he dropped his shorts, rolled on the condom and joined her on the bed. He took his time, tracing the underside of her jaw, tickling with his nose the tips of her breasts. He stopped to suckle. His fingertips trailed over her rib cage, and he bent to kiss her navel. Going lower, he licked her intimately.

"Beck, no. Come up here. I want you inside me."

He obeyed. He lifted one of her knees and moved to kneel between her legs. Instead of putting her leg back down, he lifted the other and braced both ankles on his shoulders.

"Try not to move. It'll be better." He rocked his pelvis and rhythmically thrust in and out of her. At the same time, his hands stroked and caressed her in a sensuous massage wherever he could reach.

Soon it became too much for him. And she was breathing hard. He increased the pressure, the pace; when he felt near to bursting, she said softly, "I love you, Beck."

His world dimmed, darkened, then a miasma of pleasure split him apart.

When he came back to reality, he eased down her legs, rolled to his side and stared at her. Tears trickled down her cheeks. She reached over. "Your face is wet."

"So is yours." He captured a renegade tear. "It's all so goddamned hopeless."

Suddenly, she turned, moved into him, buried her nose in his chest. And cried harder. Big, heaving sobs that rocked her body. He closed his eyes and just held her.

• • •

THE DOORBELL WAS *ringing. Lela got up from the bed and rushed to the door. Maybe it was Beck, coming back, saying he'd make it work. Instead, Len stood outside her house covered in blood.*

"Lela…Lee, honey, your phone is ringing."

She startled awake. "What?"

He held out her cell. "You have a call. It's two in the morning."

Clicking on, her heart in her mouth, she said, "Hello."

"Lela, I'm sorry to wake you." The voice belonged to Joe, Len's father. Oh, dear God, don't let anything have happened to them and the kids. Please. *Please.*

"We're fine physically, but Josh had a bad nightmare. He woke up screaming that somebody was yelling at him in the car and he was scared. Tommy climbed into bed with him, but the poor boy was scared, too, and upset."

"Joe, I'm so sorry."

"Josh wouldn't stop crying until we agreed to go back to Hidden Cove right away. We just got them in the car and are about to leave the Adirondacks."

"Oh, okay." She glanced at Beck. "I'll be home."

Her ex-father-in-law paused. Uh-oh. What had she given away? "Fine, we'll see you in about four or five hours."

When she disconnected, she faced Beck. She told him what had happened.

He said simply, "Reality bites, doesn't it?"

"Yes," was all she replied.

And just like that, their only time together was over.

CHAPTER 12

FROM UNDER HOODED eyes, Len scanned the room. Twenty vets gathered in the common area of Warrior House, the new VA Rehab Center on the outskirts of Hidden Cove. When he'd looked up the place on the internet, he'd expected a dump, but his new home for six months wasn't half bad. A vet with money had died and set up the center to help guys like Len. He'd spared no expense with comfortable meeting rooms like this one, consisting of padded chairs, some couches and slate-blue paint on the walls. There were plenty of windows.

"Welcome, all of you." A clean-cut man of about forty stood up in front of the assembled group of deadbeats. He wore jeans and a shirt, casual like Len's, and didn't seem overly eager to enlighten all of them. Len hated when people closed in on him with their success stories and you-can-do-it advice.

"I'm Roger and I'm an alcoholic."

"Hello, Roger," Len mumbled along with several others, repeating the required, if trite, response.

"As you know, I'm from an AA group over in Camden Cove. I've volunteered to come here once a week to run a regular Alcohol Anonymous meeting—the kind you'll go to when you're released."

He got that right—*released* was the operative word, as in kept here. Imprisoned.

I told you not to let that cunt talk you into this.

His demons were right. Lela had convinced him to admit himself to the program. He'd already been worn down by his parents, and Josh, who'd climbed on his lap and looped his arms around Len's neck. His boy had said, "Please, Daddy, do what Mom wants you to so you can get better."

Len hadn't known the kid knew so much. And it stirred something inside him that he thought dead—an empathy for Josh and those who loved Len. Then, too, sober and in the cold light of day, the suicide thing had blown him away, pun intended!

You should have done it. Ended this.

Go away, he told the inner voice that had checked in right alongside him.

The group started out with readings, the kind Len had heard a million times before and hadn't helped him. The topic that day was guilt. A woman who was a Colonel in Fallujah read in clear, clean tones, obviously having led troops her whole life.

When she finished, Roger asked, "So, I imagine as veterans, you have a lot of guilt?"

A drumbeat began in his heart. What? Guilt over an encampment of the enemy (who were really just kids like him) he'd been partly responsible for massacring? Guilt for the collateral damage of women and children blow apart by land minds? Guilt for all the crap he'd put his family through while he was in theater and when he got back home?

You're right, asshole. Look at all the shit you've pulled. Who can forgive that?

175

Despite the voices in his head, Len sat through the meeting. When it ended, he got up and hurried outside to the smoking area, where he didn't have to talk to anybody. There were a ton of people always around and sometimes he wanted to be left alone.

"Got a light?"

Damn! Len turned to find a big hulk of a guy with tats all over his arms, a scruffy beard and a red bandana around his neck, like a biker. He was holding a cigarette, probably waiting for another vet. Len handed him a lighter, then shook out a cig for himself. The guy lit his, too.

"Manny Perkins." He took a big drag and blew out rings of smoke. "Afghanistan."

"Len Allen. Same. National Guard, 104th."

"How long you been out?"

Despite his resolve not to care, Len could feel his face flush. He was embarrassed to still be screwed up this long. "Two years. You?"

Manny glanced away. "Just about the same. Got better for a while, then the little woman divorced me."

"Huh. Me, too."

The guy's fists clenched. "Fuck. I thought, nice reward for goin' over there."

Len nodded. He didn't want a friend, but they had something in common.

"Play cards?" Manny asked after a few more drags.

"Excuse me?"

"You play cards? We got a euchre tournament that meets twice a week. This afternoon. Wanna come?" Something about his eyes seemed off somehow. "Can guarantee you'll get something out of it."

Say no. You aren't like these guys.

Len heard his demons loud and clear. They were always right. But suddenly, he saw Josh, in his lap, begging him to get better. Maybe, just maybe…

So ignoring the whacky vibe he got, Len shrugged and said, "Yeah, sure, I'll come. What time?"

• • •

NICK STARED OVER at Amy, who'd invited him for lunch today. Julie, the shelter's director, had encouraged him to go, Lela had pounced on the idea and even Beck had happened to call today and advised him to *extend himself.* So one of the other vets who worked part-time had given him a ride. To his house. Which he'd come home to for a week but couldn't stay at because the neighbors stared at him with pity when he went out to get the mail, and Amy's grief slammed into him every single day.

They'd had a nice meal, and he'd relaxed some. Then Amy had excused herself. He sat in the kitchen and looked out the window to the small backyard. They'd planned to have kids who'd climb that tree. His buddy Billy and his wife, who were their best friends, had the same plans. He and Billy would have built a sandbox and a wooden swing set. No kids were being made these days. And Billy was dead. Nick also took in the deck, in need of repair, the garden, which should be weeded, and cursed himself for the jobs he couldn't do.

Just when the grief of that loss and inadequacy began to swamp him, Amy came back to the dining room. He glanced over to the doorway.

"Nicky, please, don't be mad." She referred to the sexy outfit that made her boobs look bigger and covered her in lace.

Dumbly, he asked, "What *is* that?"

She fingered the pink strap. Her blond hair fell softly to her shoulders. "It's called a teddy. I bought it for you."

Jesus. He stood and limped to the sink. "You wasted your money." One of the hardest things for Nick when he saw her in Kuwait and then got back here was he couldn't get it up for his wife.

"I thought we'd try today." She bit her lip. "When you're relaxed. No pressure."

"There's always pressure on a guy, sweetheart."

He heard her come up behind him. She touched his shoulder. "Things have been good between us. We've had a few dates. I just thought you might want to take this to the next level."

Fuck, why was everybody pushing him? First Beck about the camp, suggesting a wheelchair. Then everybody saying he should try to make some inroads with his wife. Didn't they know that every time he disappointed her, he felt like such a piece of crap he wanted to die?

Hit your wife? Hurt your kid? Endangered the lives of those you love? Yeah, Nick, I've done it, too. But you gotta manage this thing or it'll win. The fucking terrorists will win. We didn't go over there to fight so they could win once we got back in the world.

He heard muffled sobs from behind him. Hell, he hated making Amy cry. So he turned. Her eyes were wet with tears and he raised his hand to brush a few off her cheeks. "I can't be the kind of man I was."

She shook her head, and gulped back emotion. "I don't believe that, but what's more, I don't care. Let's just move on."

God, he wanted that more than anything. Still, try this again? He pulled her to him, kissed her head, always surprised that she didn't flinch when she came in contact with his face. "I'm sorry, I'm just not ready. Go change so you can take me back to the shelter."

As she fled up the stairs, Nick watched her with an overwhelming sense of grief, like he'd just given up something very rare and very precious.

• • •

"THIS IS DECADENT." Sophia Ramirez wiggled her bright red toenails as the woman who'd done her pedicure reached for her hand. "They're beautiful, Marta." She grinned over at Lela. "I can't remember when I last had a mannie and peddie."

Lela smiled at her friend but said nothing.

Her friend eyed her. "Don't tell me. You've never had either?"

She'd never been into this kind of pampering. She'd agreed to come out with Sophia today because Lela had spent two weeks crying over Beck—*I love you, Lela* still haunted her—and she'd decided today was the time to reenter the real world. The hardest part was keeping her overwhelming sadness from Josh and others around her.

Sophia sniffed. "I even like the smell of this place. It's so girly."

"By all means, let's be girly today."

"That's good to see."

"What?"

"Your smile. There haven't been many on your face in a few weeks."

So much for hiding her feelings.

"Time to join the living." She'd told Sophia about the spilt with Beck. Lela had been so upset she'd cried, which she never did now, except over Beck. When she looked in the mirror every morning, she saw the bloodshot eyes and the lined face of a woman who'd lost something she'd never find again and almost couldn't bear it.

Her friend squeezed her arm. "I'm glad you're getting better. But I'm sorry how it all turned out."

"Yeah, me, too."

As Lela's attendant, Nancy, painted her nails a bright coral, she thought back to how she and Beck had parted. They'd climbed out of bed in stunned silence after Joe Allen's call. They'd dressed somberly, not daring to touch, having nothing to say that could ease the awful situation. And when he'd walked Lela to her car, he'd brushed his knuckles down her cheeks in that way he had and stared into her eyes. His were as bleak as a February dawn. "Good-bye, love. I'll never forget our time together."

Swallowing back her emotion, she said simply, "I love you, Beck."

That was the last time in nineteen days she'd seen him.

Her cell phone chimed, indicating a text. She looked apologetically to Nancy. "Sorry, I have to get this."

"Be careful with the left hand," Nancy chided.

Lela picked up the phone from where it sat on the chair next to her and clicked into messages.

Hi. Need to know if you're going to Sophia and Tony's party tonight. And if you'll be alone. B.

Tony and Sophia had been married twenty years last fall, but with the birth of their new baby in November, they'd postponed their celebration until this summer.

"Oh."

"What is it?" Sophia asked.

"A text from Beck."

"I thought you weren't in contact."

"Only through texts, and then just about the boys." Who'd been together four times since her and Beck's spilt.

"Is it something about Josh?"

"No." She sighed. "He wants to know if I'm going to your anniversary party and if I'll be alone."

As if she could handle a date with another man. The memories of how Beck touched her, of his sweet whispers of love, of what it felt like with him inside her had haunted her midnights. Would she ever be able to forget that and have fun with another man?

"I told you, sweetie, you don't have to come. All the fire-fighters from Group 7 will be there."

"I know that. Beck and I can't stay away from each other forever. He already skipped one PTSD meeting and me the next. We said three weeks of no contact at all. Time's up to face the music."

Sophia frowned. "The music sounds pretty grim to me."

"No, we have to get better. We have no choice."

Sophia watched her as if she was deciding whether to say something. "Then I guess I can tell you this. Christian Singer asked me about you. When he was up in pediatrics yesterday."

"What on earth did he say?"

"He didn't pump me or anything. He's too nice of a guy to do that. He's concerned about you."

"Since our one ill-fated date he's asked me out twice and I found excuses not to go."

"Well, there's nothing like letting one sexy hunk take your mind off another one."

Hell, maybe she should. She really did like Christian, and as Sophia pointed out, he was a great guy.

She texted Beck back.

I'm going. Alone. It's time to face each other. I'll only stay an hour or so. She pressed send.

His return was quick.

See you there. Alone for me, also. I'll be the one with the phony smile.

Me, too, she replied.

And that was that. Tonight she'd see him in the flesh. Though it wasn't an ideal situation, they'd both make the best of it.

They had to.

• • •

HOT, SWEATY AND ornery, Beck yanked the nearly dead bush out of his backyard—Patty's now—and bees shot out from behind it. When he went to shoo them away, a swarm of them stung his hand. "Jesus." He raced to the house, into the kitchen, knowing as an EMT that bees released a scent when in danger and more would come to feast on him.

The door slammed hard as he crossed to the sink. Four welts were already visible. Carefully, with tweezers he found in the drawer, he removed each of the stingers.

"What happened?" Tommy had come into the room.

Biting back all kinds of obscenities, Beck got out, "Bee stings from behind the bush your mom wanted dug out."

"You okay?"

"Yeah, but you could get me an ice pack from the freezer."

Once he'd dispensed with the stingers, he took the ice pack and put it on his skin. Luckily, the bites were on the back of his hand. Sitting at the table, he glanced over at his son. They'd been distanced for nearly three weeks, since the PTSD attack that had ruined his life. The only time Tommy seemed happy was when he went out with Lela and Josh. Beck hadn't been allowed to see Josh alone again. Rightfully so, he guessed, but he was pissed about that, too. He was pissed about everything these days.

Tommy dropped down in a chair across from him. "Not your day, Dad."

A smile flirted with his lips. "You can say that again."

"It was kind of funny upstairs."

He'd volunteered to do some home repairs when Patty was at work, and earlier, he'd been trying to fix a pipe under the bathroom sink, which was leaking. He'd hit his head hard getting out of the cabinet, then slipped and fell on his ass in water that had seeped onto the tile floor.

"Easy for you to say, kid." He watched the redness spread over his hand. Tiny prickles of pain shot up his arm. He'd take ibuprofen as soon as he was done with the ice. "You know the procedure for treating bee stings?"

Tommy shook his head. "Tell me."

He reviewed the process for caring for stings and was able to pretend for a little while that he was a good father. He hadn't felt good at much lately.

Nor had he really felt like a man again. He remembered how his heart had soared bringing pleasure to Lela, hearing her compliments for his body and performance — hell, he was a guy! Since then, he'd been morbid and miserable.

"You been sad, Dad." Huh. The kid had read his mind.

He grunted.

"Since, you know, the time in the car wash."

They'd never talked about the incident. Tommy had refused. Having to come home early from the trip with Josh's grandparents was icing on the cake. So he stared the boy right in the eye. "I am sad, Tom. Every time that happens."

"You didn't have a lot of attacks before that for a while, did you?"

"Nope. That was the first in months."

His child peered up at him from beneath shaggy bangs. "Was it scary?"

"Yeah, son, it was. And for you and Josh, too, I imagine."

Again Tommy shrugged. "More for Josh. He was afraid you were going to yell at him."

"Me? Yell at *him*? Why would I do that?"

"His father always does when he gets sick. That's what Josh calls it."

"Well, that's not good."

Tommy waited and Beck adjusted the ice on his hand.

"That why can't you see him? Why won't his mom let you?"

"Lela and I decided it was best for me to stay away from Josh a while."

Tommy's eyes narrowed.

"What?"

"Me and Josh. We liked doing guy things with you."

The knife in his heart twisted as painfully as if Beck had gotten a hornet's nest full of bites. "I'm sorry."

"Could we try it again? Maybe we could talk Mrs. Allen into it."

"I don't know about that. Or even if it's a good idea."

"I think it is. You can be cool, Dad, sometimes."

A swell of parental love welled up inside him. Damn it, Beck wasn't going to give up with his kid, especially not after Tommy had given him an opening. Beck might have lost Lela, but he refused to concede defeat with his son.

"We both want to go to the batting cages at Play Station." Making an on-the-spot decision, Beck nodded. "Tell you what. Mrs. Allen is going to be at the same party as me tonight. I'll bring it up."

The kid's eyes brightened. "Okay."

"Can I ask you something?"

"I guess."

"Why did you and Josh become such good friends?"

Tommy said easily, "It's like having a brother I can protect." He stared through the window. "And his dad is — you know — a lot worse than you. It makes me like you more."

Beck should say the sentiment was unkind. That liking somebody because their misfortune made you feel better wasn't good. But he was in such a funk over Lela, he decided to take whatever comfort he could from here, in this sunny kitchen.

• • •

FIVE FEMALES WERE flaunting their wares on stage at Gallagher's party house when Lela walked in. Sophia had told her there would be karaoke at the party tonight and Lela hoped the performances would occupy everybody's mind, including hers. It was all she could do to dress up in the silky, peach pants and top Sophia and she had bought to match her nail polish. She dreaded facing Beck, and the more distractions, the better.

The women sang, "Don't Mess with Me, Baby," which had just been released by a teenage-favorite band.

A group of men dressed up in suits stood below them on the floor, cheering wildly. Lela didn't check to see if Beck was among them, but she guessed they were all firefighters, because she recognized most of the women singers as HCFD members.

Wearing a slinky, blue dress, Sydney Sands held the mic and ran a hand down her hip. "Don't mess with me, baby, I'm warnin' you."

One of the guys called out, "Yeah, what're you gonna do about it, sweetheart?"

She handed the mic to Felicia, a delight to look at in gold sequins. The woman bent down and sang—to her hubby, Lela guessed, "I'll cut you down with my charm."

Hoots and hollers.

"I'll beat you up the ladder and over the roof." Oh, Lord. That was Rachel Wellington, strutting around with a huge belly, also encased in silk.

"Hey, those aren't the real words." This from Gabe Malvaso, who was cheering the loudest.

The women sashayed, flirted, and snubbed the men. When they were finished, raucous cheers filled the room.

"Hi." A pretty woman in a sage-green dress came up to her. "That was cool, wasn't it?"

"Yes. The place looks great, too." Lela motioned to the array of white tables, with red napkins and blood-red roses, set up for diners.

"I'm Emma O'Malley."

"Oh, Brody's wife?"

"Yes, have you met him?"

"He's around the hospital sometimes. I'm Lela Allen, a nurse there."

"Oh, you're the war medic. Brody sings your praises." Emma took a sip of her drink. "It was very brave of you to go to the Middle East. He said you joined right after 9/11."

Nodding an acknowledgement of the compliment, Lela asked, "What do you do?"

"I'm a fourth-grade teacher."

"That takes its own kind of courage."

Emma laughed. It made her pretty face startlingly beautiful.

Lela gestured to the now-empty stage. "Who were the other two women up there? I've met Rachel, Sydney and Felicia."

"Casey Malvaso and Megan Hale Malvaso."

Something triggered. "Hale, as in Hale's Haven. The camp for kids."

"Yeah." She winked at Lela. "They always need medical personnel."

"I heard. I'm thinking about volunteering." For one of the overnight camps. *Don't go to Junior Hale's Haven.*

Dinner was called after fifteen minutes. It was then Lela noted there were place settings. *Please don't let Sophia have put me near him.*

She hadn't. Finding her tag, Lela sat down and was introduced to the fire chief and his wife, Noah and Eve Callahan, Mitch and Megan Malvaso, and Eve's brother, Ian Woodward. His wife, Lisel Loring, was stunning. And famous.

"I've seen you on stage, Lisel," Lela said to the woman. First, they'd gotten the wheelchair for Ian in place, and then Lisel took a chair next to her.

"Which show?"

"A special revival of *Longshot*."

Ian grinned broadly. "Yeah, isn't she spectacular?"

"Was." Lisel touched her stomach. "After the baby, I've definitely retired from the dance world."

Ian's blue eyes burned with love.

They talked about babies and Broadway, then dinner was served. Lela managed several bites of the lobster, steak and accompaniments as small talk went on at the table. Then the time came for toasts.

Standing, Noah held up his glass while several others clinked theirs with spoons for quiet. "I'm not going to talk about what a good firefighter Tony is. We see that every day. Instead, I'll tell you what a good role model he is for husbands. His and Sophia's relationship is a strong statement to us all about the enduring nature of love if two people are willing to sacrifice anything for each other." He smiled down at his wife. "I try to emulate him."

An older Hispanic woman rose from the head table— Sophia's mother, with the same statuesque build and thick, black hair. Lela had met her at the hospital. "My girl and my boy have gone through so many hardships since they were fifteen. But no matter what problems they had, they stayed together to fix them. *Felicidades a mis hijos maravillosos.*"

By the end of the toasts, Lela's stomach had cramped painfully. She pushed back her chair. "Excuse me, I need to use the ladies' room."

"You all right?" Megan asked from the other side of her. "You look a bit pale."

Lela had to get away. "I'm fine. Be right back."

Instead of heading to the ladies room, she detoured to a side exit. She needed some air, some relief from the smothering knowledge that other people could make their relationships work, but not her and Beck.

• • •

HIS HAND HURT like a bitch, the ache from the bump on his head had worsened, and his butt was sore, so Beck thought it totally fucking *unfair* that he had to sit through accolades about how two people can overcome anything if they love each other enough. So when he caught sight of a streak of peach scurrying across the floor behind the group of diners, he got up and followed it.

He found Lela outside, leaning against the brick wall of the side entrance. The night air was warm and sultry, and moonbeams kissed her hair. At first, he didn't say anything, just absorbed the way the outfit clung in all the places he'd kissed three weeks ago. Finally she sensed his presence and glanced over. "Hi."

He watched her. "I couldn't take it, either."

"The solemn swearing that you can beat any odds?"

"Yeah, must be they never heard of the effects of PTSD on kids."

She shook her head, sending her fall of hair swirling around her shoulders. His hands itched to touch it.

Instead, he searched her face in the dim light coming from inside. "You okay?"

"As well as can be expected."

He nodded.

"I've never seen you in a suit."

Jesus. It didn't help that she devoured him with her gaze. Eye-banging, the guys in theater crudely called it.

"How are you?"

"The same."

She frowned at his hand. "What happened?"

He filled her in on his bad luck today.

"Sorry."

"Something good came out of it. Tommy's talking to me again. He seems to have gotten over...you know."

Without thinking, she reached out and squeezed his arm. "Oh, Beck, I'm so glad."

He stared down at her touch. His throat clogged at the intimacy of the one simple gesture. Best to break the mood. He stepped back. "Tommy also told me something about Josh you should know."

"What?"

He explained about the way Len reacted to Josh when he had an attack. Beck knew a lot of men with PTSD who took out their frustrations on the families, but the notion made him sick.

"I'll try to talk to him about that. He never said anything to me about Len's reactions."

"He, um, also asked why I never took them anywhere now."

"I guess this was inevitable."

"Lee, do you think you could trust me to take them for just a couple of hours to the batting cages at Play Station? We won't go often, but I'd like to try it for Tommy's sake. If this doesn't happen, our relationship might get stalemated again."

"Oh, Beck, there's more to it than that."

He cocked his head.

"Do we really want to encourage them to spend so much time together? School's out next week and they're going to want to see each other a lot."

"I'm not sure we have a choice."

She leaned against the wall again. "Maybe not. I'll think about it and let you know what I decide."

"Good enough." He angled his head toward the room inside. "So, you think they're all done with the mushiness?"

"I hope so."

"Ready to go back in?"

"Sure."

He stopped at the entrance, turned to her and brushed his knuckles down her cheek. "I miss you."

She leaned into his caress. "Me, too."

Feeling a little better, Beck let her go first into the room. But the tableau that greeted them made them both stop dead in their tracks.

Tony was on stage with the microphone, staring down at stunning-in-a-red-dress Sophia, who was seated and looking up at him. In a deep baritone, Ramirez sang the first bars of Elvis Presley's famous love song, "I Can't Help Falling in Love with You." When Tony got to the part about the inexorable nature of love finding a way, Beck sensed Lela move. When he looked over, she turned away and headed back outside.

This time, he didn't go after her.

CHAPTER 13

WITH HER ARM around Josh, who clung to her side like a toddler, Lela stared at the coffin in front of the Allens' church and choked back her own grief. She'd had to be strong for a long time now, but no more so than when she'd gotten the crippling news.

A few days ago her husband, her *ex-husband,* had been found dead outside the Warrior House four weeks after he'd entered treatment. Not from booze, which she knew all along might kill him, but from an overdose of cocaine that he'd taken right there in his room at rehab. How on earth could he have gotten the drugs? How had he avoided detection with the regular drug testing?

The coroner's findings were *inconclusive.* No one could say if the father of her child had accidentally ingested too much of the drug or if he'd killed himself. Did it even matter? The results were the same. Len was dead. Josh was devastated, and Lela was simply hanging on.

A terrible dirge from the organ played as people filtered into the church, mostly Joe and Marsha Allen's friends but also a few guys she recognized as Len's boyhood buddies. Some people from the rehab center had been bussed over. One guy, a crusty vet who looked like the stereotyped Vietnam veteran, seemed to be pretty broken up.

"Lela?" She glanced up to see Christian Singer standing in the empty pew in front of her. He looked big and strong and unbreakable.

"Hi."

"I don't mean to intrude."

He wasn't. After the searing loss she'd felt at seeing Beck at the anniversary party, after Lela had realized that her life was in a shambles over him and she needed to move on, she'd accepted a date with Christian, then another and another. She'd been with him when she'd gotten the news. He'd been a godsend this last week, giving her advice, consoling her.

"I have a seat in the back with some other hospital personnel. We just want you to know we're here to share your grief."

"Thank you so much. I appreciate your coming. Tell them for me."

He glanced at Josh. Interestingly, Christian and her son had become friends. The two of them had taken their kids places three times, and the young ones had fun together.

"You doing okay, buddy?" Christian asked Josh.

Nodding, the boy burrowed deeper into his mother's side. He'd said practically nothing to anyone since Len had died.

With one squeeze of her arm, Christian whispered, "I'm here if you need me," and sidled down the pew to the aisle on the left.

Leaving her alone with her grief. And the obscene knowledge that she'd done little to preclude Len's death. Guilt, big and ugly, swamped her, making black spots swim before her eyes. She thought he'd been getting better at Warrior House but didn't know for sure because she'd never visited him there. Instead, she'd divorced him, controlled his visits to his son and cut him out of her life.

A priest appeared in the pulpit up front, dressed in a white robe and a black stole, the Catholic garments for a funeral mass; candles and incense surrounded the church. "Good morning, everyone. Thank you for coming. I'm sure your presence provides great solace to Len's family."

Absolute quiet among the gatherers.

The man continued, "I know it's difficult to understand, let alone accept, what's happened to our friend and loyal soldier. Len Allen was a good man with unfortunate issues when he came back from war. You might be thinking, "Where does God fit in with this?""

As the priest began to talk about death and the existence of God, about war and trauma and a Supreme Being's role in such awful things, Lela only half listened. Her gaze strayed to the other side of the church, where Joe and Marsha Allen huddled together. Since their son's death, they'd become *diminished* somehow. They seemed smaller in their grief, beaten down. They'd done so much for Len and it hadn't been enough. The notion pierced her like a scalpel to the skin. When Lela had gone to see them, after the rehab center called them, they'd been cold to her…

Marsha had snapped, "You did this to my boy!"

Joe had shaken his head. "No, Martha, she didn't. Our boy was sick. The war did this to him." He'd raised the bleakest eyes to Lela. "But you understand why we don't want you here." It had been a statement, not a question.

"Of course I do. I'll leave you alone."

When she'd gotten outside, Joe caught up with her. "We can still see Josh, can't we Lela? He's all we have…left." The last word came out on a sob.

"Of course, whenever you're both ready," was all she managed to say before she stumbled to her car. Once in the front seat, she laid her forehead down on the steering wheel and sobbed.

After the priest finished his eulogy, there were no requests for friends and family to speak. Len had alienated most of his acquaintances and the circumstances of his death hung like a pall over the attendees.

They sang "Amazing Grace" and the flag-draped casket was wheeled out of the church by the priests and acolytes. Behind it, the Allens made their way from the pew and began the morbid creep down the aisle.

"Lela, you exit next." An assistant in the church motioned for her to follow the Allens.

"Come on, baby," she said to Josh. His face still hidden in her side, he held on tight to her.

During the procession to the back of the church, she kept her gaze on Josh or on the floor, to avoid anyone's gaze, afraid the slightest show of pity would cause her to break down. They were almost to the end of the interminable aisle when Josh started sobbing uncontrollably. Oh, God. Dropping her purse on the rug, she reached down and picked him up. At almost eight, he was heavy, and she hadn't eaten or slept, so the weight of him, of all that had happened, made her stumble. Suddenly, someone was at her side.

"I've got him, Lela." Christian's soothing voice, his taking Josh from her and cuddling her son to his chest, let her regain her footing, if not her composure. They finished their trek, and finally got outside. The bright July sun made her head hurt, and she shielded her eyes. People were waiting to talk to the grieving family. Oh, no, she couldn't do that. She just couldn't.

"Get us out of here, Christian, please."

"My car's on the street. Only a few spaces beyond the church. Let's go."

Before they could start away, something touched her arm. Her purse. "You dropped this, Lee."

The husky baritone could belong to only one person.

Beck had come to the funeral.

• • •

BECK DUG HIS fingernails into his palm as hard as he could, steeling himself against the ragged emotion on Lela's face. And the sight of Josh cuddling into another man. He wanted to rage to the world that he should be the one helping them, but of course, that wasn't true. He was the last person she wanted with her. After all, he'd failed Len, who lay dead in a coffin because nobody could help him.

"I'm so sorry about Len."

She swallowed hard. "Thank you. And thanks for all you did for him."

"Not enough."

"No one did enough," she said miserably.

Though he'd visited Len at the shelter twice, Beck had no clue Len was using drugs, that they might become the instrument of his death. *One out of every eighty returning soldiers kills himself on their return to society.* If only society could have done more.

Lela looked over his shoulder. "Oh, oh! Nick? I didn't know you were here."

The sad man with the scarred face eased closer. "I'm so sorry. I just wanted to say that."

It was then she noticed many of the residents of the Veterans Outreach Shelter where she volunteered behind him, including Julie, the director. Tears sprang to her eyes, but she asked, "What did you do, rent a bus?"

"The shelter has one," Nick answered. "But I came with Beck."

Beck had failed with Len, he knew, but he might be able to help this soldier find his way. He *vowed* to do that.

Lela's gaze transferred to Beck. "That was sweet of you."

Josh chose that moment to lift his head from Christian's shoulder and say, "Mommy, I wanna go." When he noticed Beck, he buried his head again.

Beck said to Christian, "Take care of them," and moved away.

Slowly, without looking back, he stood close to Nick as the trio descended the rest of the steps, feeling as if somebody had cut out a piece of his heart.

• • •

DARK CLOUDS HOVERED overhead, a fitting setting, as Lela stood at the cemetery with Christian. Josh was on the other side of her, hugging his arms tight around Joe Allen's neck. When he'd seen his grandpa, he'd lunged from Christian toward Len's father and now wouldn't let go.

The Allens wanted a military burial for their son. Lela listened as shots were fired from big rifles. She witnessed the flag being folded and then presented to Marsha, who stood like a statue next to her husband and sister. And Lela prayed for this to be over. Her nerves were stretched tight, anyway, and seeing Beck had shattered any composure she might have found inside herself. When "Taps" ended, she turned to Joe to take her son.

Joe held on to him. "I, um, was wondering if Josh could come to our house for a while. Our friends are gathering. Our church brought food." He looked chagrined. "I can't ask you, Lela, because of Marsha. Because of a lot of things."

Joe blamed her, too.

"If he'll go with you, Joe, certainly."

Len's father glanced at Christian, disapproval etched on his face. It took her a minute to realize Joe thought she'd come with Christian. Then he said to his grandson, "Honey, Grandma and me want you to come back to the house with us."

Josh raised his head, nodded, then buried his face back in Joe's shoulder. Intuitively, he must have needed the connection with his father that Joe represented. The older man put his hand on Josh's head. "I'll bring him home when it's time."

After they left the gravesite, Sophia and Tony approached her. She hadn't seen them earlier. Somber faced, Sophia asked, "How you holding up, honey?"

Lela practically flung herself at her friend. Sophia held her. "I'm so sad."

"We are, too, for you, *carina*," Tony mumbled.

After a few seconds of precious comfort, she pried herself away from her friend and they greeted Christian. "What are you going to do now?" Sophia asked.

Lela hadn't thought about the rest of the day. Truthfully, she hadn't thought about the next hour, even the next few minutes. "I, um, don't know. I left my car at the church."

"You drove yourself to the funeral?" Tony asked, "*Dios mio*."

"I brought her here from the church," Christian told them. "I can take her home and make arrangements for her car."

Grasping on to Lela's hand, Sophia said, "I have a better idea. Our kids are with Mama. My house is empty. Why don't you come back with us for a few hours?"

"Maybe." She turned to Christian. "Would that be okay with you?"

"Sure." His face was kind, full of understanding, but she could see he felt bad for her. "I told you I didn't want to intrude."

"You're not." She took his hand. "Come with us."

"If you want me to."

"I do." She turned to the Ramirezes. "Is that okay?"

Sophie gave her a sad smile. "Anything for you, *mi amore*."

As they made their way to the car, Lela saw a figure standing alone on the hill behind the cemetery. Was it Beck? No, she couldn't think about him now. She couldn't think, really, about anything.

• • •

"HERE'S SOME TEA. It might soothe you." Christian set a mug on the coffee table in front of her. The liquid's lemon scent was strong.

She looked up. "Thanks." They'd left Sophia's after an hour and when they'd returned to her car, Christian had asked if he could follow her home. She'd said yes. He seemed tired, too, with lines around his classic features, but he'd been taking care of her since the funeral. Depleted, she'd let him.

"What's that you have there?" He pointed to the book on her lap.

"An old photo album." Something had driven her to find it and peruse the pictures inside.

"Of Len?"

She nodded.

"Aren't the photos making you sad?"

"Some. But I want to remember the good times, too."

Tell me something good about Len. All we hear about is the shit that goes on with veterans.

Beck had been right. Good memories did help.

"Can I see?" Christian asked.

"Sure." She patted the cushion beside her and he dropped down close. It wasn't unpleasant. His nearness made her feel safe. His masculine aftershave increased the sensation.

After he studied a page, he said, "That's a strange one."

The photo showed Len in a chef's hat in the mess hall of an army base, a year after he and Lela were married. He was grinning at the pathetic little thing in front of him.

She smiled at the memory. "You know how couples eat their wedding cake's top layer on their first anniversary?"

"Uh-huh."

"Of course, we couldn't save ours. We were in theater when we got married. So on our anniversary, Len tried to bake me a wedding cake. *Tried* being the operative word."

"It's lopsided. And the kitchen area is a disaster."

That was true. He'd been covered in flour—even his hair— and every pan in the kitchen was dirty. His buddies ragged on him for weeks about his culinary skills, and being pussy-whipped, she guessed, but he took the razzing with good humor.

"Did it taste good?"

"You know, it did." Again she smiled. "We ate it in bed."

"Ah, then that is a good story."

"There were a lot of fun times before he came home." She turned the page. Pictures of them in Abu Dhabi, on leave from the base. Photos of them with groups of other combat personnel. "He was a good soldier."

"And you were a good army medic?" He pointed to a picture of her in army fatigues. "You even look good in those."

She remembered another conversation with Beck....

After about a month, Len remarked that he'd never seen me in anything but army green and combat boots. When I told the other women that, they put together an outfit...It was a simple, flowing, white skirt and dark top, which was...a little tight. That was the first night we slept together."

"*Lucky Len.*"

Christian's arm went around her now and rested gently on her shoulders. "Was it scary over there, Lela? I'm not sure I could have done what you did."

"It *was* scary. But you can do whatever you have to if you're committed."

He raised her chin. Stared into her eyes. "You're a remarkable woman."

"Why, thank you."

"This probably isn't the time to bring this up, but I hope you'll keep seeing me. That Len's death won't preclude that."

She shifted uncomfortably on the couch. "Len's death won't."

He must have caught her tone. "What would?"

"If we do date from here on out, there's something you should know." *I'm in love with another man.*

But she didn't say that.

His dark blond brows furrowed. "That sounds ominous."

"I don't mean it to. I was involved with someone else for a while before you. It's complicated...we weren't really dating...I don't know how to explain it."

He brushed his knuckles down her cheek, which only made the situation worse because that was Beck's gesture. "You don't have to. All I need to know is if it's over."

"It is. Very over."

His hand went lower, over her heart. "Here, too?"

"Not quite there yet, Christian; I have to be honest."

"Okay. I'm glad I know. I still want to see you."

"Good, because I'd like that."

And in the midst of her sorrow and loss, Lela meant the words. Life was definitely too short to waste. She had to move on.

CHAPTER 14

BECK RETURNED TO work on the Fourth of July, almost a year to the day since he'd been hired by the HCFD. He'd gotten through the forty-eight hours after the funeral by working at the veteran's shelter. He knew Lela wouldn't be there, so he'd thrown himself into helping out with some chores that needed doing and getting acquainted with more of the guys. He'd also spent a lot of time with Nick. Though Beck was grieving over Lela's situation with Len and the stark reality of knowing he'd never have her in his life, Nick seemed somewhat lighter than he had before. Go figure!

As Beck entered the station for the beginning of his tour and walked down the hall, his senses went on alert. It was too quiet in the house. Usually, he could hear the banter as soon as he arrived. When he reached the kitchen, he found the cause of the silence. The cabinets were decorated with American flags and red-white-and-blue posters that read "Support Our Troops and Our Returning Soldiers," "Hire our Heroes," and "Thanks, Beck, for your service. We love you!" (The last had to be Sydney's work.)

His entire crew, standing around the coffeepot, sported American-flag decals on their sleeves. They all clapped when he entered the room.

"What's this?" he asked, not in the mood for a party, yet not wanting to offend anybody. Besides, no one here would suspect his outlook was so bleak. They didn't know anything about Lela. And how the sight of her with another man had almost leveled him. Forcefully, he banished the image like he used to blank his mind in the Middle East.

Gabe approached him and held out his hand. "This is a way for us to say thank you for what you've done for your country."

"You don't have to —"

"Hey, give us a break," Brody put in, pouring another mugful of coffee and handing it to Beck. "We got a hero working with us and you never let us do anything for you. It's the Fourth; this time, we insist."

Felicia's eyes twinkled. "*And* you've only got twelve hours left of being a probie." The probationary time for a new hire was a year, though he knew he'd be watched carefully and would still get the crap jobs for a while.

"Then, thanks. Is there anything to eat?" He added the latter to lighten the moment. In truth, he was touched by the sentiments.

"Rachel baked you something." Gabe nodded to the table, where a huge cake with a flag in the middle sat. "She can't see her toes and the kid's huge, but she still manages to whip up these things."

"It was nice of her, Gabe, but she's gotta stop doing this." He patted his belly. "I need to go on a diet already."

Amidst some joking about his physical fitness, they cut the cake and settled to eat it. Before he picked up his fork, Beck noticed a small package and a scroll of some kind by his plate. "What are these?"

"Tokens of our appreciation for having you on the squad and a one-year anniversary present." Felicia donned her sternest lieutenant's voice. "Now shut up with the you-shouldn't-haves and open your gifts. Start with the scroll."

"Yes, ma'am."

He opened the paper. It was titled, "Our Own War Hero."

When he must have looked confused, Felicia explained. "Our firefighter website did a special blog for the Fourth of July."

"Tell me it's not on me."

"Yeah, it is, Beck. We try to feature at least *some* good things about the men in our unit." She scanned the guys. "Not an easy task."

O'Malley snorted. "What are we, White? Chopped liver?"

His joking eased the tightness in Beck's chest.

Beck had heard about *Fire Belles*, the blog set up by women firefighters initially to combat Parker Allen's criticism of the department. Even though the woman had married the chief, and was now in PR for the department, the girls kept up the blog.

Beck scanned the document.

"Once in a while a good guy comes along in our personal lives, and professional ones, too. The women of the HCFD are thrilled to have a new firefighter who is a war veteran. If you think our job is hard, imagine his. Imagine the heat *over there*. Imagine fighting blind *over there,* where sandstorms are common."

Beck swallowed hard at the comparison of army life with the elements of firefighting—and acknowledging he had it harder in war. These people could be really magnanimous.

What followed that statement were a list of his war achievements and the people he'd saved in fires.

He stared down at the writing for a minute before he could compose himself enough to look up. "Thanks guys."

Sydney said, "Open the present."

Beck tore off the red-white-and-blue paper and found a small jeweler's box. It was heavy. What the hell?

Inside, nestled in a bed of red velvet, was a silver key chain with a good-sized circular medallion hooked to it. He ran his finger over the bright red background with the raised Maltese Cross. The traditional symbols of firefighting — a set of axes, a ladder and a fire hydrant — were engraved on the top and two sides of the cross. The bottom had been scripted with *Firefighter Beckett Sloan.*

Beck swallowed hard. Once again, he was moved. "Very nice. Thanks."

"Turn it over," Sydney told him.

On the opposite side was another shield — the medallion for the US army, with a bald eagle in the middle. The background was deep blue, with *United States* scrawled across the top, *Army* on the bottom. His heart started to beat fast with emotion.

Sydney added, "It's so you know we'll never forget what you did over there."

Again, he couldn't speak for a few moments. "How, um, where did you find this? It's unique."

"We had it custom made." This from the chief, who'd walked in at some point and spoke from behind him. "Sorry I'm late. I got caught up at home." His face was flushed, but he looked young and happy.

"Yeah, we don't wanna know what you were doing at home, Chief," Brody teased. "Pregnancy hormones and all that."

Erikson laughed and joined them at the table. "Seriously, Beck, we wanted to celebrate your time with us. Your service to us."

"Thanks, everybody. I'm…moved."

Gabe slapped his hand on the table. "Enough mushy stuff. We always have a big Fourth of July party at our condo. House 7's crew, some of our family and friends. Tonight, right after work." He added, "Be there, probie."

"I won't be a probie by then. But, yes, sir." He reiterated the rookie response.

And felt a little better about life in general. Some socializing might take his mind off all that wasn't right with his world.

• • •

MEMORIAL HOSPITAL THREW a Fourth of July party for the kids in the children's ward every year. Lela usually worked at it and brought Josh along with her. He enjoyed the company of the sick kids and she always wondered why. Since his father's death two days ago, he'd hardly said three words to her. Which was why on the morning of the holiday, she was surprised to see him come downstairs dressed in red, white and blue and ask, "What time are we going to the party?"

Lela was still in her pajamas, sipping coffee by the window, keeping the sadness at bay as best she could. "Oh, honey, I'm not working at the party today. I, um, assumed you wouldn't want to visit with the kids, because of your dad."

"They have a clown. I like how he ties balloons into animals."

"I know you do, sweetie." She patted the chair next to her. "Come over here a minute."

He joined her at the breakfast nook. His eyes weren't red from crying as they'd been all day yesterday. "Do you *want* to go?"

"Uh-huh. Can we still?"

The last thing *Lela* wanted was to be around people, but as usual, good mothering won out. She brushed his hair back from his eyes and said, "All right. It's at lunch time. We can leave about eleven thirty."

Three hours later, dressed in jeans and a simple, black T-shirt, Lela held Josh's hand as they walked into the pediatric ward's common area. The sight made her smile and Josh say, "Oh, cool. A dinosaur theme."

The ancient animals prowled the room—posters on all the windows, cardboard cut-outs bigger than the kids scattered on the floor, along with a myriad of stuffed animals all the children would be allowed to keep. The clown hadn't set up yet.

"Mom, look. Even the food's made out of dinosaurs." Josh pointed to the table right next to the entrance. Sure enough, sandwiches made with bread cut into the shapes of tyrannosaurus rexes were the mainstay for lunch. The cookies were shaped like pterodactyls. Even the punch was labeled Dinosaur Brew.

"That is so cool, Josh."

Nodding, he sipped some punch and watched the room. "Look, there's a boy from last year. Jimmy. Mom, is he still sick?"

Lela knew some of the kids would never leave here or had been released only to come back again. "Must be. Do you want to go talk to him?"

"Okay." He looked up at her. "You won't leave, will you?"

"Of course not. I'll just get some punch."

As she turned to the table and reached for the ladle, someone else went for it at the same time. "Oh, sorry," the woman said.

Lela looked at the gorgeous blonde in scrubs. She thought she'd seen her around the hospital. "No, go ahead."

"I'll pour you some, too."

Lela accepted the glass and smiled. The woman smiled back. She had beautiful, hazel eyes, which seemed tired but held warmth and friendliness.

"I'm Lela Allen. Trauma nurse downstairs."

"Oh, I thought you looked familiar. I'm Lexie Wellington, pediatrics." She studied Lela's outfit. "Come in on your day off?"

"Uh-huh." It felt good to be talking about something other than Len. "My son attends every year." She pointed across the room. "He's talking to the little one in the wheelchair."

Lexie's expression turned sad. "Jimmy. He's back here every few months. Leukemia that keeps recurring."

"I'm sorry to hear that."

"Makes you want to live your life better, doesn't it? My sister and I were just talking about that."

"Sister?" Now she recognized the woman. "Would that be Rachel?"

Lexie grinned ear to ear. "Yep. You know her?"

"I've met her at some fire department gatherings. I'm friends with a nurse whose husband works there."

"Sophia, right? I adore her."

"Huh. Funny having so much in common with a stranger."

"Yeah, it is. I'm glad we met up, Lela."

"Me, too." Her pager beeped. "Oh, damn, that's me." She took it out. "Gotta go."

"And miss the party? Too bad."

"Take care, Lela. Hope to see you around."

"Yes, me, too."

After a few minutes, Josh came over. "Can I eat lunch with Jimmy, Mom?"

"Of course."

"Alone?"

"Sure, if you want."

"Will you get our food?"

"Uh-huh. Find a table. Be sure there's room to wheel him up."

She was filling plates when someone touched her shoulder. Christian's blue eyes smiled at her when she turned around. He wore his white coat, with some kind of T-shirt beneath it. He looked good. "Hungry?"

"What? Oh, no. This is for Josh and his new friend." She nodded across the room where the boys sat at a round table.

"I'm surprised to see you here." His voice pitched lower. Intimately. "How are you?"

"Better being out of the house." She nodded to Josh. "Him, too. He wants to eat with Jimmy. Just the two of them. I guess he's had enough of me."

"Ah, my lucky day." Christian squeezed her arm. "Join me for lunch, Nurse Allen. *I'll* never get enough of you."

Lexie's words echoed in her head. *Makes you want to live your life better, doesn't it?*

"Why yes, Dr. Singer. I'd love to."

• • •

BECK SLOUCHED BACK in the chaise, drinking a beer, staring out at Hidden Lake. The moon kissed the water, making the surface glimmer like a halo. Next to him, Lexie Wellington sipped from a glass of wine. Rachel, who seemed more tired tonight than usual, had gone to bed halfway through the evening. Gabe joined her when the rest of the partygoers left, and Beck had stayed behind to have a drink with Lexie.

"It's beautiful out here at night, isn't it?" he commented.

"Yeah. Romantic."

Beck shot her a glance. Her blond hair was fluffy and fell softly down to her shoulders. She'd worn a sage-green outfit that…he noticed. "How come nobody's scooped you up yet, Lexie Wellington? You're beautiful, smart, fun."

"Why thank you. Back at ya, by the way." She was quiet for a minute. Had he said too much?

Finally, she answered. "I made a big mistake in my life that's left me a spinster."

He snorted. "I highly doubt you'll ever be a spinster."

Pivoting in the chaise, she looked at him squarely. "Seriously, you want to know?"

"Sure."

Even in the half-light, he could see her brow furrow. "I had an affair with a married man for years. A doctor. Truthfully, I wasn't looking for a commitment because I'd just started my residency. So I was okay with his circumstances. I felt guilty in some ways, especially when I had contact with his wife and kids, but I was young and self-absorbed, so I did it, anyway." She shook her head. "Jesus, it sounds like an episode of *Grey's Anatomy.*"

"You mean the show where the docs spend most of their time in the on-call room?"

Her laughter was sultry. "I'm surprised a guy like you ever watched that."

"My wife Patty liked it."

Again, Alexis waited. "Is she the one who has you tied up in knots?"

Beck stilled. "Excuse me?"

"I asked if she was the one who has you pretty wrecked."

He waited a beat. "It shows?"

"I knew when I first met you."

"Not my ex. Someone else."

"That you can't have?"

"That's right. I really can't have her. Not married, but the situation is out of our control."

Reaching over, she grasped his arm. "Then I'm sorry."

They sat in companionable silence for a while. At one point, Lexie said quietly, "Maybe we should date."

"You think that's a good idea?"

"Well, my misadventure with the married guy has been over for years. You're obviously still hurting. Maybe hooking up with someone else will help both of us. No strings or expectations."

"Hooking up?" He knew one meaning of the term.

Lexie laughed. "Yeah, Beck, some recreational sex might take the edge off for us both. After we get to know each other, of course."

He thought of Lela standing so close to Singer that their arms touched and her lovely auburn hair brushed his shoulder. He thought of Josh clinging to the doctor. And he thought of the anniversary party for Sophia and Tony. So he grabbed Lexie Wellington's hand. "You know what, I agree. I'm all in."

"Then let's see where this goes."

Because Alexis was staying overnight in the spare room at Rachel's condo, she walked Beck to the door.

"So, you think a good night kiss is in order?" he asked, staring down at the lovely woman before him.

"I do."

She went up on her tiptoes, and he lowered his head.

A scream, loud and curdling, came from within the house. Alexis jerked back. "Oh, my God, that's Rachel."

• • •

BECK FOLLOWED ALEXIS down the hall to the master bedroom. She whipped open the door and found Rachel stiff and sweaty, sitting up, pillows behind her. Gabe bolted off the bed.

"She's in labor." Hoarse emotion claimed his voice. "She said she's had pains all night but didn't want to ruin the party. She fell asleep and woke up like this."

Calm and cool, Alexis strode to the two of them. "Are you in labor, sweetie?"

"No," Rachel huffed out. "The baby's going to come. I need to push, Lexie. I know what that means." Rachel was an EMT, trained to deliver babies. "Oh, God, will she be all right?"

As he rushed out of the room, Beck heard Lexie say, "Of course. I've delivered plenty of infants. And we've got two of America's Bravest to help us."

He strode to the linen closet in the hall and grabbed several towels and a blanket off the shelf. "Oh, man, God is watching over us." He took a box of plastic gloves off a lower shelf.

When he returned, Gabe was coaching his wife. "Breathe, honey. That's it. In and out." They'd turned Rachel on her side.

Beck handed Lexie towels, one of which she slid under Rachel. Then she donned gloves. When Alexis began to pull Rachel's pajamas bottoms off, he asked, "Do you want me to leave?" He worried about his friend's modesty.

"Absolutely not. Put on some gloves. You're going to help me. Gabe, keep massaging her back."

"It's okay, love," Gabe said soothingly, rubbing the lower part of her back. "It's okay."

"I know." Another contraction hit and Rachel rode it. "She's coming."

"Let's get her on her back, sitting up against the pillows." They complied and Rachel bent both legs.

Calmly, Alexis said, "I can see the head. Lots of dark hair, sis."

"Lexie…"

"Everything's fine. Now push. Don't yell, use your energy to get her… Oh, her head's out."

Beck gasped at the sight of this wonderful event. He'd never delivered a baby.

Rachel strained and her face got red.

"Now stop for a sec. Okay, I've got her shoulders. All right. One more push, honey."

"Arrgh…" Rachel pushed and out slid a beautiful, red, wrinkled bundle.

Beck was awestruck.

"I want to see her." This from Mom.

"Stay still for a minute, honey."

Beck noted that the umbilical cord had wrapped around the child's neck and his pulse quickened. Alexis didn't miss a beat. Slowly, she loosened the cord enough to form a loop and slipped the baby through. Alexis put her fingers in the baby's mouth and cleaned out mucus. Then she massaged the baby's back and a lusty cry filled the air. Had he ever heard a more beautiful sound?

"Beck, take the baby in a towel. Dry her off, but don't pull on the cord. You'll have to stay bent over."

He took the tiny bundle, who'd stopped screaming and was staring up at him. After she was cleaned up a bit, Lexie said, "Put her back on Rachel's stomach. Careful of the cord."

Gently Beck placed the little miracle on Rachel's tummy. "Now cover them with a blanket. Keep your knees up, Rach. I have to deliver the placenta. Beck, get a pan for this."

Still reeling, Beck hightailed it to the kitchen, grabbed a round bowl from a cupboard and rushed back just in time to see the sac come out. Meanwhile, Rachel held the child with tears in her eyes and Gabe looked poleaxed. "Oh, Gabe. Our little angel is here."

Alexis placed the placenta in the bowl, keeping it near Rachel.

"Now, get scissors. Where, Gabe?"

"In the kitchen. Drawer on the right of the sink."

"Boil some water and sterilize them."

Again, he raced to the kitchen, did what she ordered and went hurrying back to the bedroom.

By now, Rachel was nursing the child. "That's right, honey. This'll offer her comfort and make your uterus contract."

Beck handed the scissors to Alexis, and she expertly cut the cord and put gauze over it. "They'll fix this up if they need to at the hospital, but it looks pretty clean to me."

"Oh, hell," Gabe said, running a hand through his hair. "I didn't call 911."

"I'll do it." Beck whipped out his phone and walked out.

When that task was completed, he reentered the room. The tableau was something he'd never forget as long as he lived. Gabe had his arm around Rachel as she nursed, brushing her hand over the baby's dark hair. Alexis sat back and watched, her face glowing, too.

Rachel looked up at him, then at her sister. "I've decided on a name."

Gabe said, "Yeah, honey, we picked Maria."

"Nope. Maria is now Alexis Sloan Wellington Malvaso. We'll call her Ali to keep things straight."

It was then that Alexis burst into tears.

And Beck grinned hugely.

CHAPTER 15

"HOUSE FIRE ON Ambrose Street. Single-family dwelling. Rescue 7 and Quint/Midi 7 go into service."

In the dark of night, twelve firefighters bounded out of bed. No one grumbled at the interruption of sleep, something Beck had appreciated from day one. He hated whiners. They donned their uniforms and hustled downstairs to the bay, where they jumped into their turnout pants and boots.

On the way to the fire, Sydney drove as Felicia, who was in charge of the group while Gabe took two weeks off to be with Rachel and the baby, rode shotgun. Felicia glanced back at them. "Simple house fire, but stay on your toes. You never know what the Red Devil's gonna do."

"With any luck, we'll be able to catch a few more zees." This from O'Malley, who was the grumpiest when deprived of sleep, but at least he kept his mouth shut about it.

"Aw, whatsamatter, Brody?" Sydney teased. "Afraid you won't get your beauty rest."

"Stop picking on me." He elbowed Beck. "They been doing this since Ramirez left. Can't help it if I'm the best-looking guy on the squad now."

The banter continued as the rig roared to the fire. Once there, the rescue truck screeched to a halt in front of a narrow three-story building. Flames licked the roof and shot out of the upper windows. Plumes of gray smoke rose from the structure. The smell of gas fumes and burning wood greeted them when they left the truck.

Erikson had already arrived at the scene. Looking up from his computer, which perched on the hood of his Jeep, he called out to the officers, "Holmes, get water on the fire. The roof looks spongy, so nobody goes up there. White, three people made it out. They say the house is empty inside, but we gotta search the place. The blaze is rolling pretty hard, so be prepared to evacuate fast."

White barked orders for her group to follow her inside.

Buttoned up to his chin, Beck began to sweat in the hot July night. He was second last and had just reached the porch when somebody ran up to him and Sands, who followed him. "My dogs are in there. My dogs… Can you get them out?"

Beck nodded and said to the young Hispanic woman, "We'll try our best to get them out. Where are they?"

"They sleep in a cubby under the stairs. I…I got scared and forgot about them."

White spoke into the radio. "Sloan and O'Connor, take the downstairs. The rest of us, up."

Visibility was poor, but Beck could see the outlines of a living room as he followed O'Connor, who was subbing for Gabe. They wouldn't split up, because firefighters always worked in pairs. The living room was empty, so they searched the small dining area, then the kitchen. From upstairs he heard through the mic, "Bedroom on right, clear," and "Second bedroom, empty." Then White, "Let's go. O'Connor, you done?"

"Yeah. We're on our way out."

"What about the dogs?" Beck asked.

"What dogs?" he asked, as he hadn't heard the conversation outside.

The house shook and rattled loudly. Immediately, the evacuation horn blew. "Never mind. We're outta here." Grady's mandate was stern. "We leave now, Sloan."

Beck never disobeyed orders. He'd spent his whole life following them and then giving them. But when O'Connor made a beeline for the door, Beck detoured to the staircase, where he heard a soft mewling beneath them. Yanking open the small door, he found the two dogs curled up into each other, barely able to make the sounds. Quickly Beck scooped them up and rushed outside.

No one seemed to notice him, so maybe O'Connor hadn't caught his little detour and delay. Unobtrusively, he crossed the sidewalk to a safe distance away from the fire — which was fully involved — and stopped under a big oak tree. Gently, he set the dogs on the ground.

The owner, who'd spoken to him earlier rushed over. "Oh, no, oh no. My dogs." She dropped to her knees and picked up the larger of the two Yorkies. "Hattie, come on girl," she said as she gently patted the dog's face.

Beck took off his mask and dropped to the ground.

"They're not breathing." The woman looked up at him with frightened, brown eyes.

Carefully, Beck took the pet from her, cradled it in his lap and placed his mask over its mouth. Not too long after, the small furry chest began to heave up and down. Setting her aside, Beck turned to the second animal. "Jesus." This one was a three-pounder at the most.

The woman grasped on to Hattie and hugged her close. "That's Huxley. He's so little, he might not—" She cut off abruptly, her voice raw.

Beck looked down. The mask was almost as big as the dog.

Still, he held the tiny mutt in one hand and set the mechanism the over him. It totally enveloped him. Soon, this one began to breathe, too. A strong sense of relief flowed through Beck; he must be getting soft to be so moved by saving animals when he hadn't been able to save some people during his career.

The owner deflated. "Thank you so much. So much. I…" She hugged Hattie while Beck cuddled Huxley to his chest. The thing literally fit in one hand.

After a few minutes, he sensed people around them. Glancing up, he saw his crew, all of them, even the chief. Sands bent down with a bowl of water. Hattie went right for it and lapped up the drink. When he set Huxley down, the tiny dog limped over, too.

"What ya got there, Beck?" O'Malley asked.

Ryan O'Malley, his cop brother, peeked over Brody's shoulder. "It's a rat? Ow…ee, Beck saved a rat."

Running a couple of fingers over Huxley's soft head, Beck shook his head. "He's a three-pound Yorkie, jerk."

"Big rescue, Sloan." This from O'Connor.

Felicia added, "Worth breaking ranks for?"

Beck endured the teasing until someone from outside the circle yelled out. "Could you all move so I can finish filming?"

When his group parted to make an opening, Beck saw the TV crew. A female reporter. And a guy holding a video camera.

"Tell me you didn't," Beck muttered.

The reporter asked, "Didn't what?"

"Tape all this."

"Of course we did. It'll be all over the news tomorrow. Now, Firefighter Sloan, is this your first doggy rescue?"

Oh, hell, Beck thought as Huxley nipped at his hand. *I'll never live this down.*

• • •

DR. CHRISTIAN SINGER bit his lip and averted his gaze from Lela's to ask the man who was face down on the gurney and moaning loudly, "Mr. Lipinsky, I have a few questions."

"Just get it the fuck out of there."

"I, um, need to know, was this a solo adventure or was someone with you?"

"What does it matter?" the guy shouted, all dignity and sense of decorum lost after he'd apparently shoved a vibrator up his rectum.

"Angle, strength of…er…insertion matter. What's with the tongs?"

"I tried to get the damn thing out with them."

And they'd gotten stuck, too.

Suddenly the guy stiffened and howled in acute pain.

"Intermittent pain, Nurse Allen. What do you think?" Christian's eyes, made bluer by his scrub cap, twinkled at her.

"Maybe the thing turns on and off with a delay timer."

Christian choked on a laugh and tried to cover it with a cough. "All right, let's get them out of here. Forceps."

An hour later, Lela sat with Christian, outside on a bench, drinking cups of strong coffee. They were still chuckling like kids instead of an experienced doctor and nurse. "I don't know why this tickles me," Christian said, "We've seen things shoved up people's asses before."

Lela threw her head back. "Well, I don't know about you, but the tongs are a new one for me. How did he even reach —"

Holding up his hand, Christian chortled. "Stop. The images are too gross to even consider."

Again, she laughed aloud.

"I like it when you laugh." He grasped her hand. Held it.

She thought back to Len's death, two weeks ago. The fallout for her hadn't been nearly as severe as it had for the Allens. Josh was making progress, though, with the Fourth of July party, but he hadn't wanted to go to a playground program he usually attended in the summer. This morning, though, he'd asked to see Tommy Sloan.

Beck's son. No, don't think about Beck. About green eyes lit with fire, a body to—*No!* As she'd done for the last weeks, she concentrated on the here and now, which included Christian Singer.

He squeezed her hand. "Lela?"

"I was just thinking about the last two weeks. And Josh. He's better, but it's slow."

"He needs time to adjust to life without his dad."

"I guess. He liked seeing Kayla yesterday."

Christian had brought his daughter over for a backyard picnic, and she and Josh had played some catch in the yard. Josh had been modestly excited when they went to get ice cream.

He glanced at his watch. "Want to have breakfast with me? We're off night duty."

"I can't. I'm going to the shelter this morning."

He set his coffee down and, turning to face her, he brushed his hand down her hair. "You work too hard. I worry about that."

"I appreciate your concern. But they need me there more than ever. The angst the vets experience when one of them kills himself brings along a lot of ailments and minor accidents. I'll cut back on my hours after the whole thing with Len settles down."

"All right." He drew her close and kissed her head.

She'd found a way over five weeks to deal with another man touching her, too. And she was beginning to like it. "Hmm," she murmured.

"Hell. Don't do that unless you want a trip to the on-call room before you leave."

She chuckled, then pulled away. His face was lined with fatigue, but he was so attractive in the light from the hospital behind them. "Nope. Not ready for that. But you can walk me to my car."

They held hands across to the staff lot. Once there, she unlocked the door. A blinding slice of memory hit her, of standing with Beck several times at her car or his... *No, no, no.*

So she bent down, pressed the unlock button, and said, in as much of a flirty tone as she could muster, "It's still dark out. Y'all wanna neck in the car some?"

"I'd love to, Nurse Allen." Hurriedly, he rounded the trunk to the passenger side.

Building up her enthusiasm, she slid in the front.

And soon, she was indeed thinking only about Christian.

• • •

AFTER HIS SHOWER at the end of his shift, Beck had just finished dressing when his text chime went off.

Done with the night shift. Poor sick kids. Caught an interesting morning news clip that I got on tape. Wanna come over and see it with me?

Beck grinned as he sank down onto his cot to put on his deck shoes and texted her back a yes. Why not? He was wired, he'd had a good night, and even if he'd saved only dogs, two little hearts were beating this morning that wouldn't have been if it weren't for him.

When his replacement arrived, he snuck out of the firehouse the back way so he didn't have to endure the night shift explaining what had happened to the morning crew.

On the drive to Lexie's house, he thought about his state of mind. He'd been in a black hole the weeks leading up to Len Allen's death. But something had changed for him after the suicide. For one thing, the incident had confirmed that he and Lela weren't going to be able to be together, despite their vows of love. Josh was in the pits of despair over losing his father, and it was ludicrous to think Lela could ever risk another man with PTSD living with her son. The truth had slapped him in the face, and he'd accepted the end of their relationship. He'd also begun to think about how he was going to live his life from here on out. Right now, he was casually dating Lexie Wellington.

The sun warmed his face and his step was light as he took the stairs up to the front porch of her patio home outside of Hidden Cove. He rang once, and she opened the door immediately.

"Hey, there, handsome."

"Hi, beautiful."

Leaning over, she kissed his cheek. She had that aftershower scent of soap and shampoo clinging to her. "Come on in."

He held on to her for a second, kissed her damp hair, then followed her inside. He'd been to her home a couple of times, but mostly they'd sat in her backyard, and so he hadn't seen much of the interior. It was decorated with modern motifs, bright colors and wood that made a statement. The kitchen was full of high-tech gadgets and appliances.

As she placed the single-cup serving in her Keurig, he watched her move around her own space. She fit here, all lithe and beautiful, upbeat and sweet.

When the brew finished, and he was sipping his coffee, he asked, "All right, how did you get a tape of the rescue?"

She chuckled. "One of the nurses had seen you pick me up at the hospital last week. She was watching the news before she came to work, and recorded the big event because she knew I was on duty."

"So they aired the clip?"

Lexie nodded.

"I'm embarrassed."

"I haven't seen it." Her hazel eyes twinkled. "But I heard what you did."

He rolled his eyes.

"Come on. Let's go watch it." She held out her hand and when he took it, she said, "Oh, by the way, my TV down here is broken. The only one working is in my bedroom."

He stilled, capturing her gaze. "I could see your bedroom today."

They made their way upstairs. She put in the DVD and he kicked off the Docksiders he wore with navy shorts and a casual, light blue shirt and dropped down on the bed. This room sported modern decor too—skylights, an arched ceiling, sleek teak. It was so different from... *Nope. Can't go there now. Can't ever really go there again.*

She slid onto the mattress next to him, propping herself up with pillows. He noticed now she was wearing light knit, yellow capris and a printed top. Were those pajamas?

"Oh!" Her expletive distracted him from her unfettered breasts. "Look at you."

God, he *looked* ridiculous. Big guy, in clumsy turnout gear, clutching the two mutts to his chest. He hadn't noticed their gray-and-white hair and russet markings. Hell, did he have to hold them so…tenderly?

You're so tender, Beck. I love that.

A voice-over said, "One of America's Bravest shows his feminine side."

"Shit, I'm not going to hear the end of that one."

"I think it's adorable." Lexie moved over and skimmed her hand down his thigh. "Besides, I know how masculine you are."

They'd had fun getting to first base, then second and third, building up to what she'd called recreational sex. Soon, he knew, they would take their physical contact to the natural conclusion. He was looking forward to it.

"My Lord, Beckett Sloan." She was watching the TV again. "You sat that little dog right inside your mask."

It *was* a cute picture. He'd removed his helmet and was seated on the ground with the distraught owner.

The screen switched to a list of emails—no wait—tweets. Again the invisible narrator. "The twittersphere has been abuzz with these pictures and praise for our brave heroes." Some of the tweets flitted by…*Bravo to firefighters who care about everything…Love that guy. Is he single?…Finally, a man who shows his gentle side…*

Setting his coffee down on the nightstand, Beck grabbed the remote from Lexie. "Hell, don't these people have anything better to do with their time?" He switched off the DVD.

Lexie disposed of her cup, too. She said sexily, "I know I do. How about you, Beck?"

Tossing the remote to the floor, he turned over and reached for her, not misinterpreting her remark. "I do, baby. Oh, I do."

• • •

"ANY INTERESTING CASES last night?" Nick asked Lela as they sat having coffee before the clinic officially opened for the day.

Lela giggled. "One that I'm too embarrassed to tell you about."

"Ah."

Her eyes twinkled. Since her husband's death, her face had been consistently shadowed. It was nice to see some brightness today. "It involved a vibrator and parts of our anatomy that we usually don't discuss."

Laughter bubbled out of him. He was feeling better. He'd been thinking a lot about how *he* was or wasn't living his life.

"Did you see the thing on TV about our friend Beck saving some puppies?"

"Um, no, I didn't."

"It was cute."

Standing, she got a coffee refill, and asked if he wanted one.

"No, I'm avoiding too much caffeine."

After she sat back down, she studied him. "You look happier these last couple of weeks, Nick."

"I feel happy, some at least." Should he tell her it was because of her husband's suicide? Was it callous or would it help her. "Since the funeral."

Her expression was questioning.

"Something happened there, for me. Something that opened my mind." He touched his face. He'd never get used to the way he looked, but he'd had some kind epiphany. "Like I don't want to end up like your ex. Is that an awful thing to say?"

"Not at all. It makes me feel better. Does this extend to Amy?"

"Yeah. I've been seeing her regularly. She doesn't seem to mind going out in public with me."

Although at the movies one day, a little kid at the concession stand had run away screaming when he'd caught a glimpse of Nick's face. He'd handled the situation, and the mother, God bless her heart, hadn't let it go. She'd corralled the boy, spoke to him, and they'd both approached Nick. Still, he'd avoided places where children would be. Though Beck was on him about volunteering at the day camp he'd become involved in.

"Of course she doesn't mind being with you. She loves you."

"I love her, too."

"Have you told her that since you got back?"

He shook his head. "I wanted to spare her a life with me. I pushed her away."

"Oh, Nick, life's so short. You have to live it. Especially after surviving the horror of Afghanistan. We owe it to ourselves, to live well here."

He thought about Beck's statement.

You gotta manage this thing or it'll win. The fucking terrorists will win. We didn't go over there to fight so they could win once we got back in the world.

He was still thinking about Lela's words—and Beck's—when Amy came to pick him up at the shelter at noon the next day. They were taking a drive out to the lake. Her little sedan swerved to the curb and he approached the car. With a lighter heart, he swung the door open, said, "Hi, there," and climbed inside. Before he put his seatbelt on, he touched his wife's arm. She looked adorable today in simple jeans and a pretty, pink blouse. "Ames?"

She turned to him with the sweetest expression on her face. "Yeah?"

He drew a deep breath. "I love you, you know. Still. I've been a bear, but that never changed."

Her throat worked and her eyes clouded with tears. "Oh, Nicky." She unbuckled her seatbelt and threw herself into his arms. For the first time in months, he didn't balk at the contact.

Instead, he savored it.

CHAPTER 16

"AND WHEN WE need to talk to you, I'll raise my hand, and you raise yours." Megan Hale Malvaso lifted her arm with her palm outstretched for the kids to mimic, and Beck watched them somberly follow orders. Though her sister-in-law ran the entire camp, including the residential part, Megan had wanted to be the one to kick off the first Junior Hale's Haven.

But ten little ones couldn't remain quiet for long. A buzz started, and Megan raised her arm again. They settled. Beck knew they were anxious to get off the bus and into the Anderson County Zoo.

"The one rule is that you have to stay with your counselor," Megan continued.

Beck looked down at his little guy: a four-year-old, still in diapers, whose dad had died in a firefight in Kandahar that had taken out his whole platoon. "Did you hear that, Adam?"

Big, blue eyes looked up at him trustingly. "Yes, sir."

"You can call me Beck."

"Mommy said you're an officer."

"I was. But I'm just Beck here."

"That's it for instructions," Megan finished. We'll walk into the zoo and go right to a meeting place." Where the director of the camp would stay for the entire visit and where kids would also gather when the time came to leave. The nurse would be stationed with her in case someone got hurt. He looked toward the front. Or in this case, the *doctor*.

A week ago, Lexie had said to him, "Gabe told Rachel the nurse for Junior Hale's Haven broke her leg. They can't get a sub. I have a lot of time off. Would you mind, Beck, if I was there for the four days?"

They'd been in bed, and truthfully, he didn't mind. He liked being with her. "No, of course not. It'll be fun...."

They proceeded out of the bus at a snail's pace. Little kids bumped one another, jumped ahead of adults, and didn't really know how to wait their turns. It took a while to get to the gathering place at the front of the zoo. Once again, Megan called for their attention. "This is Dr. Wellington. If you feel sick or fall down, she's going to patch you up."

In the bright sunlight, the two women looked alike in blue camp shirts and denim shorts, both with blond hair tied back. Lexie was slimmer and taller, but they resembled each other.

"Go ahead, now," Megan told the group. She cupped her hands around her mouth as they started away. "And stay with your counselors."

After much coaxing and some tough love, Beck had convinced Nick DeBlasio to volunteer with him. Megan had assigned him to Beck as an assistant, but he'd had doctors' appointments this morning. Nick would join them at the movies after lunch, which was probably a better way for him to start off.

Beck walked away, holding the hand of his camper. "So, Adam, where do you want to go first?"

"The penguins. Mommy and me watched *Happy Feet* on a tape. I liked the movie."

"To the penguins, it is."

Adam chatted nonstop as they passed the playground, a couple of food stands and a section with snakes. When they reached the penguins, Beck boosted Adam up on his shoulders so the boy could see. "They're small."

Suddenly, Beck was catapulted back to Lela, telling him how Josh had loved the zoo, too. A stab of pain surprised him as he wondered how Josh was doing.

In the last two weeks, since he'd been sleeping with Lexie, he'd forced Lela from his mind. The PTSD meetings were over, so he didn't have to see her there or make arrangements about who would attend which session. But at odd times, someone would say something, or he'd catch a certain scent, and his mind derailed right to where, deep in his heart, he wanted it to go.

And he'd seen her a few times. Once at the Veteran's Outreach Shelter, where he'd gone to visit Nick. And once at an ice cream stand. She'd been with her doctor boyfriend. Christian Singer had been holding Josh's hand and Beck had steeled himself at the sight. He'd also had to introduce Lexie to them…

"Lela, Christian, this is Lexie Wellington."

Lexie grinned, not knowing the dynamic between him and Lela. "Lela and I have met. At a hospital thing. Nice to see you again."

Lela croaked out a reply, obviously affected by the sight of the two of them together. He wondered briefly if she had told the doctor about him.

Lexie added, "Chris and I know each other from the hospital. How are you?"

The guy slid his arm around Lela and Beck's throat felt like somebody had stuffed a sock into it. "Just great. You?"

Lexie moved in closer to Beck. "Me, too."

He'd caught Lela's gaze and they'd watched each other for a few moments. Messages had passed between them. The main one: *We've gone on with our lives....*

"Can we go to the monkey cage now, Beck?"

Swinging the boy to the ground, Beck said, "I'd love to. Do you know that there are 264 species of monkeys?"

"I like the spider monkeys the best. They're called that because of their long arms and legs and tails."

Laughing—this one was going to be hard to impress—Beck again took his hand. Fuck it, Beck decided in the beauty of this day, he was going to enjoy himself and not think about what he couldn't have.

• • •

HALE'S HAVEN, LOCATED on Hidden Lake, was absolutely beautiful. In the week Lela had been on the lake campus, she'd fallen in love with what the organization had done for the children of slain firefighters, police officers—and those of war veterans, thanks to Beck. They'd managed to sign up the latter for all the camps, not just Junior Hale's Haven, which she had avoided working at even after the scheduled nurse had broken her leg.

Instead, five days ago, she'd come to help out here. She'd tried to appreciate the smell of the water, the sun sparkling like diamonds on its surface, the crisp blue of the sky, and the chatter of kids at the picnic area behind her. It had been a wonderful, if exhausting week. Though the counselors took the brunt of the responsibility for the kids, Lela had managed to participate in many of the activities, hence the fatigue. A good kind of fatigue, though. And she only had to get through this last day; she could sleep for hours as Josh wasn't coming home until tomorrow. The Allens, who'd kept him all week, were taking him to visit Marsha's sister in Camden Cove today.

But a complication in her well-planned schedule had occurred. It turned out the little kids from junior camp were visiting the main camp and were about to arrive at any time — an event she hadn't known would happen when she'd signed up. And Beck would be with them. She could still see him with the beautiful Lexie, standing close, as lovers do, when the four of them had met up at a local ice cream stand. Swallowing hard, she battled back the desolation she experienced whenever she thought about Beck and Lexie together.

"Penny for your thoughts."

She turned to find Christian standing there, looking young and healthy in the blue camp shirt, his bathing trunks and flip-flops. His dark blond hair caught the morning sun. "Hi."

Leaning over, he kissed her head. "You seem far away."

He'd volunteered, too. But got her permission first…

"What would you think of me volunteering at Hale's Haven the week you do?" he'd asked.

She'd been caught off guard and blurted out, "That would be great."

"I'd like to be part of the whole endeavor. Everybody in town is so excited about it. Besides, I want to be with you.…"

And she wanted to be with him, too, most of the time. It was only when she saw Beck — or, okay — she thought about him other times, too, like when she'd first slept with Christian. She'd gone into the bathroom and cried afterward.…

"Honey, what is it?"

"Oh, sorry. I…I always feel nostalgic at endings, I guess. My mother said I used to cry on the way home from summer camp every year."

"I like that about you. As a matter of fact, I like everything about you."

He did, and that helped in her split from Beck.

"This was fun, wasn't it? The week here?"

"Yeah, I feel like I did something good."

"It's different from hospital work. I know we do good there, too, but this is something more."

He surveyed the pavilion. "I'm glad we included the kids of veterans."

"Me, too."

She heard behind her, "Okay, everybody. Heads up." This from Jenn Malvaso, who appeared happy and healthy, her face glowing and her dark eyes sparkling. Her husband, Grady, was here, too, with their kids, and the five of them were staying at Mitch and Megan's house. "The little ones have just arrived," she said brightly.

She and Christian glanced up the hill to see fifteen counselors and other administrative personnel reach the pavilion, the kids seeming shy, the counselors showing the same signs of exhaustion that Lela felt. Off to the side, she caught sight of Nick DeBlasio in a wheelchair. She'd been shocked when he'd told her he'd taken Beck up on his offer to be an assistant counselor. Shocked and so, so glad. He was going to make it.

She didn't search for Beck.

"Okay, everybody." Jenn spoke into the megaphone. "Take seats. We're ready for lunch." Already the scent of hamburgers and hot dogs filled the air.

"Sit with me and my kid, okay?" Christian asked, leaning into her. He felt solid, safe.

"Sure." She watched as the campers greeted each other, but when they selected a table, a small child approached the three of them. A small child holding Beck's hand.

"Buddy!!" the kid shouted as he threw himself at Buddy Sampson, Christian's camper. "I missed you."

Buddy rolled his eyes but hugged the boy.

"Hi," Beck said easily. God, he looked good, with his hair longer, his face tanned. He seemed bigger, more masculine. Though it couldn't be possible, she swore she could smell the spicy aftershave he used. "This guy here is Adam Sampson."

Damn it to hell! Christian's camper and Beck's were brothers? Once again, Lela bemoaned how cruel fate could be.

"Good to see you Beck," Christian said. "Have you had a good week?"

"The best." He shrugged. "Except that I'm whipped."

Christian grinned. "We are, too."

We. Beck's eyes flared at the pronoun.

"I didn't know our two camps would coincide," Lela commented.

Beck sighed as if he meant it. "Me, either."

Lela grinned over Beck's shoulder and smiled genuinely. "Look who's here."

Nick wheeled toward them. When he reached Lela, she bent down and kissed his cheek. "I'm so glad to see you."

He angled his head at Beck. "This guy badgered me so much, I did it just to shut him up." He nodded to Jenn Malvaso off to the side. "She must have talked to the kids about" — he touched his face — "because they only stared a little."

Buddy stepped forward. "Does it hurt?" he asked, pointing to Nick's face.

"Only in here." Nick put his hand over his heart. Lela's eyes misted. Then he wrinkled his nose. "Sometimes it itches."

Satisfied, Buddy turned to Christian. "Can I show my tie-dyed T-shirt to Adam?" He motioned to a few yards away, where the shirts the kids had made this morning hung on a clothesline to dry.

"No fair," Adam whined. "I like tie-dye."

"I made you one, dummy," Buddy said with affection.

Christian reached out his hands for both boys. "I'll go with you." To Beck he said, "Take a load off. We'll be in watching distance." Then to Nick, "Want to join us?"

No, please, no. Lela didn't want to be alone with Beck.

But nobody answered her silent plea. Christian led the boys and Nick away.

And Lela and Beck were by themselves.

"Just like before," he said in a hoarse tone. "We can't seem to get away from each other."

"We've done pretty well, don't you think?"

His throat worked convulsively. "Too well."

"Beck…"

"Sorry I said that." He jammed his hands into his pockets. Stared over at the lake. "I miss you, still."

She caught sight of Lexie Wellington talking to Jenn. "You've gone on with your life, Beck. It's what we agreed to."

He shot a glance toward Christian. "So have you, Lee."

Lee. Images of them in bed when he called her that bombarded her.…

You feel so good, Lee, when I'm inside you…Hey, Lee baby, slow down. We have all weekend. And maybe the worst, on that tiny side street in New York. *I love you, Lee…I love you, too.…*

But he was with someone else, sleeping with someone else, and so was she. It was over between them.

"I'm sorry," Beck said, intruding on the memory. "I can see my comment upset you."

"No, Beck. Having to cut off our relationship upsets me. And it's a hundred times worse when I see you." She shook herself. "Talking about this isn't helping. How's Tommy?"

"He's had a pretty good summer. He appreciates the time he gets to spend with Josh."

"So does Josh. They seem good, both kids."

"Well, I wouldn't know, as I'm not allowed to see your son."

Lela stepped back at the harshness of his tone. Just after she'd decided that they could try letting Beck take the boys alone, Len had died.

"Hey there, handsome…oh, Lela." Lexie glanced from Lela to Beck. She wore short, shorts, and her camp T-shirt was cut off at the arms, making her look young. And sexy. "I'm sorry if I'm interrupting something. You both seem so somber."

"No, not at all. Good to see you, Lexie."

Alexis nodded to the line of shirts. "I see you got your boyfriend to volunteer, too."

The foam cup Beck was holding crushed in his hand. Coffee spurted up. Lexie gave him a searching look. "What… what happened?"

But Lela knew the answer to that question. Lela knew full well why Beck's temper had flared. And damn if it didn't send a little thrill through her.

• • •

AS ADAM SLEPT in Beck's lap on the bus ride home at the end of the day, Beck cursed the images that flitted through his mind. He wished he didn't have this time to think. Nick had gone home in a van, and so he had no one to talk to. Maybe if

Nick were here, Beck could forget about the sights etched too clearly in his mind.…

Of Lela and her *boyfriend* climbing the rock wall. Of Singer boosting her up, his hands on her hips, flirting with her ass.

Of Lela with Adam when he fell and Lexie was tending to someone else. Lela had grasped the boy to her chest, let him cry, then said, *We'll fix you up good as new, sweetie.* Adam had kissed her face, a face Beck had held, kissed, loved, all those weeks ago.

And of Beck lifting Lexie off the sandy beach to twirl her around after they'd beaten the other team in a volleyball game. He'd caught site of Lela, a few yards away, staring at them. The longing on her face had cut him to the quick.

Fuck! Why did today have to happen?

"He's out like a light." Lexie dropped down in the empty bus seat next to them. Her face was tanned and her nose a bit sunburned. She looked less tired than him, though.

Beck motioned to the seats ahead of him. "Most of them are. It was a fun day."

"You think so? You seemed ready to spit nails for most of it."

"Nah. I get cranky when I'm tired. I think I'm too old for chasing around a kid this little."

Her eyes turned sultry. "Too tired to stay over at my place tonight? I have to work the late shift tomorrow night. All those days off I took. And you're on days this week, right?"

"I am." His mind spun. He knew what she was asking. Jesus, how could he sleep with her when, after seeing Lela today, he couldn't get *her* out of his brain?

"Beck?"

"Not tonight, babe. I…promised Linc and Sally I'd have dinner with them. Tommy's away until tomorrow, so I wanted to take this opportunity to see my brother."

"Oh." He could ask her to go along but didn't.

The bus rumbled down the road and an uncomfortable silence sprang up between them. Finally, she said, "Beck, is something wrong that I should know about?"

He shook his head. He was unable to utter a lie, but not saying it didn't make it any less true.

• • •

SINCE THEY'D DRIVEN out to the lake together a week ago, Lela and Christian rode back to town together. Christian pulled his Mercedes into her driveway and shut off the engine. Then he faced her. He put his arm on the back of her seat and brushed a hand down her hair. "Nice week, wasn't it?"

"Very nice." She smiled at him. "I'm glad you came along."

"I need to ask you something. I hope I'm not overstepping here."

"You can ask me anything you like, Christian." *Please don't let it be about Beck.*

"Beck Sloan's the guy, isn't he?"

She didn't shy away from the question because she remembered their talk the night Len died…

"I was involved with someone else for a while before you. It's very complicated…we weren't really dating…I don't know how to explain it."

"You don't have to explain it. All I want to know is if your relationship with him is over."

"Yes. It's very over…"

The last thing she wanted now was to talk to Christian about Beck. She was feeling raw and vulnerable after having seen him. But she owed Christian the truth.

"Yes, it was him."

"Mind telling me what happened?"

"Why?"

Christian removed his arm from the seat and sat back. "Because he's still in love with you. It showed every time he looked at you, and me, I'm afraid."

In her heart, she knew that was true.

"I don't want to go into detail about this, but if what you say is true, it doesn't matter. Nothing can ever happen between us again."

Christian waited some long seconds. "If you tell me that, I'm going to believe you." He leaned in closer. "I want to believe you."

Please don't let him ask if I'm still in love with Beck.

"I'm telling you that."

"All right." He nodded to the house. "When's Josh coming back?"

"Len's parents are bringing him over as soon as I call them." The lie just slipped out.

Shaking his head, he ran his knuckles down her cheek. "I wish we could be together."

Oh, God.

"Soon?"

"Absolutely, soon!"

He walked her to the door and kissed her deeply before she went inside. Like an automaton, she let herself in, climbed the stairs and headed straight to the shower. Turning on the faucet as hot as she could stand it, she stepped into the stall.

The hard spray stung her skin, but it didn't help. This was all too much. She couldn't tolerate the feeling of loss. For the first time since Len's death Lela slid to the floor, put her head in her hands and cried over the loss of Beck.

• • •

NICK WAS PROUD of himself, proud of the monumental accomplishment he'd achieved this week by going out in public, being around kids, being himself. Maybe it was time to tackle one more thing, which was why he'd asked the director of the shelter to give him a ride.

"Thanks, Julie," he said as she dropped him off at his home. *His and Amy's home.*

"My pleasure." Julie nodded to the house. "Did you call first?"

He probably should have. "No, I wanted to surprise her."

"All right. I'll wait to see if Amy's there." She poked his arm. "If she is, should I sign you out for the night?"

His smile came easily. "Yeah, Julie, sign me out for the night."

Feeling like he could scale mountains—well, maybe that was an exaggeration—he made his way to the house. Was he limping a little less today?

She answered on the first ring of the bell. "Oh, Nick, I…" She clutched her robe tighter. "I didn't expect you tonight. You said you were whipped from the camp."

"Actually, I feel great."

She smiled. "Come on in." When he stepped inside, she moved back from him. Probably because he'd been such a jerk about physical contact. "I'll just go change."

Playfully, he grabbed her arm like he used to, before he went overseas. "I don't think that's necessary, doll."

"Why?"

"Because I'll just have to take *those* clothes off you, instead of these." He ran his fingertips over the lapel of her bathrobe. She smelled fresh from the shower, of powder and lotion and shampoo.

242

"Nicky, do you mean...?"

"Yep. I want to make love to my wife."

Tears sprang to her eyes and rolled down her face. He felt bad because he'd hurt her so much. But no more. If he could handle being with all those little kids, in public, for four days, he knew he had options in his life. Choices.

He pulled her to him, holding her close, relishing in the once-familiar curves of her body, the soft silkiness of her hair. "Don't cry, baby. Everything's going to be all right now. I promise."

• • •

SHE WAS UNDER him again, joined with him like no woman had ever been before. "Lela, love, I can't let you go."

"You have to."

He thrust hard inside her. "How can you say that to me? Now. When we're here like this."

He began to push...hard, harder...

"Tell me you still love me."

"I still love you. I'll always love you. That'll never change."

They came together, an explosion that blew the top of his head off. When consciousness returned, he rolled off her and she slid out of bed.

"Where are you going?"

She stuffed her legs into the trousers of her scrubs. Then donned the top. "I have to go."

"Why?"

"Because I came over tonight to tell you something." She motioned to the bed. "This shouldn't have happened."

"Why?"

"Because." Dressed now, she looked down at him. "Christian asked me to marry him."

"What?"

"I said yes."

"No." He bolted upright. *"No. I won't let you do that."*

"You have no choice, love. It will end this thing between us. Finally."

No, no, no....

He was shouting as he ricocheted off the bed. "No, no, no." Stunned, he looked around the room. He was alone. Fuck. He lay back on the pillows. He'd dreamed of her, of losing her for good. Jesus.

He glanced at the clock. Seven a.m.

Getting out of bed, he stood stock still and thought about the dream.

An hour later, he rang Lexie's doorbell.

She opened it, looking fresh as the proverbial daisy in yellow shorts and top. "Beck, what a nice surprise. I was just about to go running." Studying him, she asked, "What's wrong?"

"We have to talk, Lexie."

• • •

LELA STARTLED AWAKE. What the hell? Her phone was ringing. She snatched it up. "Hello."

"Lela Allen?"

She didn't recognize the voice. "This is me."

"It's Amy DeBlasio. We've only met a couple of times, but I don't know who else to call."

"Calling me is fine, Amy. Is something wrong?"

"Nick...Nick..." She started to cry.

All Lela's instincts went on red alert and she forced herself into nurse mode. Swinging her legs out of bed, she sat on the edge and asked, "What about Nick?"

"He's gone. Missing."

"What do you mean?"

"He came over last night. He had a great experience at the camp. He wanted to…but he couldn't…oh, Lela, he left here in a black mood. He didn't go back to the shelter. I called Julie. No one's seen him."

"How long has it been?"

"Several hours. He's really missing. I'm so worried. Julie says he has to come back on his own, and she believes he will. But I don't. Can you help me look for him?"

Her heart was beating at a clip. "Of course, Amy. I'll come right over to your house. Give me your address."

As soon as she took the information down, Lela clicked off. Gripping the phone in her hand, she considered the unthinkable, remembered when Nick had told Beck that sometimes he didn't want to live anymore. Remembered the suicide watch imposed on him at the shelter. Remembered how her husband had died. No, no, this couldn't happen again!

She stared at the phone. She couldn't do this alone. She just couldn't. Forcing herself to calm, she punched in another number. He answered on the second ring. "Hello."

"It's Lela. Beck, I need you. I need your help."

"Are you all right? Is Josh?"

"Yes. It isn't us. It's Nick."

"I'll be right there."

"No, meet me at his house." She gave him the address. "I'm afraid; his wife's afraid. I think maybe Nick is going to hurt himself. Or maybe already has."

"I'll be right there. You can tell me everything then."

"All right. Thanks."

"Any time, love. Any time."

CHAPTER 17

NICK SAT ON the grass staring at his buddy Billy's headstone. He hadn't visited the gravesite since he'd been back from theater. But what did it matter now? Again, he wished he'd died with his friend. Died when that fucking IED exploded and marred Nick's face forever. Took his foot. Drained his dignity in drips and drabs.

Dignity that he thought he might have a chance to get back had been lost forever last night. He cringed at the memory…

Amy had been on top of him, naked and beautiful; his hands had cupped her breasts. She'd run hers over his chest. He'd reveled in her touch, in how hot he was for her.

"I miss this so much Nicky." He wasn't inside her yet, but he was as hard as a rock. And it felt damn good.

"Me, too, baby. Me, too." He grasped her hips. "Now lift up on your knees."

She grinned. "I remember how to do this." It had been a favorite position of theirs before the war. She raised up to her knees and started to impale herself on him. It was so good… until it wasn't.

"What?" Her eyes were full of shock. "What happened?"

He was mortified at losing his erection. He'd thought if he could just get it up…

"Oh, fuck."

Amy tried to lean over, to cuddle onto his chest.

"Don't!" He shouted hard at her. "Get off me."

Meekly, as if he'd slapped her, she obeyed. As quickly as he could, he got out of bed, found his clothes and left the bedroom. He grabbed his backpack from the floor, and after making a stop in the bathroom, he stumbled downstairs. She must have thought he needed time, because she hadn't followed him; she'd just let him go. But he'd heard her muffled sobs as he'd quietly opened the front door and let himself out…

"What difference does it make anymore, Billy?" he said to the headstone with the little plaque beneath it, touting that twenty-three-year-old William J. Greene was an American serviceman. "What fucking difference. I can't do anything." His laugh came out ugly. "I thought I could. I thought I'd turned a corner this week." He shook his head. "But I didn't. I couldn't…" Tears formed in his eyes as he recalled his complete failure as a husband. "I can't keep going on like this, Bill. I can't."

Slowly, Nick reached off to the side, into his backpack, and pulled out the pill bottles he'd stolen from Amy's cabinet. Old painkillers he'd left behind. Sleeping pills she'd told him she'd been taking. Now he rattled the brown glass. There were enough.

Why not, he thought. Why the hell not?

• • •

"AMY, TRY TO calm down. We need to make a list." Beck's voice was even, reassuring. Lela needed that now as she sat next to Nick's wife and held her hand. "Start with the shelter and work from there. Where might he go?"

"I...don't know. He never goes anywhere except with me. Unless you two brought him out."

Lela asked, "Where did he go when he first got home and stayed here for a week? You had to drive him wherever he went."

"He didn't want to leave the house. He was embarrassed by his face. His foot." The woman started to cry again into the ragged tissue she held to her nose. "I tried to get him to go out."

"Where did you want to go?"

"To the store. Or to a movie, where it was dark inside. He eventually did that. But no movie theaters are open all night here. He wouldn't be at one now."

This was no help. And Lela knew every minute they wasted Nick could...

No, no, not again, reiterated in her mind.

Beck continued to talk to Amy, lead her in various directions that might reveal where Nick could be. Lela left the room to make coffee. While she was in the kitchen, she looked around the cute little space. Nick and Amy should have had a happily-ever-after. But Lela knew all too well those didn't exist for some people. For her. And maybe for the DeBlasios.

As she leaned against the counter, listening to the drip... drip...of the coffee, just its strong scent perked her up. She caught sight of some frames on the little bar next to the table. Three photos. She crossed to them.

The first picture showed Nick and Amy on their wedding day. God, he was handsome, and the realization made her throat close up, thinking of all the war had taken from him. The next—a split frame—caught Nick and another guy wearing graduation garb. Next to it, the two men sported fatigues and hooked their arms over each other's shoulders, caps tilted up on their heads.

Grabbing the frame, she hurried into the living room. "Amy, who's this man with Nick?"

"Billy Greene. We all grew up together; he and Nick joined the service together."

Beck grasped Amy's hand. "He's from Hidden Cove?"

"Yes."

"Did Nick stay in contact with him? Maybe Nick went to see him."

Amy shook her head. "No, he didn't. Billy died in Kandahar six months after he got there."

• • •

MORE EXHAUSTED THAN he'd ever been in his life, Nick fished the water bottle out of his backpack and unscrewed the top. He stared down at the drink. Morbid calm had descended on him. This was right. This would end Amy's pain and Nick wouldn't hurt her anymore. Maybe some others would miss him—Lela, the people at the shelter. Beck.

Thoughts of Beck shamed him. The guy was so strong, so able to deal with what had happened to him. Nick could never live up to that standard. Once, maybe he could have. But no more. Suddenly, he remembered a conversation they'd had when Lela had called Beck to come over, after they'd both had attacks in the same week.…

"I can't do it." Nick had meant, go on like this anymore.

"Yes you can. You don't want to be the statistic that says every eighty hours, a vet commits suicide."

Nick had stared down at his hands. "I understand why."

"Are you suicidal, Nick?"

His head had risen and he'd met Beck's gaze straight on. "I think about it."

"Most vets think about it, especially initially. Do you have a plan?"

"No. I just want to die sometimes…"

What did it matter? Beck was alive, he was even a hero again, doing good things for the world. Nick only hurt people. Shit, shit, shit. *Don't think about Beck.*

Carefully, he shook the pills onto his hand so they filled his palm. For some reason, he started counting them out. Lining them up on the small, rectangular plaque in the ground. One, two, three, four…

• • •

AS BECK'S SUV rumbled through the early morning, Lela sat across from him, stunned, scared and sad. He reached out and she took his hand. Held tight. "We'll find him, Lee."

"I know we will. It's just a question of getting to him in time." Right after they'd figured out Nick could have gone to the cemetery, Amy had bolted up and flown to the second floor. She came down sobbing. *They're gone. All the pills in the medicine cabinet are gone.*

Amy had stayed home in case Nick returned, and Lela and Beck had set out on the macabre journey.

To comfort Lela, to give her some hope, he said, "Try to think positively."

They reached the entrance to the cemetery and drove under the big, white arches. Lela gasped. "This is where we buried Len."

"Hold on, honey. Don't jump to conclusions until we know for sure where he is and what he's done."

Beck gripped her hand even while negotiating the narrow, winding roads. They had no idea where Billy Greene was buried, but the day had dawned clear and bright, the grounds were deserted and the place was small. Lela watched out the window as they drove down the gravel paths. He wondered if his words sunk in, if she was hopeful they'd find Nick in time. Truthfully, Beck didn't believe any of the things he'd said to console her. He thought probably Nick DeBlasio was dead.

"There, Beck." Lela pointed to some plots off to the left. "He's there, but he's lying in the grass."

Beck stopped on a dime and they both sprang out of the car. Rushed across the grass to Nick. "Jesus," he said as Lela bent down.

Pills were lined up like little soldiers on the iron plaque. Nick sprawled out, on his side, head resting on his backpack, with a bottle of water falling out of his hand. His eyes were closed and Beck couldn't see if his chest was rising and falling.

Then he caught sight of the three empty prescription bottles, lying like evidence on the grass.

Beck had been right. They were too late.

• • •

SOMEONE WAS SHAKING him. He heard muffled sounds. Talking. "Beck. God, Beck, he's
    still breathing."

A slap across his face. Another. Then cold water splashed on him. He coughed.

"He's coming around. Dear Lord in heaven, he's coming around."

Nick opened his eyes and the sunlight stung them. His gaze adjusted; Lela and Beck knelt on either side of him. Where the hell was he?

"Help me to get him to sit up," Lela said. "Maybe we can make him vomit."

Beck sat behind Nick and eased him into a sitting position, supporting his back. "The ambulance should be here soon."

"Whoa," Nick said, his head clearing. "Hold on, you guys. I don't need an ambulance."

"He's coherent." Lela looked to Beck. "I don't understand."

Nick caught sight of the pills on the ground. Now he got it. Now he understood.

• • •

LELA HAD COLLAPSED with relief when they took seats in the waiting room. Nick had been brought here by ambulance and taken inside, regardless of his denial about swallowing any pills. Though he didn't display any signs of an overdose, either, the ambulance had brought Nick to the hospital in case he'd lied to them. He'd also said he'd thought seriously about taking them all but had gotten so tired he'd lain down and fallen asleep. The doctors needed to do their own evaluation.

"This whole thing is amazing, Beck."

"I know. He didn't take any of the pills. Not one." There was disbelief in his tone.

"Yes, but would he have taken them when he woke up, if we hadn't found him?" Lela asked raggedly.

She felt his lips brush her hair. "I don't know, honey. He said he didn't think so."

By tacit agreement, they'd put their differences aside to concentrate on Nick. But once again, being together during a traumatic time had them behaving like lovers. Nothing had changed between them, but she didn't have the energy or stamina to stay distanced from him.

A nurse Lela worked with came up to them, and both she and Beck stood.

"Hey, Lela. I'm on Nick DeBlasio's case. Dr. Martin said to come out and tell you what we found. Your friend did *not* take any pills."

"He told us that, Joan."

"Martin talked to him. He said the guy is seriously depressed. But, Lela, you know as well as I do that a suicide attempt is so much different than thinking about taking your own life or even preparing for it. If, in the end, the subject doesn't swallow the pills or pull the trigger, there's a lot of hope for him."

"I'm glad. Can we see him?"

"Not now. Martin's insisting Psych be the first to talk to him. Other than his pretty little wife who won't leave his side. He wants her to stay. Another good sign."

Beck smiled. It was a beautiful smile; he was a beautiful man. Lela didn't know what she would have done without him today. "That's good to hear."

"Are you gonna stick around? It might not be until later this afternoon that he can have visitors."

"We'll talk about it. I'll let you know." She reached out and squeezed the woman's arm. "Thanks, Joan. For the news and the encouragement."

When Joan walked away, they sat back down and Lela sank into Beck's shoulder. She felt his arm go around her again and his other hand tuck her head into his chest. "That's not the only thing we have to talk about, love."

Lela was about to respond when she heard, "I guess that makes two of us."

Pulling away from Beck, Lela looked up. "Christian, what are you doing here? You weren't supposed to work today."

His face was lined with fatigue and something else. Anger maybe? "I was called in about two a.m. on an emergency. I'm just going off." He glanced at Beck, his eyes narrowing at their positions. "What's going on, Lela?"

• • •

CHRISTIAN SET DOWN two cups of coffee on the conference-room table in his office at the hospital and stared over at Lela. She stood near the window. "Come over here. Please."

She did her best not to squirm as she crossed the room and took a seat across from him. "So, did you lie outright to me, or did something just snap inside you?"

"I didn't lie outright." She ran a hand through her hair. "I thought it was over between me and Beck. It *was* over. Then something happened with Nick DeBlasio."

"The man you work with at the shelter?"

She explained Nick's night and their subsequent morning.

Christian didn't say anything. "That's not all of it, though, is it?" he finally asked.

"No, it isn't. Seeing Beck at the camp…talking to him. I'm sorry, Christian, so sorry. I thought I'd gone on with my life, without him in it."

"And you obviously haven't. If you called him and not me."

She thought about saying Beck was the logical one to call, that he knew Nick, but that *would* be a lie. The only person she'd thought of was Beck.

"I'm sorry, Christian," she repeated.

His blue eyes darkened. "From what I saw out there, it doesn't seem this was a temporary relapse."

"What do you mean?"

He waited several seconds as if he was weighing his words. "Lela, if you can sit here and tell me you want to be with me, you could get over this guy you can't have—and I don't even know why—I'd...I'd consider continuing yours and my relationship."

In her heart, Lela knew she couldn't go back to the way things were with Christian. "That wouldn't be fair to you."

"I've heard those words a lot lately."

"What do you mean?"

Rising, *he* crossed to the window and looked out. Finally, he turned to her and said, "Melissa called me just before we went to camp." Melissa was the wife who'd cheated on him. Who'd hurt him, Lela knew. "She wants to get back together. She said she hadn't been fair to me and had spent the last year getting her act together."

"Why didn't you tell me about her call?" Lela asked gently.

His brow furrowed. "I needed time to decide how I felt about her offer."

"Christian, you told me once you would have stayed if she'd asked you to, despite the infidelity. You believed you could salvage your marriage and keep your family together."

"I know. But then...you came along."

"Oh."

"It's over between us now, isn't it?"

"I'm sorry. Even if Beck and I can't be together, you and I should stop seeing each other."

He shook his head. "Lela, life is short. I just lost a patient. Your friend came in after a close call. Think hard about forgoing what you want in life. I know I'm going to."

He was such a good man. So generous and giving. Standing, she crossed to him. He took her in his arms and hugged her. "I'm sorry it didn't work out," he whispered hoarsely.

"So am I. Really."

• • •

HER EYES WERE red-rimmed when she returned to the ER. Beck had watched the exchange between her and Singer, watched the woman he loved go off with another man and wondered if there was any future for her and Beck.

He stood. "You're not okay."

"No, I'm not. I want to go home."

"All right. I'll tell the nurse we'll be back this afternoon."

In ten minutes, they were in his car, heading toward Amy's house to retrieve her vehicle. Beck couldn't stand the suspense, and damn, he shouldn't have to. He'd just helped her through a horrible ordeal and she goes off with some other guy? Jesus. So he said abruptly, "Did Singer know about you and me?"

"Only that I'd been involved with someone and the relationship was over. Before today, that is. I can't believe how much I've hurt him."

Beck bit his tongue but he stayed silent. He didn't know whether to push her to decide what she wanted right now, yell at her or leave her the hell alone. Maybe his anger was irrational but Beck was sick of wanting her and not having her. And this emotional yo-yo was getting to him.

When they reached the DeBlasio house, he shut off the engine and faced her. "Where do we go from here, Lela?"

"I honestly don't know."

"Are you going to keep seeing the doctor?" Sarcasm filtered into his voice.

"No. That's over."

Relief swamped him. "Why?"

"Damn it, Beck. You know why. Because I'm in love with you."

"But after all we've been through, you still don't know where we're headed. God damn it!"

"Well, excuse me if I don't have any answers. In the space of four months, I've fallen in love with another man with PTSD, my husband committed suicide, another person I care about almost died. To boot, I'm exhausted from camp. Give me a fucking break."

He hadn't expected a tirade. He'd never seen Lela lose it like this before. Her eyes were fiery and her whole body stiffened.

"All right, you've got all the breaks you want, sweetheart. Get out of my car. Go home and get some sleep before Josh gets back."

"And?"

He shrugged, not wanting to be a pushover. "Call me when you *figure things out*."

She just sat there. "Well, there's one piece of information I need, soldier." Still angry. "Are you going to keep seeing Lexie Wellington?"

Hallelujah. "No, I went over this morning and told her I couldn't see her anymore. And why. She was hurt. Like Singer."

Lela blew out a heavy breath, making her bangs puff up. "We've made a mess of things."

"I guess we have. Now, really, go, before I say more stuff I'll regret."

She surprised him by leaning over and kissing his cheek. Then she slid out of the car. He watched her, watched the woman who held his fate in her hands, get in her own vehicle and drive off.

And Beck was pissed. Really pissed at her.

CHAPTER 18

"HAPPY BIRTHDAY TO you, happy birthday to you, happy birthday dear Jo-osh, happy birthday to you."

Lela watched her son blow out eight candles on the Spiderman birthday cake she'd made for him. Not only had she re-created the super hero and webbing perfectly, but the buttercream frosting was sugary and smooth.

She'd wanted to make the cake and everything else special because he'd surprised her by asking for a party. Glancing around the backyard, with its pretty rose bushes and geraniums still very much in bloom and smelling heavenly, she smiled. The party was a small one, with Sophia and Tony's two kids, Eddie, of the party Josh had left that night so long ago, his Grandma and Grandpa Allen and, lo and behold, Tommy Sloan.

"Time to open presents," Josh called out right after the cake was cut and devoured. Sophia, who'd left the baby with her mother, had brought Marianna and Miguel and stayed around to help. She'd been talking to the Allens but stood now and crossed to Lela.

"Kids can do anything they want on their birthdays. Even go from one thing to another in a flash."

Lela rolled her eyes. "I've never seen him like this. He's come out of his shell so much."

It had been almost six weeks since his father died, two since Nick had the episode at his friend's gravesite, and fourteen days, four hours and maybe twenty minutes since she'd last set eyes on Beck. He'd dropped Tommy off today but hadn't come inside. His ex, Patty, was picking her son up later.

"Josh told Mari he's looking forward to school."

"Yeah, he's thrilled they'll all be together." Because of some redistricting, it turned out that the Ramirez kids, Tommy and Josh would attend the same elementary school this year.

"And his meetings with Jack Harrison have helped."

The very generous-with-his-time, fire-department psychologist had offered to meet with any of the kids from the PTSD support group who might benefit from his expertise. To her surprise, Josh had agreed to see him. It was later that she'd found out Tommy was having a few sessions, too, so that was probably why Josh had acquiesced so easily. They had something else in common now.

"I'm so happy about the change in him," she told Sophia as they cleared cake–and–ice cream plates and the Allens hustled the boys to the picnic table where the gifts were placed.

"Then how come you look like you've lost your best friend?"

She stared at Sophia. "Because I have."

Sophia leaned against the deck railing. "Lela, you've got choices. Maybe now that Josh is better…"

"Oh, Soph, I don't even know if Beck still wants to see me. I went off on him that day in the car; he was already angry, anyway. I haven't heard from him since."

"You told him you needed time. You haven't said much and I've left you alone about it. But it's you who needs to make a decision now. Call Beck, or move on."

She watched the kids across the yard. They were stacking the presents in a semicircle around Josh. "I'm still trying to get my head on straight, Soph. Accept what's happened to Len. Make peace with what happened with Nick. And what I did to Christian."

"Rumor has it Christian's gone back to his wife."

"I'm glad. I hope it works out for him. He was devastated when they broke up."

"And you told me Nick's a lot better."

In a surprising turn of events, Nick's near suicide attempt had scared him onto a path of genuine healing. He was also getting counseling and seeing Amy regularly.

"See, everybody's moving on, Lee."

"Except me?"

"No, I think you're making progress. I just wish the pace wasn't so slow."

Her son called out, "Mo-om, come on. I wanna open presents!"

Josh enjoyed the rest of his party, and at three, Eddie's mom picked him up, and the Allens left at the same time Sophia packed up her kids and headed out. Patty called to say she'd been held up at the office and would be a half hour late, so Tom and Josh were upstairs playing with Josh's birthday gifts. Lela sat in the living room, watching the news but thinking about Beck. Was he still mad? Sad? Was he moving on?

"Mom, I wanna see Beck." Caught up in her thoughts, she hadn't heard Josh come downstairs.

Her mouth dropped open. "Excuse me?"

"Tommy and me decided. We want to do some guy stuff with Beck. That's what we been talking about."

What to say? Should she bring up the past? "Oh, honey, don't you remember what happened with Beck in the car wash?"

"Yeah, but that was ages ago. I'm eight now. Bigger. And he didn't yell at me like Dad used to. He was *sorry*." Josh raised his chin. "Dr. Harrison says we can't let bad stuff in the past ruin the good stuff we could have now."

"Okay, baby. I'll think about it."

Lela was considering Josh's request when the doorbell rang right after Patty picked up Tommy. She swung the door open to find Nick and Amy on the porch, holding hands. Nick was standing erect, his shoulders squared, his chin up. Amy glowed.

"Hi, you two. Come on in."

"We'll only stay a minute." Nick led Amy inside. When they sat, he spoke first. "I came to say good-bye."

"Good-bye?"

"Well, not really good-bye completely. I'm moving back home, so I won't see you at the shelter anymore." Though his face was marred irrevocably, his eyes were sparkling—something she hadn't seen before, in the several months he'd been at the shelter.

"Oh, Nick, I'm so glad."

"We are, too." Amy grinned. "A lot of thanks go to you, Lela. And Beck."

"Beck?"

"Yeah, he's spent time with Nick. That and the counseling Nick's getting from the center has helped him so much."

Nick looked at his wife with such unconditional love, it hurt Lela's heart. "I'm gonna be all right, babe. I promise."

She offered them coffee, but they had things to do—and a lot to look forward to. After they left, and while Josh was still upstairs, Lela stayed in the living room, staring out the window. She remembered the night she'd spent on this very couch with Beck. She remembered how he'd held her, cuddled her close, without expecting anything in return. He'd always been so unselfish, so giving to her and Josh. He couldn't change the fact that he had PTSD, but he didn't let the condition destroy him as it had Len. She thought about Nick and Amy, too.

Everybody's moving on with their lives.

Everybody but her.

• • •

TWO WEEKS LATER, Beck stood in position to rip off the hood of the car after Sands had cut through it with the Jaws of Life. Smoke still billowed from the fire in the trunk they'd put out, but the day was clear, so he could see what he was doing through the goggles he wore. Felicia took the other side and together they tore back the aluminum and handed it off to O'Malley and Malvaso.

Gabe had been back to work for over a week and was so happy that sometimes Beck had to leave the room when his friend walked in. Now Gabe jumped up onto the car; Beck and Felicia cleared the way for him. To the victim, he said, "It's okay, sir. We're getting you out." The man grunted, and closed his eyes. He was conscious but barely. Beck heard the sirens and, out of the corner of his eye, saw the ambulance arrive. Since every minute counted, he took the neck brace from O'Malley and handed it to Gabe. They hefted up the backboard next. After they fitted the guy onto it and slid it down to the ambulance crew, all of them climbed off the car.

Beck glanced at his watch. The entire rescue had taken seven minutes. God, he loved his job.

There was banter and good cheer inside the rig as they returned to the firehouse—the shift ended shortly—but before they dismounted the truck, Gabe turned to face those in the back. "Buy you all beer at Badges?" Since the baby's birth, Gabe hadn't had time or energy to spend with his crew outside of work.

"What, wifey's letting you out finally?" O'Malley asked. He was all bluster, though. In some conversations with O'Malley, Beck had discovered he and Emma were trying to conceive, too. And Beck suspected he'd been the one to post right-after-birth pictures of little Ali all around the firehouse.

"Yeah, my in-laws are back from their cruise and at the house. They've loosened up some, stopped criticizing Rach, but she told me to go out with the guys tonight."

Felicia said, "I'm in."

"Love to." From O'Malley.

"Not me." This from Sydney. "It's our second anniversary. I got plans with my guy."

"Jesus, Sands. Aren't you out of the honeymoon period yet?"

"Shut up, O'Malley. Or I'll tell Emma you said you weren't."

Some things never change, Beck thought as they reached the house and waited for replacements to arrive. Not long after, they all headed for Badges.

The place was busy with customers double deep at the bar. Some old songs rang out from the jukebox. Beck liked the bustle of firefighters and cops letting down after long days and almost-always tense situations. But he hadn't been here much lately, either. He'd been spending time with Tommy, working with Jenn O'Connor on the next year's camps—apparently, he'd been put in charge of the veteran recruitment of both kids of vets and volunteers—and hanging out with Nick. Anything to avoid thinking about Lela. But when he caught sight of the dance floor, where he'd held her close that night and realized he was getting involved with her, his heart felt hollowed out again. God, he missed her. Giving her space was hard. It had been almost a month since they'd parted ways after Nick's near-fatal night and he'd heard nothing from her, except for Tommy saying she'd seemed sad when he'd seen her at Josh's.

"Play some pool?" Gabe asked him after they bought beer.

"Sure."

The table was in a smaller room, which, for once, was deserted. Gabe set the balls in the center of the table and said, "You break."

Beck chalked his cue, leaned over and took the shot. He made a clean break, sinking both the red and green balls. "Yellow in the left-hand corner," he called out for the third.

He sunk three more before he missed.

Gabe didn't approach the table. Instead, he set his cue's end on the floor in front of him and took a bead on Beck. "I know about you and Lela Allen."

"What?"

"Lexie told Rachel. Rach told me, of course."

Jesus, Beck hadn't expected or prepared for this conversation. "I'm sorry if I hurt her, Gabe. It's why I didn't want to talk to you about our relationship."

"Lexie's fine. I don't think she let herself fall for you. She knew all along somebody else *had your heart,* I think she told her sister."

Though he hated confiding his inadequacies, he said to his friend, "I screwed things up."

"With Lexie?"

"And Lela." He explained about the PTSD. About Josh.

"I understand that even more, now that we have Ali. I guess people would do anything for their kids. I stayed in my marriage long after I should have for Lilliana and Joey."

"I did the same for Tommy." He thudded his own cue on the floor. "I just wish it hadn't been her that I fell for. I could have picked somebody with no kids, who had no experience with that goddamned condition. But no, it had to be her! And I'm not ever going to get over her."

Gabe waited a beat before he said, "Maybe that should tell you something."

"What?"

Gabe shook his head. "You're a smart guy. You figure it out." Leaning over the table, Gabe added, "Blue ball in the right-hand corner."

• • •

"HEY, MOM, WHY'RE you wearing that raincoat? It's hot out."

Because I'm an idiot. "Um, I felt chilled today." Lela tugged the khaki coat more tightly around her as she led her son to the car to take him to his first day of school.

Once on the way, she longed to turn on the air-conditioning but knew that would raise even more questions. "Are you excited about school this year?"

"Uh-huh. My teacher seems nice."

The teacher, Mrs. Bell, *was* nice. She'd called Lela when she'd found out Josh's dad had died in July and offered her sympathy. She also promised she'd keep an eye on Josh's moods.

"And Tommy said he'd eat lunch with me today." Josh's tone was excited.

Lela hoped Tommy, a fifth grader, would keep his promise. Sitting with a third grader might not go over big with his buddies. But then, the two boys had formed a bond this summer, one that hadn't been broken when she and Beck had split. At least they'd done that right.

You did things right with Beck in bed. Remember those two nights in your apartment before the call from the Allens?

She did remember, when she was awake and when she was dreaming. Nervous, she fingered the belt of her coat. It was one of the things that had driven her to today's decision, after missing him for weeks.

And she was scared as hell. She could keep her calm in the face of terrible trauma and even death, but premeditating this one action that would determine her future had kept her up all night.

• • •

BECK GRABBED ON to the railing of his porch and forced back the growl he wanted to emit. He was a wreck, and it was clouding what should be a good day. Patty was on her way to pick him up so he could see Tommy off for the beginning of school—which he'd never done before. But Beck was finding it hard to enjoy the precious moment. He'd dreamed of Lela almost every night since he'd last seen her. When he'd dropped Tommy off for Josh's birthday party, he'd had to use every ounce of willpower he possessed not to walk up to her front door, kiss her senseless and make her admit they belonged together. He hadn't believed they could be together before Len's death and Nick's incident, but since then, he wanted to make a relationship with her work, damn it.

Patty's van pulled up and he hustled toward it. He hopped into the front seat. "Hi, son. Ready for the big day?"

"Yep. Can I go to Josh's after school?"

"Oh, honey," Patty put in. "First days are important to moms and dads, too. We'll want to hear about what happened."

"Oh."

Beck said, "Maybe we can work something out for tomorrow."

He exchanged glances with Patty. She rolled her eyes. Once again, he recognized the good in his life. He and his ex were friends and agreed on important issues concerning their son.

While Lela had dealt with an alcoholic, suicidal husband for months. Shit, he should be more patient with her.

At the school yard, the three of them exited at the same time. They'd only taken a few steps when a little whirlwind flew up to them. "Hi, Tommy."

"Hey, Josh."

Josh turned big eyes on him. "Beck, holy cow. I didn't know you'd be here." In a move that Josh was still too little to know was taboo in front of others, he threw his arms around Beck's waist and said, "I missed you so much, Beck."

Dumbfounded, Beck simply held on to Lela's son.

· · ·

OH, NO. HE was here. Why hadn't she expected this? *Because Len had never showed any interests in first days of anything.* She'd also noticed the makeup of the group every year. A few fathers came to drop off their kids, but mothers having the job were in the majority.

And what was he doing with his ex-wife?

Well, she'd just find out.

Gathering the self-confidence she knew she'd need today, she marched over to them. Beck was squatting down, now, talking to both boys. When he looked up at her, his eyes revealed nothing.

"Hi, Lela." He stood. "Patty, you know Josh's mother."

"Of course. Lela, how are you?" The woman's gaze darted briefly to her raincoat—Patty wore capris and a sleeveless top— but neither she nor Beck remarked on her outfit. Man, maybe this had been a bad idea.

A bell rang. "Okay, guys," Patty said. "Looks like it's time to go in."

"I'll go with you, Josh." Lela wanted to escape these two.

"No, Mom. I'm eight now. I can go in by myself."

Oh, dear, her little boy was growing up. She watched the two of them walk away with tears in her eyes.

"Beck, are you ready to go? I have to get to work." To Lela, Patty said, "I picked him up at his house."

Turning, she faced Beck. Patty's statement gave her information about the two of them, as she'd probably meant it to. "I'd be glad to drive Beck home. I want to talk to him about something, anyway. If that's okay."

Patty's gaze transferred from Lela to Beck, and he nodded.

"Sure. Nice to see you, Lela. Beck, you can come over about three to get him off the bus."

Beck just grunted and didn't take his eyes off Lela. Soon they were alone in front of the school. "So, you want to talk to me now?"

"Yes, I'd planned to come over to your house after I dropped Josh off. Sophia checked for me. You're not working this tour."

Still he watched her. "What's with this?" He reached out and ran his finger along the lapel of her coat.

Smiling, like a siren, she hoped, she leaned over and whispered in his ear.

• • •

SHOES FLEW OFF first—her high strappy sandals, then his Birkenstocks. Beck plastered Lela up against the door and kissed her deep and hard. He couldn't wait to have her. Her taste was sweet, her scent claiming him.

"Wait, don't you want to talk?" she asked, but there was mirth in those beautiful, brown eyes.

He cupped the silky smooth skin of her face. "You told me not to all the way home. Now I don't want to."

"Not even to know what I've decided?"

He ripped open the buttons of her coat and yanked it off her. "I think this says it all. Jesus, you weren't kidding." She'd bought a why-bother, one-piece thing that revealed more than it covered. Her breasts were nearly falling out of it. He captured her gaze. "You wore this for me, right?" He touched the strap that he was already easing off her.

"Yes."

"Then that's my answer."

"But—"

"Will you just be quiet, woman?"

She giggled until his mouth closed over hers.

Too bad the strap broke in his haste to get to her.

Too bad she scratched the hell out of his chest in her haste to get to him.

Too bad that the wood would be cold on her back.

He hoisted her up and took one of her breasts into his mouth. Suckled. Then repeated the action on the other.

She said raggedly, "Now, Beck. I'm ready."

"No condom."

"I don't care. I can't wait."

"It won't matter, anyway," he murmured and plunged into her.

Once…

Twice…

Three times….

They came together in a cataclysmic burst of light and color and sound. She slumped against him when they were done. Pivoting so *his* back was against the wall, he grabbed hold of her and slid down to the floor, cuddling her on his lap. For a few minutes, they just sat there, melding themselves into each other.

She spoke first. "What did you mean, the condom wouldn't matter, anyway?"

He brushed his hand down her hair, savoring the thick feminine locks. "Did I say that?"

"Uh-huh."

Drawing in a breath, he took a big chance and said, "Because I'm going to marry you, anyway. Another kid would be okay by me."

"Oh, Beck, I–"

"Look, it's okay. We'll figure it out. Get counseling. Find a way to work with the PTSD."

"I know."

"It doesn't matter how long… You know?"

"Yes." Reaching up, she cradled his face. "We have to be together. We'll find a way. Josh is already doing that."

"How?"

She told him what he'd said about Tommy. About Jack Harrison.

"Harrison's been a busy guy. I've seen him alone a few times."

She didn't pull away when she asked, "Have you had more attacks?"

"No, none. But after Len, then Nick, I decided I had to get a better handle on this, if only for my own sake." He grinned. "Now I have you again, to sweeten the pot, so to speak."

"Pretty sure of yourself, soldier."

He laughed out loud. "What did you expect when you wore this...told me about this...in the goddamned school yard?"

"I thought I'd learned not to expect anything. But you proved me wrong, Beck. For some reason, it was you that I fell in love with, no matter how much I fought it."

"You sorry about that?"

"No, not if we can be together." Reaching down, she palmed his still-hard groin.

He growled, "Speaking of which, I'm not done here."

Slowly he eased her to the floor. And slowly he started kissing his way down her body. Since he planned to be doing this when they were eighty, he took his time.

• • •

For notification of Kathryn's new work and information about her books, be sure to sign up for her newsletter at http://on.fb.me/1bLS0bN.

AUTHOR'S NOTE

AS I'M SURE you can tell I have a soft spot in my heart for firefighters and veterans. I worked for years with a big city fire department in order to write books about them, and I've been drawn to veterans since I wrote COP OF THE YEAR, about a Vietnam vet. (See poem below.) When I read about all the initiatives the government was implementing to hire our veterans, a story simply sprung to mind. Two people on each side of the PTSD condition. Truthfully, I didn't have a clue how I would solve this problem. PTSD is manageable, not cured. So how could a woman who'd been through the tortures of the malady risk her heart on another sufferer? The answer came as I wrote the book, and it's an answer that I end up with frequently in my work: being apart is just too painful, and it's worth any risk to be together.

Did you cry as you read the book? While proofreading it, I did. When Beck comes to the funeral and sees Lela with someone else. When Nick, who finally feels like he can handle his life, is dashed by his failure in bed. And when Lela realizes it's truly over for her and Beck.

I loved these people. They don't have a lot of flaws, which my characters usually do. They are good people caught in an unfair an untenable situation. The conflict is external, again rare for me. But I tried to mix it up, give them negative character qualities, and I couldn't.

I'm proud of this book in a way I'm usually proud of my work—and more. I think I've called attention to a social issue prevalent in society today framed by a poignant love story. I hope you liked reading it.

Visit or Contact Kathryn at www.kathrynshay.com www. facebook.com/kathrynshay www.twitter.com/KShayAuthor http://pinterest.com/kathrynshay/

If you liked this book, you might want to post a review of it at http://amzn.to/U4NHlt

Other Kathryn Shay firefighter books

After the Fire
After being trapped in a fire, the Malvaso brothers and sister decide to make changes in their lives. Follow Mitch Malvaso as he struggles to get closer to his kids and out of a doomed marriage. Jenn, his sister, wants to have a baby and asks Grady O'Connor, her best friend, to be the father. http://amzn.to/fwxJBS

On the Line
Fire Chief Noah Callahan and Albany Fire Investigator Eve Woodward butt heads while she investigates the cause of accidents at Hidden Cove fire scenes. Who knew they'd fall in love? And watch Zach Malvaso become the kind of man he wants to be with feisty firefighter Casey Brennan. http://amzn.to/hu66kz

Nothing More to Lose
Injured 9/11 firefighter, Ian Woodward (Eve's twin), and a disgraced cop, Rick Ruscio, struggle to salvage their lives with the help of the women who love them. http://amzn.to/h5QpxS

America's Bravest—Six novellas
The men and women on another Rescue Squad in the Hidden Cove Fire Department have complicated personal relationships due to the nature of their jobs. Each of the six novellas details the love and work of one firefighter, but the stories are tied together with an arson case and a blogger out to discredit them. http://amzn.to/vy6mUx

It Had to Be You
Beckett Sloan is an Iraq and Afghanistan veteran who comes home with PTSD. He joins the fire department and finds the love of his life in army nurse Lela Allen, but his demons keep them apart. http://amzn.to/U4NHlt

Chasing the Fire—Three Novellas
Inanother set of novellas, CHASING THE FIRE, the past catches up with three brave firefighters and they must wrestle with it to find love and contentment. http://www.amazon.com/dp/B00DU1QBTA

And you might want to read COP OF THE YEAR, Kathryn Shay's novel written in the nineties, about a Vietnam Vet. http://amzn.to/1aGrrFW

To browse Kathryn's impressive list of titles go to http://www.kathrynshay.com/books/.

EXCERPT FROM *CHASING THE FIRE* BOOK 6 OF THE HIDDEN COVE SERIES

BACKDRAFT

"Hey, Gallagher, I hear your cutie's subbing on the Rescue Squad tonight. You gonna bunk with her?"

Riley looked up from a copy of *The Heart of Hidden Cove*, a magazine produced by the husband of a firefighter he liked. "Say one word against Jane and I'll deck you, Decarlo."

"Ha! You and whose army?"

The retort was accurate. He'd need a battalion to subdue Rocky Decarlo, *the Rock,* a hulk of a guy, with hands like baseball mitts and a body as big as the trunk of a tree.

Riley snorted back. He liked Rocky and knew the guy was wholly supportive of the women in the department. Besides, Jane Phillips could take care of herself. That trait was one of the many things he loved about her. Really, he'd been crazy about his childhood friend, turned high school sweetheart, turned fiancé for literally half their lives.

The magazine article on Hale's Haven, a camp for the kids of firefighters and police officers that was held every summer, kept his attention until she walked into the kitchen.

Rocky greeted her with a big hug. "Wish you were on this shift more often, Phillips. We'd rather look at your beautiful face than Gallagher's ugly mug."

"Yeah, I can understand that."

Janie wasn't drop-dead gorgeous and they both knew Riley was, but they joked about it. He dug her dark, short, sassy hair, chocolate-brown eyes and her five-foot-eight sturdy build. Also, Jane possessed an inner beauty, which he'd seen when she was a gawky nerd in high school and he was a star football player. He'd fallen hard in that tenth-grade science lab and was still madly in love with the woman.

She glanced over and winked at him. "Hi, hotshot."

"Sweetie." He smiled, grateful all over again that she was part of his life's work.

The only thing he cared about as much as Janie, his mother and a sister who'd given him two beautiful nephews was fire-fighting. He scowled. Too bad one of the boys was named after Riley's degenerate father who'd once been his idol.

The captain of the Rescue Squad, Nick Evans, walked in. "Gallagher, your fan club's outside. They came right from school."

"Oh, fun. I love those kids."

"Yeah, that's why they keep bugging us."

Ever since House 7 had gone on a call at an elementary school to put out a simple fire, the kids had rallied around Riley because he'd found a couple of little ones hiding in a closet and carried them out. He'd told them to stop by the fire station anytime—and they did.

A staticky voice crackled out from the PA. "Fire on First and Liberty. Rescue Squad 7 and Quint and Midi 7 go into service."

It was as if somebody had turned on a switch. All teasing evaporated and the men and women assigned to the three trucks in the house bolted up from wherever they were and met in the bay; the smell of gasoline and smoke was strong.

Three feet from the rigs, eleven sets of turnout boots and pants waited for them on the concrete. Riley kicked off his shoes, tugged on his boots and pulled up the bulky, blue pants, securing them with yellow suspenders. Just before he hopped on the truck, he caught a glimpse of Janie heading toward the Rescue rig. *Be careful,* she mouthed.

He nodded to her. *You, too.*

They were lucky that way, having vowed not to worry about each other on the line. But it was easier to dismiss the danger she put herself in when she worked at her home firehouse and out of his sight.

A shiver skittered through him, a feeling something bad was going to happen today. Shaking if off, he noticed the kids out on the pavement. "Sorry, guys," he called out. "Next time."

Openmouthed, they watched him climb on the truck, where his turnout coat and self-contained breathing apparatus, commonly called SCBA, awaited.

Adam Langston, another firefighter on the Quint, drove the truck from the bay at high speed on the mild April night.

Lt. Tony Ramirez, seated next to him, warned, "Careful, Langston, we wanna get there."

Sirens blared and horns blew as they rumbled through the April night, the streets crowded with traffic. And Riley did what he always did on the ride to a call. He closed his eyes. Centered himself. Focused on the task ahead. It was one of the many things his father had taught him. *Be prepared. Get into the zone. You need all your wits about you to fight a fire.*

In minutes, they arrived at the abandoned clothing store in the center of Hidden Cove. Since it was a one-alarm blaze, Company Seven was the only one called. The Rescue Squad would search the building, the Quint would gain entry and slap water on the fire, and the small Midi's job was to deal with medical issues. It had recently been replaced with a truck that had a bed area in the back so the paramedics could drive victims to the hospital.

Their battalion chief was also on scene. Mitch Malvaso was the town hero, a top-notch firefighter, and an all-around great guy. He made his way to them from his setup of Incident Command on his department Jeep. "One-floor building. Fire's contained to the front, we think. Smoke color says no chemicals are in there, which makes sense, because the building was a clothing store. But be on your toes. You never know what the Red Devil's gonna do."

Another shiver ran through Riley. He ignored it and focused on the instructions shouted by the officers.

Captain Evans gestured to his crew. "Once the fire's contained, the five of us will head inside and scour the back." To the Quint, he added, "The rest of you'll search the front."

Though the building was abandoned, Riley knew that every section needed to be thoroughly searched. Since the structure was in the center of town, homeless people might have taken shelter inside. Hell, the fire could have been started by druggies freebasing in there. Even the idyllic town of Hidden Cove, an hour outside of New York City, had its share of social problems.

While the Rescue Squad circled around back, Ramirez huddled with his crew. "Gallagher, follow me with the rabbit tool. Decarlo, take the hose in behind him and the rest of you follow *them*." Langston, the driver, would stay with the truck.

Even the paramedics went inside, as they were fully certified firefighters.

After he yanked the pry tool off the rig, as the others were unfurling the hose, Riley followed Ramirez to the building.

The doors were double-wide and padlocked. "Shit," Riley said. Someone from behind nudged his arm with cutters. Firefighters never left the truck without a tool. Riley snapped the thick chains and, over the mic pinned to his collar, heard the lieutenant speak into his radio. "Door's chained. We snapped it but the Rescue Squad should know that nobody got in this way."

Riley put the tip of the rabbit tool — a hydraulic hand held manually operated tool — between the door and frame. He pumped the pneumatic unit so the two interlocking jaws exerted enough force to pop the doors. They opened inward.

Inside the building, they were met with a gray curtain of smoke that they couldn't see through. The Rescue Squad had a thermal imager for use when the flames were out, but Riley's group would work blind.

His crew slapped water in the front rooms, which *was* the point of origin. The noise was loud and hissing; he could hear it, even through his facemask and helmet. In ten minutes, the fire was doused. Next, two of his guys would take axes to the walls to make sure no flames were hiding.

The lieutenant's voice came over the mic again. "Gallagher, go down the left hallways with Duncan. Me and Decarlo will take the ones on the right."

Again over the mic, Riley heard from Evans from the rear. "We're in the back of the store and searching these rooms. We already found two guys and dragged them out so there *are* folks inside."

"Make sure you're thorough." Malvaso's voice came next. "We don't want to lose anybody because of neglect."

Thinking, *Nobody will be left behind on my watch,* Riley turned left with Duncan behind him. Because of the heat, they dropped to their knees and ran their hands along the wall to find their way. Their progress was slow, but this was how fires were fought.

• • •

JANE PHILLIPS WAS glad she kept in shape. Even so, her arms ached with the weight of the four people she'd dragged out of the building. She was heading back inside when Evans stopped her. "You okay to go in again, Phillips?" he asked. "You been in and out four times."

"Since I heard you ask Bilky that, I won't consider it a sexist question, Cap." Her tone was teasing. She knew Evans was fair and generous to women and had gotten some on to rescue squads.

"Then ladies first, Phillips." The remark was also made in good humor. Man, she loved her job.

Jane led the way through the door, and Evans nudged up to her side. The smoke was lessening, but she still couldn't see her hand in front of her face. Evans held up the imager. They walked quickly through the sectioned-off areas they'd already checked. The rank smell of decay and the stink of smoke seeped in through her SCBA mask.

"There's an area at the end we didn't cover, Phillips. Stay close."

They'd taken only three steps when a loud cracking noise rent the air, and the floor opened up. They fell through fast. Before Jane could internalize what had happened, she landed on top of the captain. He hit his head and his face mask flew off. Loss of air made him cough.

When she got her bearings, Jane thrust off the burnt wood that covered them and climbed off Evans. He wasn't moving. She began to feel around, running her gloved hands along the floor. Finally, she touched metal. "Thank God."

"What's going on there, Evans?" The voice came over the mic.

Jane ignored Malvaso's question and grabbed the helmet, felt the cap's face and managed to secure the hat and breathing device on him. Then she said into her mic, "Chief, me and Evans fell through the floor. Northwest quadrant of the building. Evans's out cold. He lost his SCBA, but I retrieved it. Oh, wait, he's moving, coming to."

"We're sending ropes and harnesses. Hang on. We'll be there in minutes."

It was quieter down here and she heard a moan come from the corner. Jesus, victims in the basement were all they needed. She rummaged around again until she found the imager and scanned the direction the noise had come from. A body was moving in the corner. Quickly checking the rest of the area through the viewer and seeing no heat-emitting shapes, she started to move toward the corner. Evans rasped out, "What is it, Phillips?"

"Victim about ten feet away. I'm going. Stay still, Cap."

The fact that he did made her realize this rescue was all on her. Slowly, feeling her way, she crawled to the body. Her hands reached the victim and she discovered he was a big lug of a man. "Whaaaa happened?"

"There's been a fire. I'm a firefighter." She took off her mask and placed the mouthpiece over his lips. "Here take some air."

The man sucked it in as she coughed like a son of a bitch. He handed her the mask back. "Make sure you take yours, Firefighter." The gravelly voice sounded surprisingly confident in his order.

They exchanged two more mouthfuls of air, then she heard from above, "Hey, Phillips, we're here."

She yelled out, "Cap's right below the hole. I'm in the corner with a victim."

"Stay there." Apparently Malvaso had decided to join the rescue with his fellow firefighters. "I'm coming down with two others, and there's a group here to pull us up top."

The smoke started to clear. She saw the outline of Malvaso shimmying down the rope. Then someone after him. Malvaso went to Evans, and two people headed to her. She hoped one of them wasn't Riley. That'd freak them both out.

It wasn't. Duncan and McCabe, both paramedics, reached her. "I have the BVM," Duncan said. "Keep your mouthpiece on and I'll fit the guy with the oxygen mask."

The victim, who coughed mercilessly, muttered something about saving somebody else first, but they ignored him.

In minutes, the paramedics put a neck brace on the guy and moved him onto a backboard. Before he left, McCabe tugged her up by the arm. "Should I check you out?"

"I'm fine, Jack. I fell on top of the cap."

As the two paramedics left, Jane glanced around; she was the only one left down here. Quickly, she walked to the hole, where megalights were shining through. Somebody threw her a harness, she stuck her feet in it, belted the waist and let herself be pulled up. She heard somebody joke, "Jesus, Phillips, you gotta lose some weight."

When she reached the top, her limbs were saturated and her head hurt from the smoke. "Okay."

"Hell, she must be in bad shape if she let that remark go." She recognized the voice of the man who helped bring her up. He grabbed on to her and held her close. "I got ya, babe, like always."

Jane removed her helmet and unbuttoned her coat—the cool air felt wonderful—then surveyed the scene. Bodies were scattered over the parking lot and grassy area behind the store. "Casualties?" she asked.

"Not a one." Riley put his face close to her ear. "You scared me, honey."

"None of that, Rye." She looked around. "The Cap?"

"Fine. His head's hard enough to withstand the blow."

"How 'bout the guy I was with?"

"Alive, they say. With a wracking cough."

After a few minutes, Malvaso approached them. "Gallagher, the man Phillips saved is asking for you."

"For me? Not Janie?"

"Uh-huh. But she should go with you."

"What? Why?"

"Just do it."

Jane and Riley headed to where Malvaso directed them. The man lay on the grass propped up against a tree. His clothes were in tatters, now covered with smoky grime, and he sported a beard which practically obscured his face.

Riley knelt down in front of him. "You wanted to see…" His voice trailed off.

Janie bent over, too. The guy smelled like body odor and alcohol. He raised his dirty hand to cup Riley's cheek. "I never thought I'd see you again, son."

Riley jerked back. Bolted up. His fists curled at his sides. "Yeah, right back at you. Which was fine with me."

• • •

For notification of Kathryn's new work and information about her books, be sure to sign up for her newsletter at http://on.fb.me/1bLS0bN.

If you liked IT HAD TO BE YOU, you might want to post a review of it at http://amzn.to/U4NHlt

Printed in Great Britain
by Amazon